"You have the life you stole from me."

Lilah squeezed the towel in her hands. "I don't know you anymore, Owen, but I don't want you near Ben. He'd be afraid of you if he saw you the way you used to get."

He turned around to face her.

Suddenly she felt as if she were vibrating. Was this shock? She couldn't control her reaction to seeing Owen again. He was still handsome, rugged.

She saw shadows of the younger man she'd loved.

She didn't want to see him, or remember how she'd cared for him. Loved him as much as she was able. She must not have loved him the way she'd thought if she'd managed to excise him from her life.

She couldn't let him back in.

Dear Reader,

Owen Gage and Lilah Bantry knew each other at a time when they were both trying to live down the secrets that ruled their lives. When Lilah discovered she was pregnant, she decided the baby was one more secret she had to keep because Owen had problems he didn't want to fix, and she was determined their child would never suffer the fear both she and Owen knew as children.

When Owen discovers Ben was born, he wants only revenge—and a chance to get to know the son he would never harm. Except his revenge can't bring Ben happiness, and he finds himself beginning to understand why Lilah made the decision he hates. It's only when Lilah and Owen give up the defenses that kept them safe before and learn to be generous with each other that they also learn to love. They begin to wonder if they can be a family...

I hope their story brings you the joy they find in each other.

All the best,

Anna

HEARTWARMING

Owen's Best Intentions

—

Anna Adams

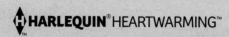

Recycling programs
for this product may
not exist in your area.

ISBN-13: 978-0-373-36740-5

Owen's Best Intentions

Printed in U.S.A.

Anna Adams wrote her first romance on the beach in wet sand with a stick. These days she uses pens, software or napkins and a crayon to write the kinds of stories she loves best—romance that involves everyone in the family and often the whole community. Love, like a stone tossed into a lake, causes ripples to spread and contract, bringing conflict and well-meaning "help" from the people who care most.

Books by Anna Adams

Harlequin Heartwarming

Christmas, Actually
(an anthology of three novellas)

Harlequin Superromance

The Talbot Twins

Unexpected Babies
Unexpected Marriage

The Calvert Cousins

The Secret Father
The Bride Ran Away
The Prodigal Cousin

Welcome to Honesty

Temporary Father
The Man from Her Past
Her Reason to Stay
A Conflict of Interest

Her Daughter's Father
The Marriage Contract
Maggie's Guardian
Her Little Secret
Another Woman's Son
Marriage in Jeopardy
Once Upon a Christmas
"All the Christmases to Come"

Visit the Author Profile page at Harlequin.com for more titles.

PROLOGUE

"HERE, BUDDY. THIS is the place." Owen Gage had to concentrate to make the words sound normal as he raised his hand awkwardly to tap on the taxi's back passenger window.

"You sure?" The driver pulled to the curb in front of Lilah Bantry's apartment building on one of Manhattan's long, narrow, building-bound streets. "This your place? Do you want me to wait?"

"No, why?"

"It's none of my business, but I'm not sure you belong here, and I feel bad just dropping a drunk guy on the street."

"A cabbie with a conscience. Thanks." The interior light almost blinded Owen. He might not have been in the best shape to see straight. "But I'm not drunk." He shoved money at the driver and then fumbled with the door handle. He was in control. He just needed to *concentrate*.

The handle gave way, and he all but fell out of the car, onto the rain-splattered curb.

After the month he'd spent in a rehab center in the mountains, just being in this city cut through the friendly warmth of his buzz. Only a buzz. He could handle his liquor.

He headed toward the uniformed doorman who stood sentry beneath a wide awning that was green by day, but looked dark and damp tonight.

"Kevin," Owen said, "how you doing, buddy?" There. He'd strung those words together like a champ.

"I'm better than you. What are you doing here like this, Mr. Gage?" Kevin had stood his post for as long as Owen had known Lilah and her family. Since the first time Lilah had taken one of Owen's carved wooden sculptures for her fancy gallery. He'd thought his work was too rustic for the Bantry Galleries, but she'd refused to give up on his sculptures, or him, for the past two years.

"I want to see Lilah. Is she home? I have news for her." Not good news, but information he was sick to death of hiding. He was tired of trying to be a different man because he loved her. Time she found out who he was.

Kevin reached for Owen as he tried to open the doors. "Wait."

He shook the guy off, looking at him with an unspoken promise to make his point more plainly if he needed to.

"Mr. Gage, she doesn't want to see you like this. Come into my office. Have a cup of coffee."

"Yeah." Coffee. "Why do people act like caffeine defuses vodka?" Owen pushed through the door.

The foyer's tiles, white marble threaded with gold, looked wet and slick. He was careful about where he placed his feet. At the elevator, he grabbed the edges of the silver doors and stepped inside. It took a couple of jabs to get Lilah's floor number, and then he backed into the wall behind him.

Kevin was on the phone at his desk, no doubt alerting Lilah.

Maybe coming here had been a mistake.

He'd climbed a fence at the world-renowned rehab center in upstate New York, hiked through the woods and found a liquor store before he located the bus line back to civilization. After all that effort, Lilah deserved to see the man she claimed to love.

The doors opened at her floor. He pushed

himself off the wall and left the car, veering to the right.

She didn't answer at first. He banged on the heavy wood with his fist, noting pain, but from a distance. It didn't really hurt.

She finally opened the door, clinging to it, her face pale. "You have another month."

"Kevin did call." He had an urge to touch her sallow skin. She didn't look right. "Are you sick?"

"You have another month in rehab."

"They tell you it won't work unless you're honest, and I'm tired of lying." He reached for the door. She held on to it and, oddly, didn't invite him inside.

"Why did you come here when you're like this?" She looked him up and down. "You couldn't think I'd be glad to see you." Her eyes were almost bruised with exhaustion.

"I asked are you sick?"

"You quit, didn't you? You walked away from rehab."

Even in his head, the big, honest announcement he'd come here to make sounded like the load of bull it was, except Lilah had to know the truth. "I don't want rehab." That wasn't it. "I've tried. You don't know how many times I've tried."

Over and over. Sometimes for a week. Sometimes for a few hours. Sometimes for a month or more, like after that first morning—at thirteen—when he'd passed out in the tree fort he and his brother had built. He'd woken with a cotton mouth and a head like a gong, and guilt that had become his oldest, most loyal friend.

Telling her about that would only make him weak. She looked away, pain pinching her face. Shame squeezed his warm buzz into a hazy memory.

"I like to drink, Lilah. So do you. We've had a good time."

"I'm not having a good time anymore." She sounded as if she might cry.

"Because you've changed?" But why? He couldn't understand what had made her different all of a sudden.

"I have changed." She pressed her hand to her mouth.

He stared at her, waiting. "Explain."

"My work suffers every time you're in town. I spend so much time watching you, waiting for you to get ready to leave this bar, or that pub." She covered her mouth again.

"Do you have the flu or something? You look like you're going to be sick."

"I wanted us to have a chance."

"A chance for what? You act as if you don't remember how many times we've headed back here at daylight. Together, and we weren't always trashed."

She laughed, but the sound cut like a piece of glass. "I wasn't," she said. "Because I can stop."

"I can stop, too." Even to him, that sounded idiotic after he'd staggered, drunk, into her home on the fumes of a fifth of vodka.

She lifted her face. Her whole body stiffened as if she were bracing for a blow. "I have stopped. I liked having fun. I liked the way alcohol made me feel different, but I was playing around. I guess I'm tired of playing, and I can't be with someone who needs to be drunk all the time."

"I can quit anytime I want."

"Like your dad."

Those three words were a shot to the gut. She was one of the few people outside of his brothers and sister and mother who knew what growing up in his house had been like. She'd compared him to the slob who'd made his family a bunch of victims. "You throw him in my face the first time you get mad at me?"

"Your father hurt you because he drank, Owen. He drank like you do. You told me yourself, he couldn't stop."

"Maybe he had his reasons." He closed his eyes for the briefest second. "I'm not my father."

"You don't want to be. I believe that." She came to him, taking his face between her hands with patience and sadness that was more painful than accusations.

She was saying goodbye. He knew it even as her touch eased the pain in his head.

"I just wanted to see you tonight." He tried to put his arms around her, but she slipped beyond his reach. Over her shoulder, he spied the silver tray that held vodka and scotch and whiskey so expensive a guy from Bliss, Tennessee, had never tasted its like before she'd first offered it.

His mouth watered. He wanted it. He couldn't help it. The thirst was a furnace inside him, a fire that had to burn. Fires burned.

Drinkers drank.

"You've seen me." She walked away from him, her mouth tight, her eyes wounded. Pale blond hair fell over her face. "Now you can go back to the center," she said. "I'll drive you. Let me change."

"I'm not going back. I tried because I care about you, and you wanted it, but I don't want it."

"What if I can't be with you if you drink?"

He moved in front of her, jostling a small parquet table he'd given her as a thank-you for his first show at her family's gallery. "What are you talking about?" He tried again to decipher her expression. "Why are you looking at me as if I've cheated on you?"

"Because that's how I feel. Every time you show me you prefer vodka to me, you cheat on me."

"You showed me the best clubs in Manhattan. You've matched me drink for drink and laugh for laugh. We've had a good time. Maybe it was just fun at first, but you matter more than…"

"You are vital to me, Owen, so I'm begging you…" He'd never heard this tone before, so earnest, so broken. Where was the woman who'd survived a childhood kidnapping to step bravely out in the world as a successful gallery owner? "I am literally begging you to promise you can stop drinking. That you will stop drinking."

"I can't." Every last moment in that place had been like marching through a desert, his mind always fixed on a glass of the only relief for the thirst that owned him. It was painful to acknowledge, but he'd needed that drink more than he'd wanted Lilah.

"I came back because I missed you." He could barely look at her as he said the words. "Why can't that be enough? Maybe it's time we stopped doing this long-distance relationship. I could move here."

At least then he could lose the title of town drunk, transferred from his father's head to his.

"No." She turned her face away, and strands of her hair stuck to the tears on her cheeks, making this whole mess worse. "I need you to commit to being sober."

He was sober now. The vodka he'd sipped all the way from rehab on a bus that had smelled like unwashed humans had long since vanished from his system.

He licked his lips. What he'd give for another fifth.

"I will not lie to you," he said.

"I don't want you to lie. I want you to be the decent man I believe in, not a man who terrorizes his family and wastes his life."

He laughed as if that were funny, but he headed for her door. "You don't believe I'm decent." He didn't believe it. "I've made my choice. When you get bored with being reformed, give me a call."

CHAPTER ONE

SOMETHING PRODDED Lilah Bantry's face. Something small and pointy and insistent. She woke, felt the smooth weave of the couch beneath her and peered through the tangle of her hair. Her son's tiny index finger poked gently at her arm this time as he leaned over her.

"Mommy?"

"Ben." She gathered him close. "Morning, buddy." She'd doubted her ability to be a good mother until she'd seen his red, scrunched-up face in the delivery room four years ago and realized she would do everything she could for this little guy. "Hey, buddy."

"Are you awake?"

"I fell asleep waiting for the ball to drop." She hugged him tight and relished the grip of his little arms around her. "Happy New Year, baby. Are you hungry?"

He nodded. "Blueberry pancakes?"

"Perfect, from the blueberries we picked last summer."

"I can stir." He tugged at the quilt.

She stood, pushing it off her legs until it fell to the floor. Her son grabbed her hand and pulled her toward the kitchen. Solemn and intent, he pushed the stool he usually sat on while she did the prep work for their meals, until it bumped into the granite island.

"Flour, Mommy."

First, she took the blueberries out of the freezer. Then she carried the baking powder, sugar, milk and an egg to the island. She ran the blueberries under water to thaw them slightly and then mixed up the batter. When she added the blueberries, and the batter turned purple, Ben clapped his hands. She'd never been a big fan of purple food, but her boy was.

"Blueberry pancakes. Yummmm."

She'd broken their griddle at Thanksgiving, and she hadn't found time to replace it yet, so she heated a frying pan and poured small pools of batter, just the size Ben liked best.

"I can eat more than three."

"I'll make you more." She grinned at him over her shoulder. His dad was allergic to blueberries. She hadn't remembered that the first time she'd given them to Ben, and she'd followed her son around for an hour before she realized he was going to survive her mistake. "Want to make a snowman on the green in town after we eat?"

"Why do they call it green, Mommy? It's white, and when the snow melts, it's brown."

"Excellent work on your colors, buddy, and I don't have a clue. I'll have to look that up for you."

"You said you know everything."

She probably had. She did that sometimes. "I will know after I look it up."

Their doorbell rang. She glanced at the frying pan. Her pancakes were puffing a little steam just around their purple, bubbling edges. She flipped them, moved them off the heat and turned off the stove.

Ben had already hopped off his stool. He hurtled down the hall in front of her while she plucked at the collar of her pajama shirt. She was decent enough. Someday, she should buy a robe.

She peeked through the sidelight, and almost stopped breathing.

Owen.

Haggard, unshaven, leaner than she remembered, but at least he hadn't been drinking. She knew him well enough to be certain with one glance.

For a moment she couldn't think. She just jerked back, out of sight.

She wished with all her heart she could magically transport her son and herself somewhere far away.

He was bound to find her someday. She hadn't tried very hard to hide. She glanced at Ben, who was staring at her as if she'd grown an extra head.

"Mommy?" His voice restored her composure immediately.

"Company." She tried to sound as if Owen Gage's showing up at her door was no big deal. "I haven't seen my friend in a long time. I didn't expect him."

Ben put one finger in his mouth and stared at her.

He would take his lead from her. If she panicked, he would be afraid, and she was smart enough to know that Owen would not just go away. Somehow, Ben's father had discovered he had a son.

Forcing herself to smile at her little boy, she turned and opened the door. A firing squad would have looked less threatening than Owen. She'd wanted to give him a chance to be a good father, but he'd been too in love with the bottle. Still, she couldn't blame him for the anger that turned his pale blue eyes to ice and thinned his already sharp features.

"What the…" he began, but Lilah stepped aside so that he'd see Ben.

So that the first words Ben heard from him wouldn't be angry swearing.

Owen sputtered to a shocked halt. His gaze softened, warmed. "I can't believe it." He squatted, still outside the door. Snow glistened behind him on the trees, the sidewalk, the pond across the street and the granite-colored roof of his car.

He was leaning toward his son, and his eagerness made her feel uncomfortable. If she could have turned away, she would have, because the moment felt too personal, and his vulnerability hurt her.

"Hi," Owen said, but then looked up at her, and the anger came back into his eyes.

He didn't know his own son's name. "Ben," she said. "I called him Ben."

"Hi, Ben."

Lilah reached back for her boy, trying to find his shoulder with her trembling hand.

Owen looked as if he half expected her to scoop up their child and run out the back door. "Ben's having pancakes," she said, trying to sound normal. She'd learned to act when she was five years old, and she'd tricked a pedophile, who'd taken her from a grocery-store aisle, into turning his back just long enough for her to escape. "Maybe you'd like to join us?"

"Join you?" Owen's voice shook slightly. She read him like a book. How could she sound calm?

Five years ago he hadn't understood why she'd demanded he get sober. He'd told her how much his own father loved alcohol, and she knew their child wouldn't be safe with him as long as he loved liquor more than he could love a family.

She stared into his eyes, searching for telltale signs that he'd fortified himself to come to Vermont to find Ben. All she saw was shock and anger. Betrayal.

She had betrayed him. But his feelings didn't matter. Ben mattered.

"We're just going to have breakfast."

Owen stood. "I am hungry."

"Blueberry pancakes." Ben waved his arm toward the kitchen, eagerly leading his guest.

He'd never been shy, but even for Ben, this friendliness was unusual. "Let me show you. They're purple. I like purple food. Grapes, yogurt with blueberries. Grape popsicles, but Mom won't let me have those very often. Maybe once in five years."

"You aren't even five years old," Lilah said, aware of the quiver in her voice.

"I remember last year and the last year and the next year."

Owen laughed. "That's the way I remember, too."

They reached the kitchen, and Lilah managed to restrain herself from clutching Ben close to her side. He patted his stool. "You can sit here, big man."

Owen laughed again. "Big man?"

Ben didn't like being laughed at. "You're big?"

Owen, who was taller than most men, nodded. "I guess I am."

"And you're a man?"

"Yeah."

"We can't say 'yeah.' Mommy says it's the wrong word."

Owen didn't even glance her way. "Yes, then. I am a man."

"Big. Man." Ben scrambled onto the stool

himself. "Maybe I better sit here because I can't see if I don't, and you're big enough to see without a stool."

Lilah slid the frying pan back on to the burner, but then remembered Owen's allergy. "My friend Owen is allergic to blueberries. I'll need to make more batter."

"Don't bother."

She turned to look at him, but he was peering around the room, inspecting. She couldn't tell if he approved of the cozy space, lined with baskets and painted pie plates and her embarrassing collection of kitten and cat figures. Ben had given each one of them a name.

"Have to eat breakfast," Ben said, looking anxious. Why should he be concerned about Owen's eating habits? She refused to believe a father-son tie could be so strong that Ben felt it without knowing about it.

She turned the heat back on beneath his breakfast and whipped up another batch of batter. Ben was halfway through his first stack of small pancakes by the time she set a plate and silverware in front of Owen, who looked from her to Ben as if they were playing a game he didn't understand.

She served him normal-sized pancakes

and made another small stack for Ben, who attacked his plate with gusto.

Owen ate every bite, and when he'd finished, Ben clambered down and took his plate. With supreme four-year-old concentration, he carried the dish to the sink. Then he came back and gave Owen a clumsy pat on the back.

"Good job, buddy," he said.

Lilah laughed, but she couldn't hide the nervous hitch in her voice.

"I'll have two more," Ben said, holding up three fingers.

"Are you really hungry?" Lilah asked him.

Ben looked down at his belly as if he could gauge how full he was. "I might not eat them," he said. "Do I have to take a shower now?"

"You could play in your room for a little while if you want."

He nodded so hard his chin must have hit his chest. Then he tilted his head to grin at Owen, who laughed. A husky laugh that made Lilah shiver. She remembered it far too well, and she could already tell Ben was going to have the same laugh when he grew up.

"Go to your room and play, then, but don't turn on the water until I come up."

"Okay, Mommy." He slid off the stool again, but offered his hand to Owen. "See you later, Mommy's friend."

"You can call me Owen."

"Own."

Ben turned and ran for the stairs, growling car engine sounds as he climbed.

Owen seemed to topple forward onto his elbow, which was braced on the counter.

"My son," he said. "And such a sweet kid. So friendly. He doesn't even know me."

He didn't move for several seconds. Lilah's worry spiked. He was either trying to hide his feelings, or planning revenge.

When he looked up, redness rimmed his eyes. "Get this through your head. I am never leaving him."

CHAPTER TWO

WEREN'T THOSE THE WORDS she'd hoped to hear? Just after he promised, "I'll never drink again." She would have told him about her pregnancy, and in her dreams he would have promised, "I won't put our child at risk."

She'd stopped dreaming when he'd admitted with heartbreaking honesty that he couldn't stop drinking. After that, there had been no room for Owen Gage in her life. He'd missed his chance with their son, and she'd heard from her brother, Tim, that Owen still had problems with alcohol. Wanting to do the right thing and actually managing it were miles apart for Owen.

"Lilah." He made no effort now to hide his anger.

Startled, she jumped. Almost deafened by the silence after Owen barked her name, she didn't answer. Ben's voice came down the stairs as he talked to his trains or his army of action figures, who were hampered by the fact that he'd broken so many of their body parts.

In the sink, the faucet dripped with annoying regularity. Lilah's own breathing sounded like someone hissing.

She had to run. Hide her son. Why hadn't she done that four years ago—made herself and her baby invisible to the one man on earth who could destroy her life?

"How did you find us?"

He reached into the pocket of his leather jacket and pulled out a large gift tag the size of a postcard. He passed it across, and Lilah read the Christmas-red text that wrapped around a photo of her and her parents and her brother. And Ben. They were sprawled or standing or slouched on the porch of the beach house at Fire Island.

"From our family to yours," the gift tag read. And her family had told Owen about his son.

She knew immediately what had happened. Her parents had arranged to send an alcoholic a bottle of good wine with this gift tag around its neck.

"I knew the second I saw the photo," Owen said. "But I got out an old picture of myself to compare Ben and me at the same age. You understand I'm not leaving him with you, right?"

"You don't have custody." She had kept his son from him. If he didn't have a reputation as an alcoholic, he might have a leg to stand on. "You can't come up here and walk off with my son. First, I won't let you, and, second, you don't know him."

"What can you do?"

"Ask anyone who knows you to testify in court that you couldn't possibly be a good parent because you're an alcoholic."

"That won't work. I've changed."

"You mean you've changed again?" she asked. "I talk to Tim. He knows you've tried to quit drinking, and you can't stop. All I have to do is ask your family and friends what you're like at home. No court would consider me the less fit choice."

He looked at her as if she were a stranger. "Why did you do it? You weren't a heartless woman. You robbed our son of his father. For four years."

She avoided that knowledge as often as she could. She'd made the best choice for Ben. "You told me you were afraid you were like your father. You told me he beat you and your brothers and sister. If you were like him, you had no place around my child."

He stared at her, his lips thin, his gaze practically expressionless. She wrestled silently with panic. What did he plan to do next? Lilah's best gift was thinking on her feet. She'd done it even when she was five, just a little older than Ben, and escaped her kidnapper.

She had the same sense of being threatened now.

And all the while, water splatted rhythmically on the steel bottom of the sink.

"I understand you're angry, but I don't know what you mean by saying you're never leaving Ben again."

"My son." He lowered his voice, coming to stand right next to her. He was too tall, too intense, his frustration whipping up bad energy between them. "Ben is my boy, whom you've hidden from me. You didn't dump me because I drank. That was an excuse to give you control. You didn't stop drinking because you suddenly wanted to be healthier. You quit because you were pregnant with Ben, and if you'd told me about our baby, I would have quit, too." He thought she was the bad guy? "You left because *you* decided I wasn't worthy of making a life with him."

"Tell me I was wrong. You still drink. The damage is all over you. You're twenty-eight, but you look years older. You think you can bully me with a raised voice and anger." She turned her back to him, putting the counter between them.

"You've had him for four years. Four years, and every day you passed up the chance to tell me the truth."

"I asked you to quit drinking. You said you liked it too much. You'd told me about your father. How could I take the chance that you'd be like him?"

"How could you refuse to let Ben know me or me know him?"

His eyes were troubled. He was angry, but deep inside those haunted eyes, she saw remnants of the man she'd known. When he was hurt, he fought back, instead of admitting he was in pain.

"I gave you as much of a chance as I could," she said. "I never told my family you were Ben's father. I never asked them to keep Ben a secret, and I didn't ask them to help me hide from you." Big mistake. "I wasn't naive." She shook her head. "Maybe

I thought that if you wanted to find me, it would be some kind of proof that I mattered to you. That Ben could matter to you. But after a few months passed with no call from you, I knew you weren't interested."

He shook his head. Slightly, as if the effort hurt. "After you told me I was a lush you couldn't trust? How was I supposed to guess you were pregnant?"

"I had Ben to think of."

"And that's why you changed?"

"Changed?" She put her hands over her eyes. They burned as if she'd been crying.

"You were paranoid. You assumed the worst would happen, just like you always do. Instead of telling me why you wanted a different relationship, you went from being my—"

"Designated driver. I got you from bar to bar and back to my place every time you came to New York. I couldn't be that woman anymore when a child depended on me. I had to do the right thing for Ben, and you told me plainly that you couldn't."

Owen froze, but his gaze cut her. "You knew everything about me, and all the while you kept your own secrets. You asked me to change because I wasn't good enough to be a father to my own child."

He was right that she only let people see the parts of her she wanted them to see. "You won't believe this, but I didn't hurt you on purpose."

He laughed, but he clearly found nothing about her funny. "You thought denying me my son—denying him his father—was the right thing for all of us?"

"I hoped there was a chance you'd understand if you ever found out." She scooped a dish towel off the counter and folded it, creasing each corner. "You saw my brother just before Thanksgiving. He said you were still drinking. Excessively."

He chose to ignore the comment about his drinking. "Did you really think I'd find out about Ben and think—well that's a mistake anyone could make? What's four years to a father and son?" His despair was a living thing that snaked around her as he pushed his fists into the pockets of his jeans. "I don't even understand the way you think." He straightened, seeming to reach a decision. "You forget I know how much you hate reporters bringing up the subject of 'Little Lost Lilah.' Either give me time with my son, or

I'll deliver that secret of yours to every news station."

He had her weakness in his hip pocket. The media had loved her story when she was five. Little Lost Lilah. Abducted from her parents in broad daylight but brave and smart enough to run away from her kidnapper. Reporters had hounded her at regular intervals when she'd started high school and gone away to college— checking in on Little Lost Lilah to see if she'd let that man scar her for life. The thing she wanted most for Ben was to save him from the horror of microphones in his face and strident voices asking for his feelings—because his mom was taken by a stranger when she was not much older than he was now.

"How can you suggest you'd set those monsters on me?" Owen had never been cruel.

"Lilah, did you think I'd be grateful? Ask how I could thank you enough for taking four years of being a father to Ben away from me? Because I drank?"

"Because you drink. I thought I was doing what was best for Ben. I don't believe you'll hurt him now to get back at me."

"That's exactly the kind of man you think

I am." He raised his eyes to the ceiling as if he could see through the floor to Ben playing above.

Blood rushed in Lilah's ears, and she considered calling the police. They'd never helped her when she was kidnapped. She'd had to count on herself.

But Owen could prove he was Ben's father. He'd never given up custody. If he chose to fight for parental rights, he'd win visitation.

On the other hand, if she played along, she'd find a way out of this. There'd come a moment when he'd make a mistake, take a drink. Prove even to himself that she'd been right to protect their son from a man whose worst fear was turning into the monstrous man who'd terrorized his own family.

"Visit Ben here, Owen. Let me keep him in familiar surroundings."

He seemed to hesitate. Fighting a battle of conscience? His fists came out of the tops of his pockets, and he flexed his fingers, and his jaw tightened. At last, he shook his head. "I can't. I have a job at home that's life and death to my career. I have to finish it."

"Your career? Who cares about a career?" Not the Owen she'd known.

"It matters to my reputation," he said. "I

didn't stop drinking when you asked me to. You're right about me, except for one thing. I'm not violent, and I would never harm another human being." His eyes narrowed until they were chips of ice that cut straight through her. "But I will do everything I can to see my son."

If she were in his shoes, if he'd kept Ben from her, would she be as angry? Absolutely. But she faced him down. "Do your worst."

"I will if I have to," he said, his voice contained, his breathing even. "I'm desperate. You've proven I can't trust you to give me a chance with my son."

"I could not hand him over to a man who told me he preferred alcohol to me."

"I said that without knowing all the facts, Lilah. I want a chance with my boy, and he'll have to come to Tennessee. I wish it could be different, and I don't want to frighten him. But I've made some mistakes, and this job may be my last chance at getting enough work to make a living."

"Why am I not surprised?"

"I'm not being dramatic," he said, but then he shrugged, as if her opinion didn't matter enough for him to explain. "When you pack, add some of Ben's toys, so he'll have familiar things around him and his favorite books. Whatever will make him comfortable while he's with me."

"This is crazy, Owen. No way will I send my son off with a stranger." She didn't trust Owen any more now than she had four years ago.

"I won't be a stranger for long," he said.

"You're not taking him, Owen. I'll fight you on this. Besides, he and I haven't spent a night apart since he was born."

"Then pack your stuff, too." He paced out of the kitchen, across the living room to the bay window that looked out on her snow-drifted backyard. "If you come along, that solves the problem."

"If you really care about him, you'd just leave him alone. Ben is a happy child. We have a life here."

"You have a life you stole from me." His voice sliced through the air.

Lilah squeezed the towel in her hands. "You said yourself you're still drinking. You have to stay away from Ben. He'd be afraid of you if he saw you the way you used to get."

He turned back to her, and his pain was hers for a single moment. She froze, but she felt as if she were vibrating. She couldn't control her body's reaction to seeing Owen again.

She didn't want to remember how much she'd cared for him. Loved him. She couldn't let him back in.

"I will not frighten my own child," he said, his voice low, controlled. "Stop dreaming up excuses to keep Ben and me apart."

"I don't need excuses. My mother loved me. She was responsible. She only looked away for a few seconds, and see what happened? I was kidnapped by a stranger." Lilah never talked about the past. She'd dealt with it and moved on, but he needed to know exactly why she'd rejected him as Ben's father. "I will never turn my back on Ben, especially to leave him with an alcoholic like you."

Owen barely glanced at her. "Give me a break, and stop comparing me to my father and a kidnapper."

A switch had turned on when she found out she was pregnant. All the years of healing had disappeared the second she'd read that positive pregnancy test. She'd become a little girl again, running for her life. How easily that man had lured her with his story of a lost kitten that needed her help. "I vowed what happened to me would never happen to my child."

"Our child. So, you let your own paranoia keep your son from his father? What kind of mother does that?"

"You told me you wouldn't stop drinking, and I told you I couldn't live with that. I wasn't going to let Ben grow up the way you did, Owen."

"I won't drink around Ben." Owen straightened with a pride she'd never seen in him before, not even when he was the star attraction at his exhibitions in her family's galleries. "I will be a good father to my son."

"Ben doesn't know you're his father."

"My name is on the birth certificate."

She clenched her fists to keep from going for his throat. "How did you get your hands on his birth certificate?"

"After I saw Ben's photo on that gift tag, I took a chance and requested a copy of my son's birth certificate. I found the announcement your parents put in the paper, and that gave me all the information I needed. I started looking for you."

"You've been stalking us?" She knew she was being ridiculous, but she was angry with herself. She'd left him a string of clues. Made it too easy for him to find them.

"Ask yourself what you would have done in the same situation. I didn't stalk you, Lilah."

"What do you call it?"

"Making sure my son knows he has a father."

"You're sober now, but you look as if you've been on a bender."

"You didn't bother to tell me the real reason I should have made sobriety stick four years ago And what about your own issues? I'm not the one who abandoned college after college because everyone I saw looked threatening. And I didn't move out of my apartment overnight because I thought a woman in my building was following me. Turns out she commuted the same way you did. We both have problems, Lilah, but we're both Ben's parents."

Her skin seemed to be on fire. She knew her face had turned bright red, but she wasn't so embarrassed about the truth that she couldn't fight back. "You told me you liked to drink, that you chose to drink."

He ignored the accusation. "So once again you packed up and walked away from yet another place, without warning, without notice, without reason. Just because of your fear."

"Ben was my reason."

"Go to Bliss with Ben and me, or I'll go to the courts and fight for custody on the grounds you're not a fit mother."

This was not the Owen she'd known. "You wouldn't bring up my past and use it against me."

"I'm asking again, how cruel would you be if I'd stolen Ben from you?"

The papers, the reporters. She'd been five years old, swarmed by curious faces and camera flashes and questions that only put her back into the bad place.

If Owen took revenge, it would be hard to keep her past a secret. It would be all over social media, complete with photos and old newspaper articles. There'd be commentary on blogs. She felt sick. She'd tried with all her might to keep Ben safe from the notoriety of her past.

She moved closer to him. "You can't. You won't. You may not know him, but you must instinctively care about Ben, or you wouldn't have come here. Making him an object for people to gawk at would hurt him."

"So, now you're using him to keep me in check?"

She'd still do anything to protect her son.

"Go ahead and push me," Owen said, with no hint of the gentleness that had once drawn her to him despite the drinking.

And he'd helped her at first. Pushed her to overcome her fears. But over time she'd grown to loathe his drinking, and hers. Daring anything to prove she wasn't afraid quickly lost its appeal as she'd pulled and pushed Owen into a taxi or through her apartment door, or dragged him out of a fight in a bar.

But at least when he was under the influence, Owen had never hurt anyone except himself.

"Show some compassion," she said.

"Like you did?"

She wanted to yell. His warm breath fanned her face. She reassessed her chances of getting Ben out of the house and making a run for it.

But that would be a ridiculously reckless decision. Whatever she had to do to keep Owen from taking Ben, she would. He could threaten her all he wanted, but she would make him see things her way. What was best for Ben would be best for all of them. "Let's calm down for a minute."

"I'm not an idiot, Lilah, and I've been played by bigger and better cons than you."

They shared one trait, a survivor's sensitivity to undercurrents.

"We both care about Ben," she said, "and you don't know how many times I wanted to tell you about him." That was true. If he'd been a different person, she would have told him. "I made a bargain with myself. If you showed up, I'd be honest."

"I showed up today." He stepped away from her. "We need to make plans."

Panic tightened her throat. "How can you be serious?"

"At least in Bliss I can make sure you'll have a harder time taking him away again."

"You want him to stay in that little cabin of yours?"

"Plenty big enough for one man and one small boy."

And no woman. She didn't figure into his plan. "What are you talking about? You don't think I'm letting him live with you."

"I'm not playing with you. I am desperate, and I don't trust you. You can take a room at my mom's inn, but Ben stays with me until we create a legally binding custody agreement. See him whenever you want, but until we have an understanding, I won't believe you'd suddenly consider I have rights at all."

She went to the sink, her mind racing. "You think legal papers will stop me?"

"Yes." Owen came around the counter, too. Stopping inches away, he touched her face with the back of his hand. Gently, to get and keep her attention. "Because you don't want Ben's name or pictures in headlines."

"You don't care about Ben. You're angry at me." She wished that were true. How else could she believe that this man she'd once loved would take away her son? She was the one who'd kept Ben safe all his life. She made the decisions about how he was raised.

"I only care about Ben. He deserves to be with his father. Your judgment is flawed, and Ben deserves better. If you'd stopped to think first, if you'd been honest with yourself, you would have known I'd love him. I'd never hurt him. I am not my father."

"You have no idea what it takes to be a parent. You've only had yourself to think about. Wait until the work starts, staying up all night when Ben's sick, listening to the stories about other kids at school who hurt his feelings, worrying about the countless things that might go wrong."

"What could be more wrong than never knowing my son?"

CHAPTER THREE

OWEN SWALLOWED, THE HEAT of anger drying his mouth. Now that she understood his intentions, he'd back off. "You're right about one thing. We both need to calm down." He could hardly suggest Ben needed his father but not his mother. "I might consider coming here for a while if I weren't in the middle of a work project. I can't get away from Tennessee."

"You never wanted to leave those mountains, but you should for Ben's sake if you want to spend time with him."

His temper snapped, but he wasn't his father. He seriously wanted revenge, but four years had given him time to realize he'd been honest and yet made a choice that had driven Lilah to break up with him. He didn't for a second believe that excused her decision to keep his son from him, but he also didn't need to hurt a woman.

He just didn't intend to let her make all

the decisions from now on. "This time we do things my way."

Her laughter was like brittle cracking glass. "This time," she said in a mocking tone. "Unlike when you first started selling your furniture and sculpture to my gallery, and you insisted on working under an assumed name."

"You should understand I wanted privacy." Crowds of people made him want a drink. Happiness could increase the thirst that never let up. Anger, loss, like the loss of his son's babyhood, made it a dull, insistent urge that gripped him. "You don't want anyone asking you about Little Lost Lilah."

She eased a deep breath between her lips. He had to make her believe he'd expose her past. She was a caged animal, pacing around the small kitchen, but she wouldn't run away with Ben again if she thought he'd use everything in his power to find them.

When she reached the coffeemaker, she picked up the pot. "Do you want a cup?"

Was she giving in? "Please."

"I don't remember how you take it." She poured the coffee into a mug and then got sugar from a cabinet. "There's cream in the fridge."

He went to the large, stainless-steel refrigerator, playing for time and space. Inside, he reached between organic peanut butter and several jars of homemade jam to get the cream. The Lilah he'd known was barely on speaking terms with her stove. "Did you make these?"

She stepped in front of him, her scent a distracting delight to his senses. He closed his eyes and backed away, making sure to look normal by the time she turned around.

"I've done everything I could to keep my son healthy," she said.

He ignored the unspoken "including keeping you out of his life" and shut the refrigerator door. "I never picked you as a home canner."

"Thanks. And while we're discussing my abilities, you obviously haven't considered that I run the gallery I opened up here. I can't leave my job."

"You don't have any staff? You did in New York. At least you talked about them. I think I remember you talking about them."

"I'm surprised you remember anything." She caught her breath. "Sorry, that was ugly. We both drank too much. I worried about

Ben at first because I didn't stop drinking until I knew I was pregnant."

"You could always take it or leave it," he said. "I did notice that you looked after me those nights we went out."

"No. I was reckless. If you dared me—if someone implied I was afraid to do something, I most often took the dare."

Even though he was angry at what she'd done to him and Ben, he couldn't pretend she'd matched him vice for vice. "It wasn't all drinking," he said, his tone dry. "Sometimes we watched movies."

Her head came up. She looked into his eyes as if she were searching for a softness he couldn't feel for her. "Think about what you're asking, Owen. Ben has never met your family. He doesn't know you."

Because she'd turned her back on him. "Maybe I would have kept drinking even if I'd known you were pregnant, but you didn't give me the chance to try for Ben's sake." Even to him, that sounded weak—but maybe, with Ben as motivation, he might have found the strength to ignore the urge that never left him. "Come to Tennessee with us, or Ben and I will go alone."

She shook her head. "He doesn't know you. He'd be afraid."

"Not if you come with him."

She shrugged, and her hair splashed across her back like a silky, blond wave that made him want to feel its softness against his fingers again. She called herself reckless when they were together, but she'd been laughing and loving, and she'd shown him the city's hidden treasures. Small parks and museums where no one looked at him with doubt that a drunk from the remotest mountains of Tennessee could appreciate art or beauty. Restaurants where the chefs made them Lilah's favorite meals, which they'd shared with love, confiding the secrets they could only trust with each other.

Deep inside, a part of him wanted to believe the woman he'd known back then was still a real part of this Lilah, who seemed to think the only way Ben could be safe was apart from his father. "I'll go with you." She didn't explain. He didn't push his luck by asking what changed her mind.

"Fine. I believe you can work from Bliss. I'll introduce you to some of the other local artisans. There are plenty of antiques stores in the mountains, and many artists produce the primitive pieces you like."

"Why are you so accepting of all this?"

Her suspicions about him only matched his own toward her. "For Ben. So that he knows he can count on both his parents to put him first." He added a parting jab. "And work keeps you happy."

"Ben makes me happy." She yanked her hair into a coil and wrapped one of those elastic things women used around it. "I'm not sure I trust you."

"You have to."

She exhaled, and he saw the first sign of guilt in the gaze she averted. "I'd be out of my mind if you kept him from me."

Anger ground through him. "Then you understand?"

She shook her head, and he remembered her young face in the faded headlines of newspapers she'd kept as reminders of her own strength. The same stubborn refusal to give in to her fear. The same determination not to let the experience break her.

"Why didn't you just tell me?" he asked. "None of this had to happen."

"For the same reason I don't believe in you now. Alcoholics want to change. Surviving depends on change, but you will always be an alcoholic."

"I'm trying to want other things more." But he couldn't deny that vodka, cold as ice, would have eased him through this day.

She looked rattled, and he learned at once to admit nothing more about his own flaws.

"Give me time," Lilah said. "A week to speak to my family and prepare Ben. My assistant will need information about the books and deliveries. I'll need to give her instructions before I can leave her with the shop."

"I can't wait around here for a week."

"I'm not asking you to, and I won't take Ben away. There was always a chance you'd find us. I'm not trying to keep him from you. You're the one who's trying to take him from me."

"You kept him all these years."

"But I didn't hide. That's proof I won't take Ben from you now."

"We tell him now, before I go back to Tennessee. If you're lying about coming, or if you run, I'll find you, no matter where you go or how hard you try to hide."

He sounded like his father. *If you leave me, I'll find you. No one will hide you well enough. No one can keep you away from me.*

That was what Odell Gage had said. So many times, Owen's mother had believed.

So had he and his brothers and sister.

"I know I can't keep you apart any longer," Lilah said.

"Before I go back to Tennessee, we'll tell him who I am," Owen said again.

She seemed to think it over, as if she had the right. "What if you change your mind?"

Incredible.

"Look at me." He didn't try to hide anything. "I'm stunned to find I'm anyone's father, and I want revenge for what you did, but most of all, I want to do the right thing for Ben." He needed to rebuild his reputation, so he could make a decent living, but he didn't want to lose any more time with his son. It had to be this way. "I won't change my mind. I want to know my son."

"O-kay," she said, with doubtful emphasis on both syllables.

THE NEXT MORNING, Owen bought a booster seat for Ben. Afterward, he stopped at the first fire station on his way to Lilah's. A uniformed man came out as Owen parked in the wide driveway.

"What's up?" the man asked, his breath forming a wreath around his head.

"I bought this seat for my son." Had he said that word out loud before? It made him proud. He'd like to say it again.

He popped the trunk open with his key fob and pulled out the huge box. "They told me at the store that you'd install it for me."

"You've never installed your kid's car seats?"

"My child is new to me," Owen admitted. "I don't mind explaining the situation to you, but do you need me to?"

The firefighter shook his head. "Sorry, man. You want to watch?"

"Yeah. This is a rental car. When we get home to Tennessee, I'll have to do it myself."

The fireman installed the seat, instructing Owen as he did. "You're sure you got the right one?"

He'd called Lilah from the hotel the night before. After making arrangements to pick up Ben and take him out today, he'd gotten his son's measurements. "I asked a salesperson at the baby store. She assured me this was right for my boy's weight and height."

"Then you should be good." The other

man stepped back and folded his arms. "If you can do it on your own."

Owen had trouble the first time, but then installed the seat correctly twice.

At last they both stepped back, Owen with a sense of accomplishment. The words "I'm a dad," repeated inside his head, but he kept silent as he dug a few bills out of his wallet. "In my town, the fire service sponsors a burn charity. I don't know if you do that up here?"

"We have a brother in ICU at the hospital right now. We've started a fund for his family. If you'd rather give the money to a different charity, I will, but his wife and children could use this."

Owen added another bill. "Thanks for your help."

He walked back to his car, ducking the fireman's gratitude. It was crazy the money his simple furniture brought him. Might as well put it to good use.

CHAPTER FOUR

HE REACHED BEN and Lilah's just as they were coming down the wooden steps of their small Cape Cod house. Lilah must have been waiting for him before she left for work. She stood on the narrow sidewalk, holding Ben's hand. They were both dressed to fight off the snowy wind in parkas and scarves and gloves.

Owen grinned at his son, who resembled the figure in one of those commercials where the spokesman is a stack of tires that look like marshmallows.

"I hadn't thought about climbing Mount Washington, but we could do that today," Owen said.

"What is that?" Ben asked. "Mommy, can I go that far?"

"Not today, baby," she said, grimacing over his head. "Owen made a lot of plans for you. He's going to take you by your day-care center to pick up your art project."

She'd agreed to let him meet Ben's teachers. "I heard you painted a poster of you and your mom, but it was still too wet to bring home last week," Owen said. "Ready to go, buddy?"

Now that the moment had come, the little guy looked up at his mother for reassurance, which made Owen resent Lilah more. But, if Lilah had been the one who couldn't stop drinking, would he have wanted to risk letting their son spend time alone with her? No. He'd have to accept that Lilah hadn't been entirely wrong.

She'd judged him and stolen the most precious gift from him, but he had to let it go. Every time he looked at her he got angry all over again, but deep inside, a voice accused him.

You aren't fit.

He would change.

"Have fun." Lilah leaned down and hugged Ben so long the boy began to struggle. "Mo-om."

She straightened, but Ben had picked up on her reluctance, clearly unsure what was supposed to happen next or if he wanted to be part of it.

"We'll have a great time." Owen took

Ben's hand and led him to the rental car. "Have you eaten breakfast?"

"Mommy made me toast and milk, but she said you wanted to have breakfast with me."

"Great. Do you have a favorite place?"

"The eggs-and-potato place."

Their first roadblock. Owen turned back, calling her name. "Lilah?"

She was standing where they'd left her, staring as if she were afraid this was her last glimpse of their son.

"What's the egg-and-potato place?" he asked.

"The Scholar's Lady. Your nav system will take you there, but I can text you the address if you like."

"No, thanks. We'll be fine."

Owen helped Ben into the booster seat. It looked a little tight to him.

"How does that feel, Ben?"

The boy was already inspecting every inch of the car within his reach. The cup holders fascinated him.

"Feels exactly like my other one. I can't move much."

"Perfect. Careful of that cup holder. I think it might break if you tug it hard enough."

"I need a cup," Ben said.

"If you like it that much, I'll have to get one like it for my car at home."

Ben sat back. "Where do you live, Own?"

The name made him smile.

"Tennessee. I live next to a big barn. On a farm with a stream and cows and goats and chickens."

Ben rubbed his nose and mouth, looking wary. "I never seen a goat. And chickens run so fast. On TV they have sharp teeth."

"Beaks," Owen said absently. Vermont had goats and chickens, but he'd bet Ben had never been near anything as fraught with danger as a petting zoo.

He backed himself up. He couldn't second-guess the way Lilah was raising their son. Lots of kids Ben's age didn't associate regularly with farm animals.

"Don't know if I like 'em," Ben said.

"We'll cross that farm when we come to it. Hold on a sec." He got into the car and started the engine. On the screen in the console, he found the navigation system. He hit the icon for voice commands. "Scholar's Lady, Barnesville, Vermont," he said.

A male voice with a New Zealand accent responded. "I will navigate you to the Scholar's Lady in Barnesville, Vermont," the man said.

Owen laughed, and Ben giggled.

"That man talks funny," Ben said. "Why did you pick him?"

"I didn't. The man or woman who rented this car before us chose him," Owen said. "He startled me."

"Me, too. Our car has a lady's voice, but the lady gets mad a lot. Mommy tries out different voices."

"The lady on my car gets mad at me, too. Maybe I'll switch to New Zealand guy."

"What's New Zealand?"

"A country way far from here, where people talk like this guy."

Ben just giggled. Owen pulled away from the curb. Lilah was still glued to the last step on her porch.

He ignored a pang of guilt. For a moment, he saw himself through her eyes, and the self-awareness was unpleasant.

"What do you want to do after we eat?" Owen asked his son, as if he got to hang out with his child all the time.

"Duck bowling."

"Duck bowling?" He made a wild guess. "There's a place called Duckpins across from my hotel. I walked in there last night." And out again when the beer taps began to sing his name.

"Did you practice?" Ben asked.

"I didn't know you'd want to play. I got a hamburger to go."

"I love duck bowling." Kicking his feet, Ben lifted an ecstatic gaze upward and pumped both fists. Then he drooped a little. "Sometimes, the ball goes too far."

"Too far?"

"When I throw the ball, it flies away and hits other people's balls. Or the floor. Really hard."

"Good tip, buddy. Thanks. Maybe we should stop for helmets."

Ben laughed. "Mommy says that, too."

BEN WAS AIMING in the wrong direction, so Owen sprang to catch the ball. Fortunately, his boy always missed to the left, so he'd moved them to the last lane on the end. So far, Ben's throws hadn't been strong enough to bust out the wall.

"You're good at catching," Ben said. "I hit Mommy in the head once. She didn't even cry."

"I might have." Owen could imagine Lilah

pretending everything was okay. "These balls are heavy and fast."

"If I practice, they'll go toward the little pins," Ben said. "Mommy knows things like that."

"Mommy's pretty smart."

"Smartest ever." Ben threw one fist in the air.

His four-year-old pride got to Owen. The little boy clearly considered his mom heroic, and his attachment to her touched Owen. He had to make sure Lilah didn't change her mind about coming to Tennessee because how could he tear these two apart?

"Ben, would you like to visit me at my house?"

"All by myself?" Anxiety pinched his small nose. "Like today?"

"No. Your mom would come with you."

The little boy tossed another ball that veered unexpectedly to the right, but landed in a chair without injuring anyone.

"Do you have toys?" Ben scrambled over a bench to grab the ball back and tried again. It went straight this time and didn't gouge a hole in the floor, despite landing with a heavy thud.

"We could take your toys," Owen said.

"And maybe pick up a few more for you to play with while you're there."

"You got those chickens and goats, too?"

"And cows. They're fun to hang out with. But you can only visit the animals when an adult is with you."

"Adults are big people."

"And a lot of them live near my house. My mom. My sister and one of my brothers. His name is Chad, and he can play football with you."

"Football?" Ben's eyes gleamed as he whispered the word. He looked so happy, he didn't have to say what he was thinking; but then he looked down, clenching his hands together.

"Do you play football, Ben?"

"Mommy doesn't let me."

Owen found it hard to imagine how Lilah could risk her life with Duckpins, and be afraid Ben might get hurt at football.

"If you come visit me with your mom, I can talk to her about football."

"Football," Ben said in another reverent whisper.

There it was. The key to Ben's heart.

Owen scooped the next ball off the return and sent it down the lane, but he wasn't a whole lot better at Duckpins than his boy, and the ball slid off into the gutter. Ben, clearly a fighter, waited no time to make his next competitive throw. Three more tries, and they'd both managed to head a ball and their scores in the right direction.

"Own, can we have a hot dog to celebrate?"

"A hot dog?"

"They'd make us bowl better. I know."

He looked so wise, Owen laughed and gave in. Maybe not the most nutritious lunch, but a celebration indeed. The Duckpins kitchen made great hot dogs.

After they ate, they headed to the day care Ben usually attended while his mom worked. The little boy seemed more comfortable with Owen. He said he wanted to introduce him to everyone, and Owen was even more eager to meet the people who'd be caring for his son during working hours when he was back here with Lilah. Because Owen had to face facts. Ben would spend substantial parts of his life back here with Lilah.

They parked in front of a small Federal-style house, but Owen had to ring a doorbell before a woman in a dark blue dress came to let them in. Smiling at Ben, she held the door.

"Ms. Bantry mentioned you'd be dropping by," she said. "Ben, will you introduce me to your friend?"

"This is Own. He knows my mommy. Own, this lady is in charge of my school."

"Thanks, little buddy." She planted her hands on Ben's shoulders. "I'm Tina Matthews. I run the day care. You'd like to see Ben's class?"

"Owen Gage." He shook the woman's hand. "If you don't mind."

"Ms. Bantry explained." She started down the hall, pulling a set of keys from her pocket. "This house belonged to my great-grandparents. My mother started a school here when I was a child. Sort of homeschooling to an extreme. She had small classes, from K to eighth grade. You know, restrictions and rules are tighter than they used to be, and we've had an influx of families with young children, so I reorganized several years ago and turned the school into a day-care center."

Each room had a half wall of plaster and a half wall of glass, giving a view into the classroom. Lilah would have been drawn to that openness.

"You've no doubt noticed Ben has a wide vocabulary for his age."

"I didn't actually know that," Owen said.

"He's extremely intelligent. This room is his class." She opened the door. "The children have gone outside to play. You can go out to see them if you want, Ben."

"You won't leave, Own?"

"Not without you, buddy." He zipped Ben's coat all the way up and tugged his knit cap over his ears.

Grinning, the boy shot through the door at the back of the classroom. Owen undid his own coat.

"Thank you for seeing me, Tina."

"Not a problem. I understand a parent wants to be sure of his son's care. Let me tell you about him. Ben can handle some books for young readers. He writes his own name and some basic words. He's learning addition."

Owen looked at her. "At four?"

"Nearly five, but we don't push him. We offer him the opportunity to learn at his own pace."

"He's pretty amazing." The surge of pride surprised him, as if he'd had anything to do with Ben's bright curiosity. Genetically, yes, but so far, Ben was a product of Lilah's nurturing.

"He's a lovable child, and he's eager to learn. I hope you'll be able to find a similar type of school for him when he visits your home."

"So do I." But he was doubtful. His brother had just dragged the town's council into the current century long enough to squeeze permission to build a medical clinic. A new day care? Probably not, and he'd never heard of anything this progressive in Bliss.

His conviction to keep Ben in Tennessee wavered. He didn't want his son to have an inferior education just so they could be together.

LILAH HAD SPENT most of the day trying to pretend she wasn't worried Owen would run away with Ben just to make her suffer through an equal amount of time without him. She came home early, hoping they would, as well.

No such luck.

After she wandered through the empty rooms of her home for an hour, she started Ben's favorite spaghetti sauce for dinner. It was Owen's favorite, too, but she wouldn't be admitting she remembered that.

The second they opened the front door, she heard Ben's exaggerated sniffing.

"Spaghetti," he said, then, "No, Own. Let me go."

Her pulse beat a little faster, but she refused to rush out to see what was going on. Fear for her son was part of loving him. Maybe it wouldn't have been if she'd had a different childhood, but she couldn't help being the mom her life had made her. She knew all too well how easily a child could get hurt, despite a careful parent's best intentions. But she didn't want Ben to learn her kind of fear.

"Can I help you with your coat first?" she heard Owen ask her son.

Lilah went to the hall in time to see Owen on his knees, peeling Ben out of his coat and mitts and hat. He barely got the coat off before Ben hurtled toward the kitchen, brandishing a thick piece of drawing paper.

"Mommy, this is my painting. Miss Katie put it on the wall, but she took it off so Owen could help me bring it home."

Lilah swung Ben onto her hip and took the paper from him. Ben had drawn the two of them in front of their house. The house had big windows, like wide, happy eyes. She and Ben were both smiling stick figures with clothing.

The psychologist who'd cared for her would have described it as a happy drawing by a well-adjusted child. Lilah smiled to herself as she looked it over, until she noticed the large brown long-haired dog with huge eyes and sharp teeth.

"A pup," she said. Ben believed if he kept inserting a dog into his life, she'd give in and let him have one.

"He's hungry." Ben tapped the paper twice as Lilah hugged him, walking toward the kitchen. "I would feed him," he said. "All by myself."

She didn't look back at Owen. She didn't want him to see how the day had unsettled her.

"Your pretend dog can sit at the table with us." She kissed the top of Ben's head, breathing in his scent because she'd been starved for the sight of him, the sound of his voice, the feel of his wriggling body in her arms. She was almost tempted to give in on the dog front.

Anything to make sure he loved her best.

She wasn't going to be good at sharing her son. Down the hall, the closet door closed.

Owen finally followed them into the kitchen, brushing his own hair with both hands. The static made his longish curls both stand up and cling to his face.

"He really wants a dog," he said.

"For a long time." She cuddled Ben, who stopped struggling and folded his arms between his body and hers, and buried his head beneath her chin. He always leaned into her like that. She wanted to hug him even harder.

"Own's eating with us?"

"I think so." Owen obviously hadn't managed to tell Ben he was his father today.

"I'd like to," Owen said, and his face, pleading despite the fact he had the whip hand, startled Lilah with his resemblance to her son. "Spaghetti. Smells amazing, Lilah."

"It's Ben's favorite," she said, defensive because she still didn't want him to know she'd remembered.

"Can we help you with anything?" Owen asked.

She wanted to just sit and hold her son. Instead, she set him down and went back to the kitchen. "Nothing left to do," she said. "I've set the table and made the salad and bread. We're ready to eat. You and Ben should wash up."

"Aww, Mom." But Ben looked at Owen and led the way to the bathroom. Their splashing and laughter unsettled Lilah even more. Her boy had missed having a man in his life. He was already bonding with Owen, and she dreaded the day she'd have to leave them together at the airport, or even just at Owen's car, and come home without her son for days or weeks.

The thought sent her back to the kitchen, where she added pasta to the pot of boiling water on the stove. She poured ice water in glasses, set the pitcher in the center of the table and tried to look self-assured.

"You didn't dry those hands," Owen was saying as he danced Ben back into the kitchen with a towel. He drew Ben to the sink and dried his little fingers and dripping-wet palms.

"Thanks." Ben scrambled into his seat at the table.

Lilah made his salad plate and added a slice of garlic bread and served it to him. To her surprise, Owen dished out salad for her and put some on his own plate, and then set them both on the table.

"The pasta isn't ready yet," she said as he peered into the pot of boiling water.

He came back to join them at the table. Ben waited until Owen lifted his fork. They chewed as one man. Lilah closed her eyes, not wanting to see them together.

"You like me, Own."

Lilah jerked in her chair at the head of the table. He'd also inherited his father's habit of speaking bluntly.

"I do like you, Ben. You know why?"

Ben had created the most natural opening for Owen to tell him about himself. Lilah dropped her fork and slid her hands beneath the table, twisting them together.

"Because I'm lovable." Ben gripped his fork like a spear. "Right, Mom?"

"Extremely right," she said, her insides shattering. Her son was about to gain a second loyalty that would last a lifetime.

"You are lovable," Owen said, "but I'd care for you, no matter what, because you're my little boy."

The fork stopped in midair, pointing across the table at Owen's face. "Huh?"

Owen's confidence didn't waver. It had to be an act, but it was convincing. He looked happy, not anxious about how Ben was going to react. She felt sick.

"You are my son," Owen said. "I'm your dad."

"I don't have a daddy. Mommy says so."

Owen still didn't falter. He gazed at Ben's face with a loving expression of reassurance. "Just this once your mom made a mistake. I am your dad, and I always will be."

"But I'm a big boy now. I didn't see you when I was a baby."

Lilah's eyes burned as her son seemed to panic. She reached for his hand, trying to make it seem as if this situation only rated a little bit of comfort, and she wasn't scared. She couldn't help feeling guilty.

She'd love to believe she hadn't set up this well of pain for her child the moment Owen walked away from rehab.

"Where's he been, Mommy?"

"Owen's been at his house. He didn't know about you."

"If I had known, I would have been with you," Owen said, and Lilah's guilt increased.

She hadn't been wrong. She refused to consider the possibility. Owen reached for Ben's hand, but Ben pulled away from both of them. He threaded his fingers together in his lap, looking down.

"We had a nice time today, didn't we?" Owen asked.

Ben nodded, looking up with suspicion in

the ice-blue eyes he'd inherited from his father. Owen had told her once that his father and all his siblings shared the same color.

"Well, we'll get to have fun together from now on. We'll have good times and bad times, but we'll learn more about each other with every day that passes, and I can't wait, Ben."

"Do I have to call you Daddy?"

Lilah bit her lower lip and leaned forward. Trying to save her son, she'd given him grief and confusion. And she still didn't know if Owen was capable of being a good father to Ben. "I thought you wanted a daddy like your friends," she said.

"How do I know he's my daddy?"

"I can help you with that." Owen pulled two small photos out of his shirt pocket, along with the gift tag her parents' assistant had draped around the neck of every wine bottle he'd sent to the gallery's artists. Owen set down the tag, folded to display only Ben's photo. Beside it, he lined up two pictures of himself, one at a beach, holding up a bright yellow bucket, the other of him perched on a dirty white picket fence, his face more solemn. "Daddies and sons sometimes look alike," Owen said. "Those two pictures are me when I was your age, and you and I look almost exactly the same."

Ben looked even more confused. He turned toward Lilah. "I don't get it, Mommy."

"You know when people say I look like my mother?"

"Yeah."

"Owen is saying you look like him, and you really do."

"But I don't want to call him Daddy. I'll call him his name. Own."

"Sounds perfect," Owen said, sounding relieved. He must have thought Ben didn't want a dad, or if he did, he didn't want this stranger who'd shown up on his doorstep.

"We're going to Tennessee," Lilah said, startling herself, as well as Owen and Ben.

"That place where Own lives?"

She nodded. "He wants you to meet his family because they're also your family. I want to go with you because I'll miss you too much if you go on your own."

Water bubbled over the pasta saucepan to sizzle on the stovetop. Lilah sprang to her feet. "I may have to start this over."

"It'll be fine." Owen appeared beside her. "Looks good."

She had a feeling he was thanking her for

making this sojourn in Tennessee look like her idea. She didn't want his thanks. She looped a piece of pasta on a fork and tasted. "It is good. Ready, Ben?"

"I'm done with my salad."

Owen collected the salad plates from the table and took them to the sink. He picked up the top plate on a stack of three for the pasta. His frozen gaze had melted a little when he looked into hers.

"Thank you," he said.

"Fighting you is pointless." She couldn't pretend she'd been wrong, and if she let him see she had any awareness she'd cheated him of these years with Ben, he'd grab back all the time he could. "We're not moving to Tennessee."

Owen glanced at Ben, but answered with a smile. "We'll work out a custody schedule. I don't mind flying to pick him up and bring him back."

She resented him all over again for acting as if he were being perfectly amenable. "You are not human."

He laughed, but the sound lifted all the hairs on her arms, while Ben watched them, his mouth open.

"You might have a point," Owen said in a

tone only she could hear. "And I still can't believe you took Ben from me. But I'm going to make sure I make things different for him."

CHAPTER FIVE

"I DON'T WANT you to go, Own." In the bright sunlight flooding into Lilah's living room, Ben clung to Owen with all his might, legs and arms wrapped around his newfound father.

"I don't want to leave either," Owen said in a voice gone thready with emotion. His face was taut with sadness, his eyes closed as if he wanted to keep Lilah out of his private suffering.

He was probably right. She didn't trust this instant love he seemed to feel for Ben, and he blamed her for the years he'd lost with his son. It didn't matter that she'd believed she was making the best choice for Ben.

"Come on, buddy." She tried to peel Ben away, but both males locked their arms around each other. Despite herself, her throat tightened.

She'd never wanted to hurt either of them. That hadn't been her goal.

Finally, Owen eased Ben to the ground. "You know what?" He straightened, blinking as hard as his son. "It'll only be a few days. Seven, before I come back to get you. And then we'll have lots of time together, and you'll meet your uncles and aunt and your grandma. They'll be so glad to see you."

"And the goats?" Ben asked. "You said the goats are nice?"

"The goats will be your best friends."

"Okay." Ben slapped his forehead with sweet, little boy exaggeration. "Wait, Own. I forgot something."

Without further explanation, he bolted toward the stairs. Owen looked at Lilah.

"I'm mystified," she said.

He took a quick glance at his watch. "I hate to leave, but I have to make the flight."

"You know, I could bring him, myself. There's no need for you to come back."

"I want Ben to know he matters to me."

"I think he'll realize that anyway."

"He'll remember how he learned about me and the rest of his family all his life. I want him to know I'll always take the extra step for him."

Unspoken was his accusation that she'd made those extra steps necessary. Lilah swallowed, pretending she didn't feel the slight-est guilt.

Ben skidded into the room, brandishing a piece of white drawing paper. He held it up for Owen. "This is me and you, duck bowl-ing."

Two happy stick figures in clothing were flinging balls at objects she didn't recognize, but the drawing was so full of happiness she smiled, until she met Owen's gaze.

His eyes looked fierce. She couldn't tell if he was touched or upset or a confused mix-ture of both. He lifted Ben in his arms and held him with tenderness that rocked her. What had she done?

And yet, she'd do it again.

OWEN WAITED IN his car until the last of his family strolled into the Pizza Keller just off the square in Bliss. He didn't want to re-peat the story to each new arrival, and he hadn't trusted himself to wait in the restau-rant alone, with the bar at hand and his worst fears taunting him about how bad he could be for Ben.

He got out as the clock on the courthouse in the center of the square tolled seven times. Snow crunched beneath his boots, reflecting the colored Christmas lights the town had yet to take down.

He crossed the sidewalk, nodding to a neighbor who greeted him by name as she walked past. Laughter and a whiff of delicious pizza aromas drifted out as he opened the door. No one had ever risked that kind of laughter around his family's dinner table when he was growing up. Dinner then had been a quiet, tense, often terrifying affair. Knowing Ben, loving him already, had somehow revived old memories Owen thought he'd long since repressed.

He shook himself mentally and waved off the hostess who came to meet him. "I hear them in the back already," he said and took the menu she held out to him.

As if to make up for all those quiet years, the Gages were now at least two decibels louder than everyone else in the joint. His mother stepped out of the back alcove, carrying an empty water pitcher.

"Hi, son," she said. "Let me just get this refilled."

"Mom, you don't work here." He took the pitcher, passed it to the server headed their way and turned Suzannah Gage back toward their small room. Noah and his girlfriend, Emma, were seated at the far end of a long bench, eyes only for each other. Owen's brother Chad was going through breadsticks as if no one had fed him in a decade, and his sister, Celia, had her tablet out and her fingers flashing over the keyboard.

"Sorry I'm late," Owen said.

"We saw you in the truck," Noah told him.

"Lurking," said Emma. Apparently, they were aware of the rest of the world after all.

"What's up?" Noah asked.

"What's your big secret?" Emma peered at him. "A girlfriend? A new job? Because you can't leave Bliss until you finish the barn."

"Clinic," Suzannah said. She glanced at the younger woman. "Sounds classier. You don't want to tell your father he'll be bringing his brand-new baby girl to have a checkup in a barn."

"Right." Emma's father had helped Noah push the clinic through the town council, just as his own infant daughter was born. "We need to keep him on our side," she said with a sweet smile, and snatched a breadstick out of the red plastic cup in front of her before Chad could grab it. They laughed at each other as if they were already family.

Celia's head snapped up. "Are you drinking again?" Her blue eyes were a little dazed from too much work. "Did you come to confess? I don't mean to be blunt, but I could really use the diary of a struggling, yet recovering addict in my psych research project."

"Is that what you're working on?" he asked.

"Making notes." An overachiever, like Noah. Her class didn't start until the end of the month.

"Thanks for your vote of confidence," Owen said, "but, no." Not that being in the middle of this family inquisition didn't tempt him. He loved those tall red cups. He loved the foam of beer climbing to the lip. "But I have a few things to tell you."

"Should we worry?" Suzannah eased back onto the bench on Emma and Noah's side.

Owen slipped in beside Celia.

"Sorry," his sister said. "But you know what you have to lose if you give up on your sobriety again."

"Lay off, Celia." He squeezed her wrist in an affectionate warning. He couldn't take it just now.

Chad offered him a breadstick, and Owen couldn't help laughing. Chad had the metabolism and the extracurricular-sports schedule to treat his troubles with food. The rest of the family laughed, as well, and for once, he didn't feel like an outsider.

"I'll wait for the pizza," he said. The server came back. Looking harried, he eyed Owen with his pen at the ready. "I'd like a tea, please."

"Okay. Anyone ready to order?"

Chad jumped right in. "Man Meets Meat special."

"Owen, will you share a mushroom and cheese and arugula with me?" Celia asked.

He nodded, and she smiled at the server, who blinked and fell a little in love with her. Owen grinned at the poor guy.

Noah and Emma said "Pepperoni" in tandem as they always did.

Suzannah shut her menu and looked into the shadows of the beamed cathedral ceiling, reeling off her memorized list of ingredients. "Artichoke hearts, feta, mushroom, and hot Italian sausage." She beamed at Owen as the server hurried away. "You can share mine, too."

Cleanup. That's what he was around here. Never stepped out on his own that his family knew of. Never made his own mark, except in ways that shamed them all.

So he didn't know how to tell them about Ben. Would they believe his unbelievable explanation about Lilah, or would they assume he'd abandoned his child?

"I have a son," he said, and the miniconversations, already building up sound and steam, ceased immediately.

"Huh?" Emma seemed confused.

"That's not right." Celia gripped her tablet for comfort.

"Oh, no," his mother said, but at least she didn't pretend everything was all right, and they'd all be fine, her MO since she'd finally excised his abusive, destructive father from their midst.

"Are you okay?" Noah asked, still the oldest brother, still the first to step up and take care of them.

Chad kept chowing down on the bread sticks.

Owen cleared his throat. He glanced back at the front of the restaurant. Where was his tea? "He's almost four years old. I met his mother when she was handling some furniture I built to sell in her family's gallery in Manhattan."

"At last," Emma said, cutting him off. "I have been dying to tell someone about that

furniture and the other pieces you've done."
She turned to Noah. "He built my stepmother's cradle for her baby."

"You knew about my son?" Owen asked.
Emma was his friend, more like a second sister. He trusted her not to keep secrets from
him. She was the only person in this town
who never seemed surprised to find him
sober.

"No, I was being thoughtless." Crestfallen,
she sat back, flexing her fingers on the table
ledge. "I just meant I wish you'd be more
open about your work. That cradle was beautiful. But I had no idea you had a son. How
did you find out?"

"It sounds ridiculous. The family who
owns the gallery sent all the artists who show
there a gift of wine." He'd expected their
worried reactions. "I poured it out," he said,
and the memory of the rich, red liquid swirl-
ing down the drain made his mouth water.
"But they left a gift tag that had a photo of
their family on the bottle. Ben's mom—Ben
is his name. Ben's mom is the daughter of
the guy who started the gallery. She broke up
with me when she found out she was pregnant because I told her I didn't want to stop
drinking."

"Owen." Celia sounded disappointed.

"I know. It's probably the stupidest thing I've done in a long line of stupid mistakes. I didn't know what I was throwing away. I just thought I had to be honest with Lilah, and I couldn't stop. Back then."

"But now?" his mother asked.

"You know I'm not drinking, Mom. Not since Thanksgiving, when I started working on the clinic." His eyes drifted toward the polished mahogany bar and the upright beer tap handles. He didn't tell his family that Lilah had been his drinking buddy. Funny he felt a need to protect her from that much, at least. "Lilah said she didn't want to see me anymore if I couldn't dry out. I assumed she meant it."

"You must not have been too attached to each other if that was all it took to keep you away," Celia said.

His sister had been talking med school, same as Noah. If she got in, she'd need to learn about bedside manner.

"Or you were so attached you decided you wouldn't beg her to take you back." His mother's empathy also put him off.

He wasn't about to bring up the fact that Lilah had accused him of being like his father. He still wondered himself if that was true, and he couldn't stand how easy his honesty about his own past had made it for her to choose the weapon that kept him away.

"Son?" Suzannah said. "Is there anything I can do?"

His brothers and sister took their mother's change of attitude since their parents' divorce at face value. He knew how easy it was to fall back into old habits, and he never managed to believe completely in his mother's reform.

"I've lost four years with Ben, so I'm forcing his mother to bring him here." Might as well admit he'd blackmailed Lilah. They'd soon realize this wasn't going to be some joyous reunion.

"Forcing?" Suzannah sat back, her eyes a little too wide. "How, exactly are you doing that? Owen, I don't want you acting like your—"

She faltered but left the word *father* unspoken. Which was a good thing. The accusation was too close to his own suspicions about himself.

"That doesn't sound like you." Celia shut the cover on her tablet. "Why would you do that, Owen?"

"Because I loved Ben the second I saw

him, and I can't throw away another day with him." He looked at his sister, and for once, he hid nothing.

"Doesn't this woman know you're staying sober now?" Emma asked.

He let himself smile. Good old Emma. She refused to believe the worst. "I've told her I'm trying, but she has doubts, and you can't really blame her."

"Why don't we know about her? Were you ashamed to bring her down here?" Suzannah frowned. "What's wrong with her?"

"She did come down, Mom. I just never introduced her to people here. We didn't have a lot of time together because she worked for her family in New York, and my place was here. I didn't want to move."

"Maybe you also didn't want anyone to know about your private life," Celia said.

He glanced at her. "When you take your nose out of your books, you're observant."

"This Lilah must not be. If she cared about you then, she must see you're sober now."

They were all so desperate to believe in him. Determined to trust the promises he'd made after the last bender only a few weeks ago.

"I guess I wasn't sober a lot when we were

together." He looked at Noah, who'd persuaded the council he could get the clinic
done without drinking. "I am now," he said.
"And I'm going to stay this way."

Suzannah reached for Owen's hand. The
moment for closeness had passed, but he let
her hang on because she needed to feel she
could comfort him. He was willing to let
her feel better. "You can promise her all you
want, but she might not be able to believe
you. She's probably anxious for her son. You
can't blame her since she saw you in those
darker days."

She sounded as if Lilah had filled her in,
but no one knew how many times he'd promised himself he wouldn't drink again. "The
first time I actually went to rehab, I did it
for her."

"Which is why it didn't work," Noah said.
"So she tried to force you to stop drinking,
and now you're forcing her to share your
son."

"When you put it like that, I realize how
ruthless I'm being." Owen recalled Lilah's
frightened expression as she'd watched him
drive away with Ben for their day out.

"I'd do the same, and I defy anyone at this

table to say he or she would walk away from a child. Ben's mother wouldn't do it," Noah said.

"That's why she's coming with him," Owen said. "At first, I wanted to just take him with me, but I was angry. When I realized Ben would suffer without her, I told her I was staying there until they were both ready to come, but she asked me to trust her not to run for Canada."

"From Manhattan?" Chad asked. "I'd be tempted."

"From Vermont."

Chad whistled. "You should go back up there before you lose your chance to be a good father."

"You think I will be?"

"I know you." Chad's conviction was encouraging. "You couldn't make rehab work and I know you don't like AA, but you love us enough to try doing it on your own. It may mean you're beating up pieces of the barn at midnight, but you just have to keep beating them up instead of drinking."

Everyone, including Owen, stared at his little brother. He'd thought his drinking battles were private. He looked from face to face. They all seemed a little panicked.

Chad actually blushed. "I run sprints at

night after the track at school is empty." His tone implied he had his own demons, but no sledgehammer. "What's this about you making furniture? I wondered why I heard you out working so late at night before you and Mom donated the barn for the clinic site."

"I can't believe you didn't tell me about that," Noah said to Emma, as if he wondered if there were more he didn't know.

"My stepmother, Megan, swore me to secrecy. That's how she met my father. He told her he was from Bliss, and she asked him if he knew Owen. Megan bought one of Owen's cribs when she knew she was having the baby, and I saw it at their house just before Thanksgiving. Dad's kept the secret longer than I have."

"Ben will be here within a week." Owen dragged them back to the topic. "Mom, I'd like Lilah to stay with you. She wants to be near Ben, which I understand, but I don't want her staying with me."

"I didn't know you cared about gossip," Suzannah said.

"I care about Ben. He can't think Lilah and I will ever be together as a couple. He's already been in a day care where children live with both parents, and I'd hate it if he started hoping he could have that, too, now that I've found him."

Suzannah touched her heart.

"Don't get all sentimental," he said. "How could I ever trust a woman who hid my child from me? Just tell me you'll take Lilah in and give her a room."

"I may understand what she did, but you're my son. How am I supposed to be polite to this woman?" Suzannah asked.

"By remembering that she's my son's mother, and all these problems are between us."

"She was not generous enough to remember you were her son's father."

"Which is why she needs to stay with you while I get to know Ben, and he gets used to having two parents who live separately."

Suzannah hesitated. "If she doesn't mind staying with your mother, I'll take her in, but how long is this odd little family grouping going to last?"

"Well, I can't go to Vermont until after I finish the clinic."

"How long can she stay here? How does she make a living?"

"She runs a gallery that's part of her family's business. She sells antiques and art pieces. She's fond of the work I do, and I think she'll find other artisans in the mountains, along with pieces in the little shops all through the area."

"Are you sure we aren't too rustic for this woman? Haven't you seen that crib Emma was talking about?"

"Mom, help me out. I built it."

"All right. I said she could stay. I find it pretty questionable that you have this whole side business of carving and cabinetmaking, and you never told any of us. As if you really were ashamed of us."

"I figured you all would doubt me."

Noah grinned an apology, as if he agreed it was true. Owen gave him a rueful smile in return. He hadn't meant to whine, but not one of them would have been surprised if they'd had to come pluck him off the barn roof, singing boozy songs while he toasted the next full moon. Why would they believe he had a successful furniture-making business?

"Why are you doing all the contracting work if you can sell your furniture?" Chad asked.

"I need contracting to afford to do the work

I love." He looked up, seeing the parade of pizzas coming. "Thank goodness. Let's eat."

LATER THAT NIGHT, at home in the small cabin his great-grandfather had built on the property, Owen settled with a cup of coffee in the recliner that was his one extravagance. He picked up his phone and stared at the icons lined up along the top. He could put off calling Lilah by dealing with work issues. Those matters, he understood.

He called Lilah.

"Owen," she said by way of answering.

"We need to talk logistics. I thought I could fly back up and help you drive down. You'll want a car."

"How long do you plan on us staying there? I didn't expect to need my own car. I thought I'd rent."

"It's going to be a few months," he said. "I'm at the beginning of this project."

"I can't stay in Tennessee for months. Are you crazy?"

"I'm determined to know my son, and—"

"I stole years from you. I know. Keep beating that drum, but I am not living in Tennessee for the foreseeable future."

"That's fine by me." His voice deepened as

his throat squeezed shut. "I'll bring Ben back to you after I finish my work on the clinic."

There was silence. Thick with anger and frustration. Hers and his, but Lilah's only annoyed him more. She never realized what she'd done, but he was willing to remind her if he had to.

"I'm not leaving Ben," she said, and her surrender was there in her voice.

"I'll fly up," he said. "You can come by plane with Ben, and I'll drive your car down, if that's okay with you."

"It's not," she said. "You can fly down with Ben so he doesn't have to spend two days in a car. I'll drive myself."

Even to be with Ben she was too prickly to accept a favor.

"Whatever you say, Lilah."

"It's not what I say. We're doing everything your way. But don't think I'll put up with this forever."

She was so desperate to keep her past quiet, she'd let him blackmail her. He couldn't imagine the pain she must fear of having her kidnapping all over social media. She knew what it was like to face public scrutiny, and this time she had Ben to think of.

His conscience made him uncomfortable

for a second. Then he remembered. Four years of Ben's life. He could never get one second back.

"I'll send you my flight details," he said and punched the button to end the call.

CHAPTER SIX

LILAH HAD ONE GOAL. To remove Owen Gage from Ben's life.

That shouldn't be difficult. He'd exited hers without looking back until her brother had put that photo on the gift tag. And who sent wine to a guy like Owen anyway? Tim had known better.

She couldn't imagine how shocked Owen must have been to see a face so like his own on a Christmas gift. But he'd never asked himself why she cut him so completely out of her life after he left rehab. He'd never even considered she must have had a vital reason to insist on rehab.

She'd been happy with their long-distance relationship for two years. It had started out as just fun. She'd never drunk the way he had. She'd known how to say enough, a feat Owen couldn't master, but she'd told herself she was just keeping him company as he continued to bend his elbow, and she'd started on water or coffee.

After she'd realized Ben was coming, she hadn't let herself care about Owen anymore. She'd given him the chance to get sober, and he'd failed. She needed to keep her son safe. That was what moms did.

So the morning after Owen left Vermont, she made a few calls. One to her lawyer. One to her parents, warning them that she hadn't been entirely honest about Owen's feelings toward their child. Oddly, Lilah's mother hadn't understood the decision she'd made and she'd ended the call with a frosty silence.

Lilah never appreciated her parenting decisions being questioned, especially not one as important as this.

Her last call was to Tennessee. It might be a hopeless cause, but she wanted to know how the children's services office felt about a known alcoholic who blackmailed his child's mother into giving him visitation.

"We've had no complaints about Mr. Gage," the caseworker she spoke to said.

"He has no other children."

"He has no record with the authorities either."

"Do you live in Bliss? How could you not

have heard of Owen Gage and his drinking?" Lilah sounded desperate, but she had to make them check him out.

"And you've never allowed this gentleman contact with his son?"

"No, because I never considered him safe for my child. He went to rehab while I was pregnant and celebrated his release by getting drunk and coming to my home to tell me drinking mattered more than me."

That much was true. That night had convinced her.

"Did he threaten you?"

"No, but he made sure I knew he didn't intend to stop abusing alcohol. What if he drinks while he has my son with him? What if my son has an accident or becomes ill, and Owen is too drunk to drive him to a doctor?"

"We can't take children from parents based solely on a series of what-ifs. If we did that, no child would live in his own home."

If that was the county's philosophy on child welfare, the woman was already on Owen's side.

"Look, I'm not trying to paint him as a child abuser. I simply need to know if he's done anything that would make your office or me think he might be too dangerous for my son to live with him."

"I've taken your information, and I'll let you know what our investigation uncovers."

"Thank you."

She ended the call with a shudder. Contacting the authorities gave her no delicious sense of revenge. She felt as if she'd betrayed Owen as the conversation replayed in her head. It was so humiliating, she hardly slept for the next week.

The night before he was due to pick up Ben, she packed for her son, who questioned her every move.

"Why am I going to visit Own?" He pulled his stuffed giraffe from the small suitcase. "I like here."

"I like here best, too, but Owen wants to get to know you better." She swallowed, choking on the words that would reassure her son. "You like him, don't you? He's a good man, and he'll take good care of you. I'll be down there as soon as I can make it. Two days. No more."

"But you come with me, Mommy."

"I need to drive, baby. I don't know how long we'll be in Tennessee, and we'll need our car. You'll have a good time with Owen. You did when he was here?"

"Yes. Will he let me play with his goats?"

She hesitated, imagining a herd of goats all raring to head butt her son. "If you're careful with them."

Ben already liked Owen, and she loved her son. She didn't want him to be afraid.

Owen showed up at the appointed time on the appointed day to pick up her son. The doorbell rang like a death knell, and Ben darted past his little bag and backpack waiting by the front door. He tugged at the door handle, not yet having mastered the dead bolt that was still out of his reach.

Lilah turned the dead bolt and covered his hand with hers on the doorknob. "Let me help you, baby."

"I can do it, Mommy."

She helped anyway and barely managed not to wrap him in her arms. They opened the door together, and her breath caught as she looked at Owen. It was like looking at a stranger. When he'd arrived before, she'd been so upset she wasn't sure she'd really seen him.

Tall and lean, but broader than he'd been when they were together. He was almost thirty now and seemed more mature. His dark hair was neatly cut. His ice-blue eyes were free of dark shadows. He'd cleaned up for this new turn in his life, and he took her breath away.

Until she remembered the times he'd cleaned up before. Let a problem arise, or boredom strike. That would be Owen's true test.

"Lilah," he said, his gaze on their son with the hunger of a father who'd been denied four years of hugs and laughter and tears.

"Come in." She stood back to make room for him.

He scooped up Ben, who crowed his name. "Own." And pressed his hands to Owen's face. "You came back," he said.

"I'll always come back for you." Owen kissed Ben's forehead. "You can count on me."

"Mommy says I'll have a good time with you."

"You will. And my mom will be there. So will your aunt and uncles."

"And the goats?"

"And chickens and cows, and a dog or two."

"Okay." Ben scrambled a little, the universal toddler's request to be put down. "I'm ready to go now."

Owen twisted back the cuff of his jacket and checked the time. "We do need to leave soon. I'm not sure of the traffic. Sorry to be so quick, Lilah."

She dragged her gaze from his and tried her best to look cheerful. "Ben." She knelt beside her child, plucking his jacket from where she'd left it, draped across his suitcase.

"Mommy, are you crying?"

She'd smile if her face broke. "Not a bit. You have a lot to learn about Owen, and I'm excited you get to spend some time with him. Hold out your hands."

After she got his arms in his sleeves, she put gloves on him. "You'll remember all this, Owen? You'll make sure he's warm."

"And that he eats, and I'll check he's covered up in bed before I go to sleep."

That brought his mother to mind. He hadn't said great things about her before, and she'd be caring for Ben while Owen worked. Maybe she was the one the child services office should look into.

"Ben, run upstairs and get your coloring books. You'll want them on the plane."

"Can't, in gloves."

She pulled them off again.

"Hurry, buddy," Owen said. "We can't hang around too long, or we'll be late."

"I'm fast."

Lilah leaned toward Owen. "You won't leave him alone with your mother?"

"My mother's changed, Lilah. I told you before she's not like she was when I was a kid, and she won't let Ben get hurt."

"She let your father hurt you and your brothers and sister."

"That was a long time ago, and she's still making up for it—she volunteered to look after Ben while I work. My sister will be there for part of the time, too."

"But your mother will be Ben's major caregiver."

"Call her tonight, Lilah. Talk to her. If you don't trust her, I'll deal with it." He looked at his watch again. "But I have to take Ben now, or we'll miss that flight."

"I don't want him to go."

"I won't hurt him," Owen said, his voice husky. He reached for her hand, and his touch was as gentle as his words. "You could have flown with us."

She eased her hand away, not trusting herself. Even though a kinder, gentler Owen would be the best thing that could happen to Ben, she couldn't let her guard down. She'd had Ben's safety in her hands since he was born, and she wasn't ready or able to give up control.

"It's better to give the two of you time alone without me as a buffer. I have to make one last stop at the shop, and by the time I get to Tennessee, you and Ben will know each other better. I can't change this, but I don't have to like giving you my son."

"Our son. He's my boy, too." He moved away from her. "Ben." He raised his voice, and they both heard footsteps running overhead.

"I got crayons and pens." Clutching them with one arm to his chest, along with his big coloring book, Ben held on to the bannister and came downstairs.

Owen took the items from him. "I'll put these in my bag in the car," he said. "Say goodbye to your mom."

"Bye, Mommy." Ben hugged her tight, and began to cry. "I miss you already," he said.

"I miss you, too." The teardrops on his thick eyelashes hurt her, but she smiled again, determined to make him feel safe. After she maneuvered his hands back into his gloves, she hugged him tight once more. "I love you. Owen will take good care of you."

"And you can call your mom anytime," Owen said. "You'll see her again in a couple of days." Despite all the anger between them, the kindness in his tone reassured Lilah just a little.

"Where's Tommy?" Ben asked.

"His giraffe," she said to Owen. "He's in your backpack. You and he can take a nap on the plane."

"Okay. You call me, too, Mommy?"

"I sure will."

She turned him toward Owen, and Ben put his hand in his father's. Owen took her hand, too, and squeezed. His drawn expression as he tried to deal with Ben's second thoughts offered her a moment's hope that he would change his mind, but he led her son over the threshold. She wished she could go with them as far as the rental car waiting outside, but if she did, she'd never let her son get in it.

Instead, she waved as Owen tucked Ben into a seat just like the one in her own vehicle. Ben was still waving as Owen got in the driver's side and pulled smoothly away from the curb. Just like that, she learned how hard it was to share her son.

She must have been crazy to think she could let him go off with Owen alone. And why did she need her car in Tennessee anyway? She slammed the front door shut and ran to her computer to book a flight.

DARKNESS HAD CLOAKED the mountain by the time Owen drove his son to the cabin on land his family had owned for generations. Ben slept peacefully in the booster seat, his eyelashes brushing his cheeks, his mouth slightly puckered, as if he had a thought he needed to share.

Owen passed his mother's inn, pale in the moonlight, its sunny yellow clapboards a faint glimmer amongst aged trees. Lights shone in the barn he was converting to be used as an urgent-care center for the remote resort town of Bliss.

He'd left his crews framing the new layout. Sometime this week, they'd start the drywall. This job was Owen's last chance to live a normal life again. He feared failure, that he'd take the drink that beckoned every day. He'd had so many spectacular failures that his neighbors and family took it as a given that work was only a break from drinking for him.

But his focus now lay with the boy in his backseat. Ben made everything else make sense. Owen had to do a good job with his son and on finishing this project to gain respect in his hometown. He wanted to be what he'd never had. A good father.

His conscience prickled. Did a good father blackmail his child's mother into sharing custody?

He glanced at the glow of lights from the inn in his rearview mirror. The son of Odell and Suzannah Gage did what he had to, to survive.

The inn fell into darkness, and the barn lights dimmed as he followed the curving road to the cabin.

Someone had replaced the bulb beside the front door. Often, with his own home, it was a case of "Contractor, heal thyself." He did careful work for all his clients, but he tended to put off working on his own house, including small tasks like replacing lightbulbs and hanging curtains over the kitchen windows.

Several images of Lilah's cozy home passed through his mind. The kitchen, with its smells of apple pie and cinnamon. The snowflake-shaped place mats she left on the table and breakfast counter, appliqued with boy things, like trucks and horses and heavy machinery.

He parked in the driveway. He'd never built himself a garage, despite the often treacherous winter weather. Maybe now was the time to take care of that, too. Lilah wouldn't love the idea of Ben tramping through the snow and mud and ice to get to his car.

Lilah wasn't going to enjoy sleeping at his mother's inn while he and Ben occupied the cabin.

At least she wouldn't be a thousand miles away. For Ben's sake.

Owen got out of the car and eased the back door open. Ben stirred, but only a little. Despite being unfamiliar with the restraining seat's fastenings, Owen managed to ease his son, still sleeping, from the car. Ben burrowed into Owen's chest, and Owen covered the little boy's face with his hand to keep the cold wind whistling through Bliss Peak at bay.

He fumbled with the key and opened the door, switched on the lights, and discovered his mother had been in the house. She'd placed afghans over the couches, added a small green children's table and matching chairs in primary colors, just the right size for Ben. He could sit and color there, or eat his meals, or maybe build one of the wooden train sets she'd managed to save from Owen's childhood.

One of them was waiting neatly in the center of the table, the box bound with different shades of duct tape.

A basket of fruit and homemade jams and canned tomatoes and green beans waited on the kitchen counter. One of her apple pies, all frilly crust and delicious scents, sat beside the basket on a glass trivet.

"I'm hungry, Own."

Startled, Owen looked into his son's face. Ben's trust got him right in the gut. Lilah hadn't poisoned him against his father. "I think we have food." Owen hugged him and then set him on the wide, plank floor. "Let's see."

"Like pie," Ben said, sniffing with a pointed look at the counter.

"Sounds good, but we should have a sandwich, or—something—first." He wasn't the world's best chef, but he'd borrow one of his mother's cookbooks. He went to the fridge and opened the door.

His mom had been there, too. She'd left sliced ham and a sweet potato soufflé she only made at holidays. A lettuce and vegetable salad of many colors and textures glistened in a bowl, and she'd stacked two other glass bowls covered with plastic lids.

"Own?"

He turned. Ben was struggling with the zipper, which was half up one side of his jacket, completely down on the other. "Buddy, what do we do about that?"

He tried first with the zipper, but that didn't work.

"I pull it over my head," Ben said. "Bad jacket."

"Good idea, though." They shared a giggle that chipped away at the tension as Ben's head emerged in a halo of rumpled curls.

"I'm really hungry." Ben went to the open fridge. "Look, cookies." He peered up again. "Why do you keep your cookies in here?"

"I don't know. Because my mom did. Your mother doesn't do that?"

"I don't think so," Ben said. "We eat them too fast. I like cookies."

Owen grinned. "We'll try those out later. Let me show you the bathroom. You wash your hands, and I'll start dinner. After that, we'll unload the car and get ready for bed."

He'd been wrong about his mother. She'd learned to care for her children, even if the effort was a decade or so late. He could count on her now, and he could learn from her, how to make sure Ben knew he could always count on him.

But he was wrong about quickly getting his son ready for bed. They ate their warmed-up dinner of ham and potatoes and buttery peas from last summer's garden. Ben somehow talked him into a sliver of pie and half a chocolate-butterscotch-macadamia-nut cookie for dessert.

Bath time flooded the one bathroom in the cabin. Ben refused help, and Owen counted himself lucky that his boy didn't fall down or drown in the tub. Ben told him, "Mommy always makes me take a shower, but I like bubble baths."

After he was dried and wearing some sort of superhero jammies, he decided against bedtime.

"I'm not tired, Own. I want to play trains." He sat on the yellow chair at the little table and began to unpack the train.

Owen stared at him, flummoxed. It was

getting late, but Owen didn't want to force Ben to go to bed. The little guy was alone with a stranger, who happened to be his father. He didn't know this new place, and he probably missed his mother.

Asking him if he missed Lilah might be a mistake.

"Okay. We'll put the tracks together. Then we have to go to bed."

Ben looked up from the box, which smelled a little musty. "You have to go to bed? My mommy doesn't go to bed until she wants to. What's your bedtime?"

"After yours, so I can make sure you're comfy and asleep."

"Maybe, after we play trains."

Owen felt a little queasy. He didn't want to be the heavy, but he didn't want to let Ben run all over him either. He'd spent his childhood balancing between no rules and bouts of tyranny. He'd hoped to give Ben consistency. But how did a man treat his son consistently when he didn't know him?

"Careful. That box is torn, and the tape will stick to you."

"You like trains, too, Own? Do you have more?"

"I do like trains. My mom found this one. She brought it over for you."

"Does your mom live here?" Ben looked around the quiet house.

Owen kept it clean, but it positively sparkled tonight. Suzannah had cleaned the TV screen. There were fresh vacuum marks in the rug. "She lives in her own house. We passed it when we were driving in."

"Can I see it tomorrow?"

"I want you to. You can meet my whole family. They're your family, too."

"I have an uncle and a grandma and a grandpa. They're in New York."

Owen began piecing the wooden track together. "I know. I met them before you were born."

"Mommy and I visit them sometimes. I never saw you there."

"I probably visited them when you were at home in Vermont." After his business with Bantry Galleries became strictly business. And everyone in Lilah's family had kept the secret of Ben—whether intentionally or not, he didn't know. Maybe, if he'd asked about Lilah, someone would have spoken up, but he'd been too hurt by her accusations that he was like his father. And he had kept drinking.

He'd made sure her reasons for sending him away hadn't been completely wrong. He had to stop being angry with Lilah.

Owen and Ben finished the tracks and then set up the train cars. Ben found a couple of trees and a station house in the box. Owen made a note to order more trains and accessories after he got Ben to bed.

That didn't happen easily. They went upstairs to the small loft that Owen had turned into a bedroom. His mother had worked magic, hanging fabric clouds and sails from the overhead beams, layering Ben's bed in pillows shaped like cars and a puppy and a kitten. She'd added a small rocker and another table.

Ben climbed into the big rocker that now sat on a rag rug Owen remembered from his own grandmother's breakfast room. All those years, his mother had seemed out of touch with reality, but she'd managed to preserve bits of their past.

"Read me a book, Own," Ben said.

Owen picked up one of the Golden Books he'd rescued from a box in the barn. Then he scooped up Ben and sat, with his son in his lap. He tried to keep his voice steady but soon found his throat tightening as he read about the little steamboat's trip to the sea. He could never reclaim all those days he'd missed of his son's childhood.

"You sound funny, Own."

"Must be some dust in this book." He faked a cough and pulled himself together. He felt full of joy, and yet he couldn't ignore the ache. They read two more books before Owen insisted on putting Ben in his soft, warm bed. The little boy wore a brave look as he chewed on his trembling lower lip. Owen couldn't shut the bedroom door.

"You know I'll be right downstairs?"

"But where's Mommy?"

"Still home. She said she'd be leaving tomorrow morning."

"She didn't call me."

Owen hadn't even noticed Lilah hadn't called. "She's probably packing." He looked at the clock on the small mantel. "And she probably thinks you're asleep."

"Mommy's supposed to kiss me goodnight."

Owen hesitated. Should he offer? Or would Ben rather the stranger-dad not kiss him? He couldn't stand there waiting all night, being afraid to act like his son's father. He crossed to the bed again and leaned over to press a kiss to Ben's forehead. "We'll call her first thing tomorrow."

"Okay."

Ben nodded and then turned over, pressing his face into the puppy pillow. Maybe the little man needed a real pup. Owen headed for the door again, feeling like the bad guy in this situation. He should have insisted Lilah travel with them and show Ben how glad she was to have him in his son's life at last.

Something—anything—to reassure Ben and make him feel certain he was safe in his father's home.

He reached for the light switch in the hall but left it on. Then Ben made a sound. Not a sob, just a small, almost-hidden whimper. Owen froze.

What would Lilah do? Did she let Ben cry himself to sleep? Why hadn't he thought to ask her?

It didn't matter what Lilah would do. Owen turned back into the room and scooped up every book he'd left on the table.

"Scoot over, buddy," he said. "I'm dying to read. Do you mind?"

Ben turned over, rubbing his eyes. "I want you to read to me." He burrowed into

Owen's side, his little fists tiny knots against his dad's chest.

Owen began to read, his eyes burning.

"Own," Ben said as Owen turned a page, "you can sleep in here if you want to."

"It's a nice room," Owen said, taking in the fresh coat of gray-blue paint and Celia's best renditions of airplanes and racing cars. He felt cozy. "Do you miss your room in Vermont?"

"I like this one, but I miss Mommy."

"She'll be here soon."

Ben stretched his legs and kicked a little. He put his hands over his eyes, and Owen wrapped his hand around his son's small wrist. Some day, Ben would feel as safe with him as he did with Lilah.

For now, a touch and more stories seemed to work. Ben finally removed his hands from his eyes and turned on his back. "Read the one about the boat again, please."

Owen read, and Ben snuggled. At last, Ben was so still, Owen guessed the little guy must be asleep. He didn't dare move, and he didn't realize he'd also fallen asleep until the chirp of his cell phone downstairs woke him.

He sat up, and the pile of storybooks slid off his chest. He barely caught them before they hit Ben. His little boy flipped over again to cuddle the puppy pillow. Owen slipped off the bed and then eased out of the room, pulling the door shut behind him.

He hurried down the stairs. It could be his brother or a subcontractor, maybe a new client who'd found faith in Owen's abilities because he hadn't screwed up the barn yet.

He grabbed the phone off the dining table.

Lilah.

Should he wake Ben?

"What's up?" Owen asked, answering her call.

"How's Ben?"

Her abrupt tone put him on edge. As if she were talking to the babysitter. Except she probably would have been more welcoming to a sitter. "He's asleep."

"That was quick. He's never slept away from me before."

"We managed." He relented because he'd want to know more when she had Ben, and he was the one stuck a thousand miles away. "It was a little tricky, but I read to him and he nodded off."

"Oh."

And that was it. Fine by him. "Talk to you later, then."

"Wait, Owen. I need to tell you something. My plans changed."

"What do you mean?"

"I'm already on the way. I made a mistake, insisting on driving myself. I was angry, and I didn't want to travel with you. I couldn't watch you being a father to my son."

No subtlety in Lilah. So they had something in common. "Too bad you weren't so honest when you got pregnant with him."

"I'm in Chicago," she said, clearly choosing to ignore his observation. "On my way to Tennessee. I go through Atlanta, but I'll be in Knoxville in the morning."

"Great. See you tomorrow, then."

"I'll rent a car and drive down."

He hadn't been on the verge of offering to pick her up. "Ben will be glad to see you." Only Ben. Her games were wearing him out, and he didn't care if she knew.

"But you wish I'd stuck to our original plan."

His temper got away from him. "Do you care?" They were both breathing hard.

"Not a bit," she said.

"Good."

"Not so good for Ben, though." Her voice was quiet, reflective. She sounded like the thoughtful Lilah he'd known before they parted, the woman he'd believed in. "If his parents can't stand each other, he'll know," she said. "Maybe we should both work harder at getting along when Ben's around."

CHAPTER SEVEN

MANEUVERING THROUGH THE mountain roads, the morning sun in her eyes, Lilah had plenty of time to reconsider the plan she'd already set in motion. She'd called her family's attorney from the hotel in Chicago, and told him to contact child protective services in Bliss County.

She didn't have to put up with being blackmailed. The night Owen had left Vermont to tell his family about Ben, she'd called Mr. Bankman and asked him about her rights to Ben.

He'd suggested she should appear to be amenable, show some remorse for having kept Ben away from Owen all these years. If Owen took her to court, remorse would look better than arrogance. She'd asked him how alcoholism would look.

Today, they'd find out. The Tennessee authorities, along with local attorneys Mr. Bankman had chosen, were supposed to arrive at the Gage property about the same time Lilah did. She'd meet them there and follow them to Owen's cabin.

Vaguely aware of the frozen waterfalls clinging to granite outcroppings and frost glittering on bare tree limbs, Lilah pressed her foot harder on the gas pedal. Last night she'd suggested they should stop fighting each other.

She didn't enjoy being a hypocrite.

But if she was right, and Owen was still drinking, it wasn't safe for Ben to be alone with him. She could end this crazy vacation from their real lives today, before they had to make any more changes. She hated being held hostage by Owen.

And yet the action felt extreme, even to her.

She felt a little queasy as she passed the rectangular green sign, pockmarked with bullet holes, that told her she had ten more miles to drive before she reached Bliss.

CLAMBERING OVER THE barn's roof, inspecting the grainy, tarred shingles to see if the materials could be recycled after they put on the new roof, Owen heard the roar of multiple car engines. He straightened, shielding his eyes from the sun as he searched the tree-lined road toward his mother's inn.

Three cars formed a caravan, tires grinding gravel, throwing up dirty snow.

An SUV led the way, followed by a sheriff's car. The end sedan bore a seal on the driver's door.

Owen headed to the ladder. By the time he reached the ground his crew had gathered around him with Ben, who'd been hanging out with one of the carpenters.

"What's going on?" the foreman asked. "Something with the job?"

"I doubt it." Owen took Ben's hand. That seal said something about children.

"That's a bunch of cars, Own."

"I think one might be your mom's."

"Mommy?"

"Let's walk over there and see."

Lilah had been too calm, far too cooperative. He would have fought harder than she had if the shoe had been on the other foot. He should have expected she'd try to prove he was unfit. His alcoholism was her best and only weapon.

His conscience pinched a little as he realized he might have driven her to alert the authorities. He just hoped these people would look closely enough at the situation to see that Lilah was as angry with him as he was with her. He had to admit there were moments in the past four years when he wouldn't have been a good father.

But he was trying. He struggled every day to stay sober.

"Maybe we should keep the boy?" the carpenter asked.

Owen shook his head. Ben would want to see his mom. "We'll be back." He let go of Ben's hand and took off his own heavy work gloves.

The cars' occupants emerged. A second SUV came barreling down the road. Owen could see it was Lilah, looking grim behind the steering wheel.

A couple of black-suited men stepped out of the first SUV. Two sheriff's deputies opened their car doors. At least Sheriff Layton hadn't shown up. That must mean Owen was getting the benefit of at least one official's doubt. From the last car a woman and man eased out, their eyes on him.

He got a good look at the seal on the open door. Department of Children's Services.

Lilah had staged her revenge. She parked and got out of the car.

"Mommy—" Ben took off, stopping only when his mother knelt to hug him close.

Lilah straightened as Owen drew near, looking less pleased than he'd expected. She stationed herself between the guys who looked like lawyers.

"Owen, I want you to meet my attorneys, Hank Sheridan, and his associate, Dan Randall." She gestured to the visitors from children's services. "This is Mary Grant and Paul Stanford."

"And our friends from the sheriff's office," Hank said.

"I went to school with Mary and Tom and Jay." He shook hands with them and waited for the others to start the proceedings.

No one spoke.

Owen turned to Lilah. "What's your story?"

She put her shoulders back, but her attitude was more brazening-out-a-bad-situation, than I've-got-you-in-my-sights.

"I explained that you have a serious issue with alcohol addiction." She glanced uncomfortably at Ben. At least she had some human kindness left. "And you blackmailed me into bringing my son down here." She flicked a glance at Mary Grant. "I was barely older than Ben when the incidents I described to you happened. Owen threatened to reveal them if I didn't cooperate with him, but I'm the only one who'll decide when to share that information."

Mary shot Owen a shocked glance—over his son's head. But he didn't feel guilty. Lilah's little surprise today proved he'd been right to take such extreme measures.

"While I don't approve of blackmail," Mary said, "Owen's behavior isn't as dangerous as his possible addiction."

"What's 'diction?" Ben asked.

Owen leveled a frustrated glance at Lilah. He'd threatened to reveal her secrets, but he would never have forced Lilah to tell Ben. His drinking was shameful, embarrassing, but she had no problem making sure he'd have to explain it to Ben.

Even she paled. "I'm sorry," she said. "I didn't think about it happening this way."

"How else would it happen? Ben's here with me. You brought all these—" He stopped himself. "People," he said.

He turned and waved at his head carpenter. As the man came to them, Owen's glance took in all the adults around them. "Ben, buddy, why don't you go hang out over at the barn with Mr. Craig, and we'll come get you after we finish talking?"

Mary's colleague looked sympathetically at Lilah. No doubt he was taken in by her beauty and the vulnerability she exhibited now. She must have realized she'd gone too far, but that didn't blunt Owen's frustration. This was supposed to be his chance to get to know Ben. Owen would be lucky now if Ben weren't afraid of him.

He should have known better. Steel determination had kept Lilah alive in a situation that might have broken most adults. Naturally, she'd fight back for her son.

"See you in a few minutes, Mommy," Ben said as Craig took him back toward the barn.

She waved, but even she looked ashamed. Owen felt sick.

"Let's get this over with," he said. "And maybe we can try not to make things any worse."

"We may decide to take the child with us if foster care is necessary," Paul said.

Owen felt the same dread he'd known as a child. Lilah twisted her hands together.

"No one's taking him," Owen said, in the odd position of comforting the woman who'd brought this trouble to the farm. "Even if you have doubts about me, Lilah's fitness as a mother has never been in question."

She looked stricken for a second but composed herself swiftly. Owen wasn't trying to defend or protect Lilah. His concern was for Ben—and selfishly, for himself. He would be a good father. He just needed Lilah to give him a chance.

"We'd make the same point about Ms. Bantry's fitness," Hank said. "We simply request that the boy and his mother be relocated to a hotel in town. We have enough to choose from, and Mary and Paul can finish their investigation of Owen Gage without interference or the possibility of unsettling the child."

Mary's brittle smile eased Owen's anxiety. She wasn't taken in by the lawyer's attempt to direct this intervention. She knew Owen, and she knew he was trying to stay sober.

"I understand what's going on here at the barn, and enough of us know Owen to know when he's failing," she said. His latest and hopefully, last attempt at sobriety had buzzed through the town's grapevine since he'd won the clinic contract. "We can't take a child who's not in danger, simply because his father might drink. Do you mind if we take a look inside your residence, Owen?" Mary asked.

"Not at all. Sorry I'm not a better house-keeper."

The place was as neat as a show cabin except for some of Ben's toys strewn around. Suzannah's work the day before had topped off Owen's nightly de-cluttering and dusting. Cleaning kept him from thinking too hard, or from opening the kitchen cabinet, where a bottle of cooking wine was shoved toward the back.

He might need to tackle the closets after he put Ben to bed tonight.

He turned to Lilah. "I should have known you were up to something. I was blind because I felt guilty, and I wanted this to work out between us."

She blushed. "Yes," she said, but she didn't try to stop this farce she'd set in motion.

"I don't see why we can't ask Ben where he'd like to stay." Hank bent down to pat the curious, chestnut-brown goat who had trotted over to tug at the knees of his pants.

Lilah's frustration flickered in her eyes. "Because Owen has goats and trains and fun? And he's new to Ben?"

"And I need time to get to know him,"

Owen said. "Lilah, he's four years old, and he barely knows me. If you ask him, he's more likely to go with you."

"I know my son. He'll see Owen as an adventure. Ben's not afraid," she said. "Not like me." She looked as if she wanted to cry, and Owen felt an inexplicable need to comfort her.

This was all so messed up. He'd tried to blackmail her because he was hurt and angry. She'd tried to smear his already tarnished name because she was angry and afraid. He didn't know what to do.

"Listen, Lilah," he said, glancing uncomfortably at their audience. "We've both made mistakes, but I'd never do anything—and that includes speaking about your past—that might hurt our son. I just want to know him. We might have addressed this with attorneys first, and we could let these people settle it for us, but between us, I'm asking you to give me some time with my son."

Someone must have waved Ben and Craig back over because the carpenter let Ben's hand go, and Owen's son ran to him.

Lilah touched her hand to her throat, and even Owen believed she was torn, but she bent to look her child in the eye, even as he held on to Owen's hand.

"Ben? Honey, would you like to move into a hotel in town? We'll only be a few minutes away, and we'll find so many fun things to do."

"Ms. Bantry," Paul Stanford said in a warning voice.

"I love you, Mommy, but I kind of like Owen."

Despite the fact he was a grown man who'd endured more than his share of battle-hardening experiences, Owen's throat tightened. He swallowed the lump, determined to look in control. He ruffled his son's hair, and Ben hugged Lilah, tip-toeing off the ground.

"What if you need me?" she asked.

"Own promised me last night we would call you if I need you."

"If Mr. Gage would like to invite you into his home," Mary said with a nod at Owen, silently suggesting he man up and do the right thing.

"Not tonight." He didn't elaborate. He and Lilah didn't need to discuss this any further in front of Ben.

"We'll just do a quick home visit," Mary said, "and then I imagine we'll be getting out of your way, unless you'd like to talk to us about some possible methods to make this transition easier on your son."

"That won't be necessary," Lilah said.

Owen stared hard at her. She set Ben back on his feet, but touched his cheek.

"I made a mistake," she said, looking only at Ben. "I won't do that again."

"Mistakes are okay, Mommy." Their little boy hugged her. "Want to see my room?"

"In a few minutes." She caught his small hand in hers.

Owen couldn't seem to breathe. So much emotion unsettled him. He'd been wrong, but he wouldn't give up even the one night he'd had with his son. He just had no more interest in hurting Lilah. Staring into her tight, sad face, he understood her pain, and he vowed not to purposefully cause any more problems between them.

"Maybe you should join us for dinner tonight. Ben hasn't met my family yet, and they're coming. Please," he added, the word like lead in his mouth.

"It would probably be good if we all had dinner together," Lilah said, and Owen's relief was immeasurable.

Mary turned to the sheriff's deputies. "You can go. We'll take it from here."

THE INSPECTION TEAM from children's services went in and came out in record time with the promise of releasing their findings as soon as possible. Relieved, Owen waited while Lilah and Ben inspected his room. Eventually, they came out together.

"It's a nice room," she said. "He seems to like it."

"I'm glad. Thanks for not making all that worse," Owen said.

"Let's go." Ben tugged at his dad's hand. "Mr. Craig and me were picking up pieces of wood Own and I can use for our trains."

"Is he safe over there?"

"Craig's the carpenter. He's not busy yet, so he's been hanging out with Ben. They're collecting blocks of excess wood that I thought we could paint as buildings for a train layout."

"I saw the trains." She nodded. "You won't let him near the actual work?"

"I won't."

"Then I'd better check in at your mother's place. That's the inn, back there, the yellow building?"

He nodded, too, and their truce held. He went back to the barn, with Ben galloping in his wake.

Ben had forgotten the morning's confusion by the time they turned off the lights in the barn and walked back to the cabin that night. He waited while Owen opened the front door.

"Own, what are we eating? I'm hungry."

"My mom's bringing dinner when everyone comes over tonight."

"Mommy lets me make my own sandwiches when I want a snack." Ben looked up at him, rocking on his sneakers as Owen stood him on the couch and began to unzip his jacket. "But I can't stand on the furniture."

"Then you should probably hop down."

Ben jumped with the skills of a stuntman, shedding his outdoor things as he ran across the family room and into the kitchen to search the refrigerator.

"Cheese," he said, "And then there's all this other stuff in these pans. My mom likes cooking. We cook a lot. Sometimes I help. Your mom must like to cook. My friend, Jason, gets to eat out a lot because his mommy and daddy both hate their stove. That's what he says."

Ben gathered Ben's coat and gloves and mittens. "My mother's like your mom. In cooking anyway."

"Where is my mom? She never leaves me with strangers this long."

Owen dropped Ben's things and knelt in front of him. "We both explained who I am," he said. "I thought we were getting along pretty well. For strangers."

How could he persuade Ben to trust him when he'd never managed to make anyone believe in him?

"I want a daddy." Ben stared down at his hands, twisting them together the way Lilah did when she was under stress.

"Maybe you're not sure I'm the right daddy yet?"

Ben didn't answer for a few seconds that stretched too long. Finally, he nodded, just one tilt of his head down and one up. "I want to stay with you, but can't I see Mommy, too?"

"You can see Mommy anytime." Owen wanted to stroke his son's hair, but he was afraid he'd scare him off. "She has a cell phone, and you do, too. Just call her, and she'll come see you whenever you ask her to."

"But where is she now?"

"At my mom's—that little yellow house we saw this morning, and she's coming to dinner. You're not worried, are you?"

Ben nodded, but with so much reluctance, Owen's heart ached.

"You don't need to be afraid of anything. I'll bet your mom is on her way here now with my mother and my brothers and sister." He allowed himself to lightly fist-bump Ben's shoulder. "With food. Excellent food."

"Are you sure Mommy will come?"

"Pretty certain. She didn't say no when I asked her."

"But she was a little mad this morning."

Owen touched Ben's back, flattening his palm against his boy's shirt. "Would you like me to call her?"

Ben nodded quickly, as if Owen had flung him a lifeline.

Owen stood. It might be easier for Ben if his mother lived in this tiny house with them, but what if he got used to them being together? They couldn't let that happen. Ben was always going to have two separate parents.

Owen pulled his phone from his pocket and dialed Lilah. She picked up immediately.

"Is he okay?" she asked.

"He'd like you to come over."

"I'm already on the way." She lowered her voice. "With your mother and all these people in your family."

He couldn't blame her if she didn't remember who was whom. "Mom's bringing something to eat, right?"

"A feast."

"Good." Sometimes he was lucky his mother worked so hard to make up for the past. "See you when you get here."

He disconnected the call and slipped his phone into his pocket. Then he picked up the clothes Ben had dropped. "She's on the way. Want to put these in your room before she gets here?"

"I guess."

Owen and Ben climbed the stairs together. They remade the sports-car bed, and Ben went to punch keys at the little minicomputer made for small children on his desk. Owen straightened the beanbags on the floor and returned fallen toys to the small net hammocks attached in two corners of the room.

"I'm messy," Ben said.

"This stuff is for you to play with. It's all yours. You'll just have to put it away when you're finished."

"You can come in here and play with me sometimes."

"I'd like that, Ben. I hope you'll invite me."

"Can I get a puppy?"

Owen laughed. "Nice try, buddy. Have you asked your mom?"

Ben's mouth puckered. "She says I'm not old enough."

"She's probably right."

"Nobody likes dogs. Only I like dogs."

Owen let that lie. He grabbed Ben's coat and cap and mittens to put them away. "After everyone leaves, we'll straighten up the rest of this."

"I guess."

The front door opened, and the sound of voices and boots being stomped free of snow drifted up the stairs.

Without warning, the past flooded back. Another pair of boots, their sound so peculiar to his father that he and his sister and brothers all knew the second Odell Gage returned home. They'd rush to hide from the monster's heavy tread and his fisted hand, but they found no sanctuary.

Was he so different from his father? Forcing Ben to visit him, forcing Lilah to let Ben come?

His siblings seemed to be working out a

recovery from the past. Chad had dealt with his anger by playing football and was now a pick for several excellent colleges. Noah had accomplished his single-minded plan of becoming Bliss's GP and was trying to polish the tarnish off the Gage name. Celia was following him, well on her way to medical school.

Only Owen seemed to remember their past. Only he still feared he might have inherited too much of Odell Gage's genetics, and when he looked at his son, hurrying to meet his mom, that fear was a huge lump in his throat.

"Mommy," Ben sang out to her as he shot down the narrow stairs.

Owen followed, just in time to watch Ben leap into his mother's arms. Lilah hugged him with as much joy as the little guy felt. Her closed eyes hid nothing. She could pretend she was stone cold and bitter, but every time she held Ben, she gave herself away. Little Lost Lilah might be covered in armor, but Ben unlocked her soft center whenever he was near her.

Owen joined his mother and Celia and Noah's girlfriend, Emma, in the kitchen, where they were unpacking a large cooler tote. They each sneaked curious glances at Owen's son.

"Where are Noah and Chad?" Owen asked.

Emma pointed an elbow at the kitchen door. "Bringing in firewood. They noticed you were low."

Suzannah was already unloading even more food from the bags she'd brought inside. "I have fresh-baked bread and cold ham and chicken, some potato salad and coleslaw, veggies for dipping. Baked beans and a few more things I've made for you that you can take from the freezer when you want."

She looked up with a grin as if he'd given her a gift by letting her be useful in his kitchen. "I've left a card with instructions for warming up each dish. There's roast and a couple of casseroles, and I don't know—a few other items you and Ben will like."

"Thanks, Mom. I'm a horrible cook. But how did you find time to make all this food?"

"Too anxious to just sit and wait." She eased him out of the way.

"Lucky for me," Emma said, "your mom's teaching me to cook."

"I thought you knew how. Thanksgiving dinner was amazing." Noah's first love from long ago, and now his last, Emma, had hosted the entire family after she and Noah had found their way back to each other.

Emma glanced at his brother, and Noah explained to Lilah, "She kept practicing her grandmother's recipes until she got them right."

"You boys leave her alone. That's the only way to learn." Suzannah shot Lilah a look. "And, uh—your friend? Is she a good cook?"

Owen discouraged his mother with his own warning glance. "Ben seems to think so. You could probably ask her yourself."

"Lilah, are you hungry?" Suzannah asked, her polite, Southern, ladylike manners firmly back in place.

"Starving." With a deep breath, Lilah let Ben slip to the floor. "Hungry, buddy?" she asked.

Ben wrapped an arm around her leg but followed. She walked as if she were wearing a splint, but without the least self-consciousness.

"Can you say hello to Suzannah?" Lilah said. "She's your grandma. I'll bet she wouldn't mind if you call her that."

"I'd be honored." Suzannah sank to his height. "I'm so glad you're here. If you come visit me sometimes, we can play with my goats, and we'll pick beans and tomatoes from my garden in the summer. I have a pool in the backyard that hardly anyone uses. I'd love to see a little boy enjoying it."

Ben perked up. "I swim good."

"But he's not allowed to swim by himself, ever," Lilah said, bringing conversation to a halt.

Owen understood her protectiveness, but the others clearly thought she was overreacting. He put an arm around her shoulders, not surprised when she froze. "We'll all have to keep an eye on Ben when he's in the pool or anywhere near it."

"There's a six-foot fence, Owen." His mother looked mystified. "And the gate is always locked."

"See?" He let Lilah go, but glanced at her to offer as much reassurance as he could muster. He didn't want to alienate her any further. "No reason to worry."

"We're in the middle of the Smoky Mountains." She must not care that his family was their avid audience. "The middle. Mountains, icy streams, rock cliffs."

"It's not the kind of suburbia Ben's used to," Owen said, "but he'll be fine, and he might even enjoy the change."

"These mountains are beautiful," Suzannah said. "Sometimes we forget and take it for granted. I've been so grateful my children haven't left here, though, of course, we didn't know about Owen's adventures in cabinetmaking."

The room went deadly silent again. Celia covered her mouth to keep from laughing. Emma headed for the door.

"I think I'll see if Noah and Chad went to harvest that wood from the forest."

Owen rubbed his chest. These women might be the death of him.

CHAPTER EIGHT

LILAH WATCHED BEN and Owen walking ahead of her on the wide sidewalks across from the town's courthouse. A slow, steady rain had melted all the snow and kept Owen from working past noon. He'd offered to take her and Ben to see some of the shops in Bliss.

Obviously, he hoped she'd be able to visualize herself in one of the small stores, selling the kind of rustic art and implements she loved best.

"Own, can I have ice cream?" Ben asked, running to stare into one of the plateglass windows. Lilah came up beside him as he tried to rub at the Santa figure still painted on the inside. "Maybe they have chocolate for you, Mommy."

"Sounds tempting," she said, "but we just ate lunch, buddy, and it's cold outside." She pulled up the hood on his jacket. "Ice cream will make you colder."

Owen had walked ahead to talk to a man

standing beside a rusted-out truck. The man glanced her way.

"Lilah." Owen beckoned her. "I want to show you something."

She tugged Ben, who didn't want to abandon his ice-cream dreams. He walked along, dragging his feet. The man held out his hand for her to shake.

"I hear you like old stuff made into new stuff," he said with the lilting Appalachian accent she found a bit tricky to follow.

"I guess I do." She tried not to see Owen's smile. As if he were giving her a gift.

"Butch, this is my friend, Lilah Bantry. Lilah, Butch Dayton. He sculpts with pig iron."

"I weld," Butch said. *"Sculpt."* He gave a belly laugh. A literal belly laugh that shook the rounded mound above his faded jeans.

Lilah smiled in spite of not wanting to be drawn to this place where Owen belonged. "What do you weld?"

"Whatever tickles my fancy." He let down the tailgate on his truck, and yanked back a tarp to reveal a writhing mass of rusted iron. "This was my kids' old swing set. The wife had been nagging me for years to haul it away." He leaned confidentially toward

Lilah. "She worried the grandkids might get a cut or something. You know how the ladies can be."

"Lilah is a lady, Butch, and she might be interested in this if we can get it out and set it upright."

"I call it Superstorm." Butch nodded at Owen to take a side of the piece.

Lilah urged Ben out of the way as the two men scooted the iron out of the truck, complete with screaming, earsplitting sound effects. As soon as they set it up, Lilah understood. The iron had been bent and twisted as if a tornado had reached down and scrambled the swing set to its own specifications.

It exuded energy and violence.

"You don't like it?" Butch asked.

Ben reached out to grip the pieces, but Lilah pulled his hand back from the sharp edges.

"I can't speak," Lilah said. "It's beautiful."

Butch looked at Owen, who nodded with satisfaction.

"See?" Owen said to his friend. "I told you."

"This mountain grows artisans," Lilah said. She'd known the same breathless excitement when she'd first seen Owen's work.

"You and Owen. I can't wait to see who comes along next."

"Owen?" Butch arched twin, bushy brows. "You taken up welding, boy?"

"I've been doing a little extra carpentry in my spare time." Owen reproved Lilah with a quick glance. "Lilah owns a gallery in Vermont. She's looking for some work to take back with her, if you had any interest in selling."

"Selling?" Butch rubbed two fingers against his thumb. "Like for money?"

"I can't promise, but we could definitely talk terms if you wouldn't mind sharing your work with me."

"Huh." Butch smacked his leg. "I was just going to ask the lady at the clerk's office if they'd be interested in this thing for the spring festival. I only brought it down because they got mad when I made my pieces too big last year."

"I'd love to take it for you," Lilah said. "Do you have more at home?"

"Give her your phone number, Butch."

"I ain't got no business card, man. I'm just a farmer."

"Do you have a phone?" Owen asked.

Butch rummaged in the voluminous back

pocket of his jeans and finally pulled out a scarred and beaten flip phone. "You want me to call her when I'm standing right here?"

"I'm going to put Lilah's phone number in your phone," Owen said, "and then you can call her tonight and set up a time for her to come out and look at the rest of your work." He tapped in her number, surprising her. How had he already memorized it? Then he looked at her, his blue eyes laughing. "Is all of this all right with you?"

"Sounds perfect." She smiled at him. She'd owe him a commission for this introduction. Butch was not just a farmer. Not that there was anything wrong with farming, but how had two such artists found themselves in this tiny mountain town?

"Wait till I tell the wife. She'll go trolling in the barn for more throwaways. My plows won't be safe."

With a smile at his happiness, Lilah shook his hand. The best part of her job was finding a new artist. "When you call, we'll arrange for shipping," she said. "I'd like to get Superstorm to my gallery."

"Unbelievable." Butch pointed at the sculpture. "Grab that end, Owen. We need to get this back under cover before it gets wetter."

Lilah hugged her boy with a lovely feeling of accomplishment. She'd done some work today. She and Ben could celebrate. "We'll be in the ice-cream shop, Owen."

"Okay."

Ben grabbed her hand. "That man's funny, Mommy," he said, in a loud voice.

It would be best not to look back. "What kind of ice cream do you want, buddy?"

"ARE YOU SURE you don't mind driving?" Lilah asked a few days later as Owen turned up a narrow mountain road.

"I was afraid Butch's directions might lead you to Key West. He was pretty excited about suddenly becoming an artist."

"I'm glad. He's ferocious. He packed so much energy into that piece." She took a quick look at Ben, drowsing in the backseat. "I still don't understand how Bliss managed to field the two of you."

"Maybe a place like this draws artists. Have you looked out at the mountains?"

She did now. At mist floating out on the far, rolling ridges. At the water rushing down below, between large, moss-speckled black rocks. "It is beautiful, Owen. I see that."

"I hope you'll come to enjoy it, that it won't

always be foreign to you—like the way we speak," he said, with a slow grin.

"I'm not staying," she said. "This will never be my home."

"But it will be Ben's a lot of the time, and if you come with him, I'd rather you didn't hate being here. I wasn't proud of blackmailing you."

"I see why you love it, but don't get any ideas."

How devious was he? Would he suddenly pretend to care for her again because he wanted Ben in his life full-time? Could he possibly believe she'd fall for a play like that?

"Are there other farmers like Butch?" she asked.

"All over the communities up here. We don't have a lot to do when winter comes." Thank goodness he'd let the subject of Ben spending a lot of time down here pass. "You'll find other artists. You just have to be willing to drive around."

"As long as it isn't snowing." She averted her gaze from the steep drop-off on her side of the car, tempted to lean toward Owen to transfer some of her weight. "You worry too much," he said, and then silence pervaded the car. "I didn't mean it about Ben this time. I meant you must drive in the snow in Vermont."

"I know you believe I'm overly sensitive about Ben."

"I don't have any right to suggest that."

"I try to control any situation that concerns him because of what happened to me." She didn't think she had ever admitted that to anyone out loud before. "I just want to make sure no one has time to hurt him. My mother turned her back for a second, and that man asked if I could help him with his kitten. He had his hand on my shoulder and he walked me away because I was worried about a cat." She barely remembered the details of the story the man used to lure her away, but the memory of him covering her mouth and pushing her into the backseat was painfully vivid. He'd bound her hands and feet with duct tape, and driven her into a hell that had seemed to last forever. She peered over her shoulder. Ben was sound asleep. "I'll do everything I can to keep Ben safe."

"I get that, Lilah, but you won't always be able to watch him 24/7."

His tight voice put her on the alert. "You think I don't know that? I also know kids get hurt—it happens, so I don't care if I annoy you by keeping a close watch over my son."

"Are you kidding? I'm not upset with you for being afraid. I'd like to dig that guy out of his prison grave and tear him apart for what he did to you. I don't want something like that to happen to Ben either, but I'm not anything like your abductor, and Ben deserves to have a father, as well as a mother."

"Not a father who drinks. I begged you to stop and you wouldn't."

"But you never told me why. If I'd had Ben as a reason…"

"Let's not go over this again," she said. "There's no guarantee you would have stopped, even for Ben."

"How about for Ben and for you? I loved you back then." He took a deep breath. She felt as if the car were closing in on them. "I never understood why you suddenly got the temperance bug and sent me away."

"I figured if you weren't willing to quit for me, then you wouldn't be able to quit for a baby who wasn't even born."

"You figured it was all right to test me, but you didn't let me know what I stood to lose." His knuckles turned white on the steering wheel, but his voice stayed low. And husky. The way he always sounded when he was fighting strong emotions. Anger or tenderness.

"I didn't know what else to do."

"I'm trying to get over this, Lilah, the frustration of those lost years, but you took my son and the life I thought you and I were making together. I have to understand why you did that."

"I really believed you'd realize how important it was to be sober. Not just because of Ben. Or me. You needed to do it for yourself."

"So you manipulated me for my own good?"

She pressed her lips together. She couldn't really argue that. "It doesn't matter anymore. We don't have to fix the past. We just have to make Ben's life happy."

"No matter which of us he's living with."

Instinctively, she stiffened and opened her mouth to tell him to stop threatening her. Instead she decided to assume he meant when they were sharing custody. Even that eventuality put her into a cold sweat. She couldn't always come with Ben to Tennessee, but she couldn't imagine trusting Owen to keep him safe.

"There's Butch's place, in that piece of bottom land."

She followed where he pointed. A neat little farm spread out before them like a painting. A man came out of the house in jeans and a thick coat, a baseball cap on his head. He waved at them on his way to his barn.

She shifted in the seat, straightening her back. "Don't let Ben impale himself on this barbed wire while I'm with Butch." Owen didn't answer. She turned her face to his. "I mean, please. He doesn't know about barbed wire, Owen."

He nodded, but Lilah could tell he didn't appreciate her lack of faith in him. She'd trusted him once. She'd also loved him, and he'd loved her. Just not enough to give up drinking.

And until she was convinced he could stay sober for life, she really couldn't trust him with her son.

OWEN GOT IN a few days of work before another morning brought too much rain to peel back the tarp on the nearly installed, new barn roof. Ben was already up watching Saturday-morning cartoons. They were the old ones, reruns from when Owen had been a child, where bunnies and pigs and coyotes created mayhem.

From his room, Owen listened as he yanked on jeans and a thermal T-shirt. Suddenly, he wondered if all the violence was bad for a little guy. He shook his head and ran both hands through his hair, all the combing it would get.

Lilah had spooked him into being hypervigilant. As if classic cartoons would harm Ben. He hadn't heard of any kids turning to a life of crime after watching a coyote repeatedly blow himself up.

He walked down the hall, buttoning a thick, flannel shirt.

"Boom," Ben said softly around a spoonful of organic granola.

Owen stopped. Maybe he was wrong. Ben looked up, chewing contentedly.

Owen eyed his bowl. The cereal looked like little rocks sticking out of milk. "You like that stuff you're eating?"

"Mmm-hmm. It's good." Not even the slightest hint of Grandma Suzannah's fat-filled, comforting Southern breakfasts for Ben. "*A-C-M-E*, Own, what does that spell?"

"Acme. They make everything a cartoon

guy needs," Owen said, squeezing his son's shoulder on the way to get another bowl.

Who could have guessed a month ago that he'd be sitting at his breakfast counter, sharing a meal with his own son? He poured some cereal for himself and ate it quickly, trying to catch up with Ben.

"I'm ready to go outside." Ben clambered down from his stool as Owen was still only halfway through his granola.

"Right behind you," Owen said.

Ben scooted off the stool and eased his empty bowl off the place mat. With his usual determination he carried it to the sink and lifted it to the ledge. Owen hurried over and caught the bowl just before it tumbled into the deep sink. "Thanks, buddy. Can you wait for me to finish?"

"You have to eat breakfast," Ben said. "Healthy, healthy, healthy."

"Did your mother tell you that?"

"My teacher. Healthy, healthy, healthy. I always eat breakfast." He knelt on the floor between the sofa and the coffee table, the better to see the television. "What are we going to do today?"

"I can't work on the roof in the rain, so I thought I could show you some of your grandmother's animals. You want to see them?"

Ben nodded. He put his elbows on the table and his chin in his hands. "Do you have any puppies?"

"No puppies, but our friend up the mountain has a big old white fluffy dog that looks after his goats." Wouldn't Lilah just love it if he gave Ben a Great Pyr puppy. "Sorry."

"A kitten?"

"Have you asked your mom for a kitten?"

Ben looked at his hands and rocked back and forth against the table. "She says maybe when I'm bigger."

"I can't give you a pet if your mother doesn't want you to have one." Not true. He could give his son a puppy or a kitten that would live in Tennessee. But how hard would it be for Ben to say goodbye at the end of every visit?

In fact, how was he going to learn to say goodbye to Ben at the end of this far-too-short stay?

"You'd better go get your jacket, son."

"Okay, Own."

Restlessly, Owen picked up his bowl and took it to the sink. He washed the few dishes and poured coffee into a dented silver travel mug. Then he grabbed a bottle of water for Ben from the fridge. "Ready to go, buddy?"

"Uh-huh." He came around the kitchen counter, already putting on his jacket. "Starting to rain again, Own."

He was a responsible little guy. "I'll get my coat, too."

After grabbing it from his room, he hurried to meet Ben at the door and snagged his keys off a peg.

The rain was coming down buckets. Owen pulled up the hood on Ben's jacket and then patted his head to make sure it stayed secure.

"Let's take the car today."

"Okay, Own, but I like when we walk."

"I like our walks, too, but you don't want to get soaked or muddy." He opened the door and ushered Ben outside. They hurried to the SUV that mostly sat unused beside his battered work truck. Owen helped Ben into his car seat in the back. "Do you have your gloves in your pockets?" he asked as he slid behind the steering wheel.

"I'm not cold." Ben leaned to the side to dig in his pockets anyway. He dragged the gloves out and brandished them, along with some pocket fuzz.

Owen started the car. "Do you want to go see what we've been doing in the barn?"

"Do you have a cow in the barn?"

He seriously wanted some animals, that boy. No cow in the barn had flummoxed him from day one. "No cow, but I have lots of tools you still haven't seen."

"No. I want to see cows today. And horses. And goats, ducks, chickens, frogs…"

"My mom doesn't farm with frogs."

"But Uncle Chad says they're in the pond."

"Don't go near the water without a grown-up, okay?"

"Mommy already told me."

"And don't wander off when you're with Uncle Chad."

"Mom told me."

"If you do wander off—I mean, if Uncle Chad gets lost—tell him to always follow a stream. Around here, they lead to roads."

"Do they?" Ben peered around as if a stream and a road would magically appear outside the windows.

"Because back when people first came to this place, they needed water and they needed roads, so they built the roads next to the water."

"Hunh."

"Look. There's the barn my mom keeps her cows in." It didn't compare in size with the barn they were rebuilding. It was more like an expanded garage, but she'd wanted it closer to the inn, so she didn't have to leave her guests as long to milk her dairy herd of three cows.

"Do they share their house with the goats?"

Owen shook his head and parked at the far end of the inn's square gravel parking lot. "The goats play around and annoy the cows, so we put the goats in a smaller barn made just for them." A black buck goat gamboled into view just beyond the cowshed. "Not that they stay in it that well. Usually goats don't like to get wet, but Gomer, over there, just loves to run."

Ben craned to see. "I think I like goats. If I can't have a puppy…" Ben broke off as Owen got out of the car and opened the back door to help him out. "Maybe I can get a baby goat."

"I'll bet your mom would just love that." He laughed at the image of Gomer kicking up his hooves in Lilah's immaculate house. "You can help me feed the goats after we take Gomer back to the shed."

He texted his mother to let her know they

were about to visit the cows, and they'd be slipping the goats a little extra food.

She texted back that he should be extra careful with Ben and the goats. He didn't want to give Lilah ammo to prove he didn't know how to be a father.

He shook his head. She sounded as wary as he did. Too many wounded souls were trying to make his small boy happy and safe.

"Gomer?" He flagged the small goat down, and Gomer followed like a frolicking puppy. He loved human company.

Ben hovered on Owen's other side, reluctant to touch and yet also, nearly rigid with anticipation.

Owen didn't push. He walked through the barn, holding Ben's hand while Gomer bounced around them. The cows were pastured out back, but they'd come inside to avoid the rain. Maybelle, the oldest, mooed a greeting. Her sister, Daphne, completely ignored Owen. The newest addition, Tallulah, nosed over to see if he had anything delicious to eat in his pocket.

Ben suddenly lost his nerve as the young cow went for Owen's pocket. He beat a retreat, completely silent.

"You okay?" Owen asked, searching his

pockets first, and then pulling some hay out of the feeder for Tallulah. He tried to look as if Ben's fear didn't make him feel guilty and a little scared. Bringing him here might have been too much, too soon.

"Did she want to eat me, Own?"

"She's hungry, but she never eats little boys. She eats hay and this feed stuff my mother gets for her. Usually, I have a little in my pocket, but today, I'm empty."

"Can I give her hay?"

"Sure." Owen went over and lifted him in his arms. Owen grabbed some more hay from the feeder and handed it to Ben, who leaned over, depending completely on his father to keep him steady.

Again, when Tallulah hurried to grab her snack, Ben sprang back. His fear ended Owen's indecision. He patted the cow's solid shoulder and turned toward the other end of the barn. "Time to visit the goats," he said. "Come on, Gomer. Time to head home."

Ben clapped his hands as if that were the best news he'd heard since his arrival in Tennessee. He kept a measured eye on his new shadow, Gomer.

"He's not as big as a cow, is he?" Ben asked with obvious happiness.

"No, and he's a lot more cuddly. Just stay away from the back end. Sometimes goats get all excited and they kick up in the air."

"I can do that, too, Own. Put me down, and I'll show you."

Relieved he wasn't too afraid of a cattle stampede to touch the ground again, Owen set him down. Ben ran a few steps and then hopped, laughing, so pleased with himself, he made Owen laugh, too.

LILAH FINISHED HER phone calls and the business she could do from her laptop at a corner in Suzannah Gage's breakfast room. She packed her laptop and slid the bag on to her shoulder, carrying her coffee cup to the kitchen.

Owen's mother turned from the sink. "Something wrong? Are you leaving already?"

"Not at all. I'm bringing my cup and saucer, and I wondered if there was anything I could do to help you while I'm here."

Suzannah took the dishes from her. "No, thanks. You're a guest, like any other paying visitor."

"Well, I'm not, really. I don't think you're charging me full price, and you don't bake special cookies and make organic granola for other guests' children." Somehow, she made those extra attentions for Ben sound bad, when she meant to be grateful to—if a little wary of—her son's new family.

"I'm a rookie at being a grandmother, but I think I'm supposed to make special treats for him and spoil him as much as I can," Suzannah said with a smile that warmed Lilah. "None of us is entirely sure how to handle this situation, Lilah, and I won't pretend my loyalties don't lie with my son, but I believe you're trying to do the right thing. Now."

"You mean after I alerted the lawyers and child welfare?"

"That wasn't nice." Suzannah washed her cup and saucer with quick, efficient movements. "But I'm giving you the benefit of the doubt. For some reason you find it hard to believe that Owen will be a good father, and you jumped at your last chance to keep him out of Ben's life. I'd have given anything to provide my children with a loving father, but I'm in no position to judge."

"I don't understand," Lilah said, marveling at how honest these Gages could be in their conversation.

"I guess Owen didn't tell you everything about his childhood."

Lilah felt her face heat up. She knew Suzannah hadn't always stood between her children and their alcoholic father. She didn't know why, and she didn't want to betray Owen's few confidences.

"I wasn't always a good mother," Suzannah said. "My children couldn't count on me, but I'm trying to show them they can now."

"I understand that."

"But you don't have to be afraid of Owen."

"You don't have to fight on his behalf. I'm trying to accept this situation, but surely you can understand why I have reservations. I do know about Owen's father."

Suzannah looked embarrassed. "Owen's not like him."

"I'm not sure how you can know that. I get the feeling that Owen left me that last time and came back here to drink himself into oblivion. I didn't want Ben exposed to that."

Suzannah pursed her lips, and in that moment, Lilah saw the strong mother-son resemblance. "Let's not argue, Suzannah. I'm not separating Ben from Owen anymore, and I won't, as long as Owen doesn't fall back into his old habits."

"How generous."

Suzannah turned back to the sink to wash cutlery with unnecessary vigor. Lilah understood her anger, but she had to look out for Ben. Still, she certainly didn't want to make an enemy of Owen's mother.

She stared at Suzannah's reddened hands, searching for a benign opening. "You don't use a dishwasher?"

"Depends on the dish. Stoneware goes in, but this is bone. I don't like to take chances with it, but it's cozier than stoneware, and I like using it."

"Your home is cozy. Thank you for making Ben and me feel so welcome." That was a bit of a stretch, but at least Owen's family all seemed to love Ben.

Suzannah nodded over her shoulder. "I don't like that you think Owen is a bad guy, but why wouldn't I welcome you?"

Lilah didn't know how to cut the tension between them.

Owen's mother shook her head as if to suggest Lilah not answer. "I'm sorry. I'm making this worse. Ben and Owen are headed to the goat house if you want to join them."

"The goat house?" Ben was so desperate for a pet, she could imagine him pestering the goats until one of them got tired of his overwhelming love and took a bite out of him. "Where's that?"

"A little wooden structure in the trees beyond the east end of the parking lot."

"I've never known east from west unless the sun's out."

"And it's raining again. Put on a coat. You can take one from the hall closet. I have spares for guests. Turn left as you go out the back door of the dining room. You'll hear Ben and Owen even if you don't see the little white house between the spruce trees."

Lilah ran upstairs and put her laptop away, slipping into her own jacket as she hurried back to the steps. The other guests had started to stream down. She overheard them making lunch plans as she negotiated a path between the small groups.

She glanced back, longing for the simplicity of a vacation. The fear of losing her son had kept her on tenterhooks from the moment she'd recognized Owen at her door.

Thank goodness she'd given up girlie shoes for boots since she'd arrived in Bliss. She hurried across the graveled parking lot, pausing only when she heard her son's happy laughter. Even Ben wouldn't sound that pleased if he were goat fodder. All the same, she rushed to see him.

CHAPTER NINE

OWEN WASN'T SURPRISED to find Lilah in the dining room a few nights later. All alone, looking far too lovely by the light of the small, battery-operated lamps his mother left on the tables at night.

The other guests had all gone to bed. His mom was probably hard at work in the kitchen. Lilah looked up as he climbed the steps to the sleeping porch. She pulled her earbuds out and glanced past him.

"Where's Ben?"

"Celia came down to visit, and she's looking after him for me."

The fragile lines of her face hardened. She transitioned to full alert faster than anyone he knew.

"What's up?" she asked, but she couldn't even will herself to look casual.

He corrected himself. Not now anyway. Just a few years ago, casual had been her way of life. Or so it had seemed to him.

"I have to get back to work," he said. "I've been keeping Ben with me because I wanted him to get used to being around me, but I'm paying crew to look after him when it's not safe for him to be near me, and I'm not paying myself for the time I spend with him."

She straightened as if he'd offered her parole. "We can go home. You could visit next time you have a free stretch of vacation days."

Had she lost her mind? "I don't think so, Lilah, but nice try. I've asked my family to help. They'll take turns looking after Ben for me."

"I'll look after my son. I feel as if I'm not allowed to have any time with him."

He frowned. That hadn't occurred to him. "I didn't mean for that to happen, but his care is my responsibility right now, according to our agreement—"

"Our blackmail arrangement."

"Maybe we've argued enough."

"I think you're still purposely trying to keep Ben and me apart."

"Why would I do that?"

"I don't know." She set down the pen in her hand. "Because you still imagine I might try to turn him against you?"

"No." He did a double take. "*Should* I worry about that?"

"No." She shook her head as if he were the one who was crazy. "Why would I try to hurt my own child? He already loves you."

Owen felt as if he were warming from the inside out, and a sweet sense of anticipation washed over him. He hadn't felt that since Lilah had sent him away, a small, annoying voice whispered in his head. The two of them had agreed to keep their relationship casual, but there was nothing casual about how much Owen had missed her when it ended. He cleared his throat. "Of course you should see Ben anytime you want. But when you're working or busy, don't worry. I've spoken to my family about your concerns for Ben. They'll keep a close eye on him."

"Okay."

Still the doubt. He tried harder. "Lilah, I'm glad you're here with him."

She chewed her bottom lip. "Are you?"

"Ben's way more relaxed when you're here."

"Okay." She picked up her pen, her expression shutting him out. "Is that all you wanted to discuss?"

"That's it for me." Except he possessed

a contradictory nature that wouldn't allow him to walk away on her terms. "Are you planning to look around some more while you're here?"

"Look around?"

It annoyed him that she was pretending not to understand what he meant. "For artisans like Butch."

She frowned, and Owen suspected she didn't want to leave Ben alone with him or his family any more than she had to.

"You're missing an opportunity," Owen said.

"I appreciate you introducing me to Butch," she said. "I really feel lucky to have access to his work, but I'm not here to scout new artists. I want to be with Ben."

"I admit I was a bully, and I'm sorry about that. No one's trying to block you from Ben, but if you can find more work you like while you're here, why shouldn't you? The folks in these mountains really could be good for your business."

"And you're not trying to get me off guard?"

"By leading you to people who do good work? I'm not trying to hurt you any more, Lilah."

She didn't answer, and she obviously didn't

believe him. Only time would show her he wasn't lying. As her stricken gaze drilled into his back, he headed out the door as if he didn't mind losing his temper and hurting a woman's feelings.

"MOM SAID YOU'RE going out." Chad spoke over a plate heaped with pancakes, eggs and bacon.

"Yes. I'm taking Owen's advice and visiting a few of the local artists." Lilah admired Chad's stamina. How any kid could put down that much food…

The smell of his breakfast, along with grits and homemade biscuits, still lingered in the air. All the Gages worked so hard they could afford to eat a huge meal in the morning.

"I get to play with Chad today," Ben said. "He's my bro-cou-uncle."

"That's right." She looked over his head at the high school senior. "And Uncle Chad is going to keep a good eye on you and show you fun things around the farm."

"I promise," Chad said, as much to her as to Ben.

"We're going to feed the goats and then take a hike up the mountain."

"How far up the mountain?" Lilah's anxiety started to kick in.

"To the chair lift," he said. "One of the resorts has a lift that glides almost to the edge of our property. It's a good walk. I figure it'll tire Ben out."

"But you won't let him run ahead of you? Out of your sight?" She tried to think what else might happen. "You won't leave him alone with the goats? Or go near those cows on his own."

"He's scared of cows." Chad speared another mouthful of pancakes. "I won't do any of what you just said. And I'll nursemaid that poor kid as if I gave birth to him." He looked at his nephew. "That'd be a good thing, buddy. I'd make an excellent mom."

Ben just giggled. "Mommy, you should come with us. We're going to feed Gomer and take a big, long walk." He spread both arms as if he were measuring it off for her.

"Sounds like fun," she said, and she was so reluctant to walk out the door, she had to wonder if Owen might have a point about her being overprotective. Her imagination ran wild too easily. "Stay with Uncle Chad, and make sure you don't get lost."

"I love Gomer. He eats food right out of

my hand, and he only tried to eat my glove once."

Did goats actually bite humans? She swallowed. It hadn't happened. It wouldn't happen. No way would she spoil Ben's fun by canceling her plans to go out for a few hours and scout for work for the gallery.

"It's almost like you have a pet goat," she said.

"Can I have a puppy?"

Chad laughed, and Lilah thought about collapsing into her own breakfast plate.

"No puppy, buddy. I'm sorry, but we don't have time to take care of a puppy the way we should."

"But I really want a puppy."

"Some day, when we have lots of time to look after a little dog, we'll do that."

"When I'm this many?" He held up both hands, spreading his fingers wide.

"When you're ten, we'll think seriously about getting a puppy."

"Okay." He pumped a fist, and Lilah got up to take her plate to the kitchen and then gather her coat and bag.

"Chad, you have my number?" She tried to remember all the things she should say to a sitter she didn't entirely trust.

"I have it. Mom has it. Even Ben has your number, but no one will need to call you."

She had to make herself stop hovering. "Have a good day, buddy. And Chad. I'll see you both when I get back tonight."

"Ben and I'll have a great time," Chad promised.

"Goodbye, Mommy. I hope you find lots of stuff."

"Thanks, baby." She kissed her son's forehead and grabbed another quick hug before she hurried to the door, hoping she wouldn't be tempted to turn back. "You can call me if you want to, anytime."

"Be careful on the mountain roads." Suzannah appeared in the hallway at the bottom of the stairs, her arms full of linens. "They're wet and slippery today. I heard we might have snow flurries this afternoon."

"I'm used to snow," Lilah said.

"Yes." Celia appeared from the living room and headed to the closet in the mudroom for her own coat. "But you're not used to Tennessean drivers in snow on mountain roads. We either creep along, or we fly like daredevils."

"That's the first thing I've heard any

of you say that isn't totally Tennessee-is-paradise."

"You mean you don't think it is?" Celia laughed. "I worry about your judgment, Lilah, but you'll fall in love with this place. No one can resist Bliss."

Lilah pulled her knit cap around her ears and headed for the door. This place was going to be part of Ben's life and therefore part of hers. She'd better see what lay beyond the inn and Owen's clinic project.

He'd lent her his truck for today. She'd never driven a truck before, but if she found any pieces she couldn't resist, it would be perfect. Driving a truck couldn't be that different from the van she usually used.

She put on her seat belt, started the engine and turned on the navigation on her phone. She was visiting a small town called Halcomb, where an artist who worked in ceramics had agreed to see her.

She drove out of Bliss, onto a divided four-lane highway nestled between naked hardwoods, evergreens glistening beneath partially thawed ice, and sheer walls of limestone and granite. For once, she let herself enjoy the mountain beauty, sinking into a feeling of contentment. It would be easy to fall in love with the primeval purity of the Smokies. She pulled into an overlook to take photos.

In the crisp mountain air, her fears slowly crept away. Ben had been on the farm for a week or so, and he already acted as if this place was in his blood, too. He treated the inn as if it belonged to him, and he explored the land around the sprawling yellow house with complete confidence. Even she could see that was a measure of his happiness.

And his increasing maturity since Owen had found them.

She put worrisome thoughts out of her head. Chad would look after him today. He'd promised.

Her navigation system led her down doubtful roads as snowflakes began to splat against the windshield. At last, she turned up a narrow lane through an apple orchard, which gave way to arbors of brown vines.

She parked in the driveway that simply stopped in front of a little white clapboard house, where a wizened man in overalls and a big, gray jacket that matched his fedora waited.

"Miz Bantry?" he asked as she got out.

She pushed her hands through the sleeves

of her coat and shoved her keys into the pocket. "Please, call me Lilah. Are you Mr. Clanton?"

"Robert," he said. "You want to look at my pots?"

"I sure do. Everyone in the shops in Bliss loves your work. In fact, they were all sold out."

"Yeah. I work when I want to. Rest when I don't."

"Sounds like the perfect job."

He stood and eased himself down the steps, holding the balustrade as if his joints hurt. "I have a little workshop out back. My wife and daughter got tired of my mess. It's funny. They treat me in town like I'm some genius, but Bella and Sally don't want to sweep around me anymore."

Lilah grinned. "I hear that pretty often."

"Now, you have a shop in New York? Can't say I ever imagined my old pots would be showing up in New York—unless some crazy tourist took them home."

"I actually run a shop in Vermont, but we'd probably put your work in the store in New York first, because we have a wider client base there. More people would see your pieces, and the word would spread faster."

As they went around the back of the house, a dog appeared from his little house beneath a walnut tree. He woofed at them, clearly uncertain whether to defend his domain against this stranger or continue his nap.

"He's like me," Robert said. "Can't really be bothered much anymore."

The dog eased toward Lilah across the tidy yard.

"Or maybe he likes you." Robert stretched out a hand and patted the dog's head as they reached a wooden shed, fronted by another small, wet porch.

A ceramic wind chime hung above the door, tinkling a joyful greeting via circles of smiling moons and glowering suns, a blowing North wind, and a crying face that symbolized rain. Hanging below all the other pieces was a flurry of snowflakes that brushed against each other in a soft song.

"I have a few of these," Robert said as she looked up. "I change them out with the seasons."

"This is beyond beautiful. If you ever make something similar, I'd love to buy one for my house."

"I can do that, but they don't always look the same," he said.

"I'm glad. I already know I'm going to love your work, Robert."

He opened the door, and she walked inside to find a storeroom of lovely pieces—serving dishes with ruffled edges, some with an inner bowl for dips. More wind chimes hanging from the ceiling. Ewers with delicate handles and matching primitive bowls.

But the pieces that took her breath away were the pots that bore faces—happy faces, sad, angry, frightened and soothing faces. Families of cylindrical pots that sat on fat bottoms or reached for the sky with long necks.

"Robert, you have a soul inside you."

"Sometimes troubled," he said. "You can see all of it in those." He pointed to the expressive faces on his work.

"Why aren't these in the stores in Bliss? They all said they'd love to have more of your work."

"I take it in when I feel like it. I haven't felt like it in a while, and these are personal. I wouldn't have brought you in here if we hadn't had a good talk on the phone before you came."

She looked at him, taking in the hands buried in his pockets, the face lined by life.

His hair, an unkempt white mess, still thick, shooting in all directions.

"Are you feeling all right?" she asked him, surprising herself. "Is everything all right with you?"

He stared at her like a kitten who'd been rubbed the wrong way. "Pardon?"

"I thought maybe you had a reason for keeping all this lovely work to yourself." She'd gone too far, stuck her nose in where it didn't belong.

"Not as I know of." Not as he was willing to tell her. He went to the end of the table. "What if I gave you five of them? You could send them to New York, and we'll see how they do in your fancy shop."

"I'd love five. Which ones?"

"You choose," he said.

It felt like some sort of test, but she didn't want to fail. She backed up and reached for one of the wind chimes, sliding her fingertips over lambs and goat kids and puppies and kittens. They were so delicate, baked to muted, beautiful colors. "May I start with this?"

He nodded. "You got a baby?"

"A boy, who'd never ask for lambs and kids

and kittens, unless they were real. He might think this is too babyish for him."

"Boys like real pets. Maybe he'll be a farmer."

Thank goodness she didn't have to worry about that for a few years. "If you make something with trucks and motorcycles or airplanes and trains, I'd grab it right out of your hands."

He rocked back on his heels. "I'll call that a commission."

She moved to the pots on the tables. She chose one that looked as if it had seen a ghost. She pulled it forward on the table. Next, she picked one that had clearly found its true love, another that had never been more sad, and one that simply looked at peace. "What do you think?"

He moved the sad one back into its spot. "You're not a lady who needs him right now." He touched the peaceful face. "Wish I had a matching set of these, but I think this one will do for you." He pulled forward a pot with a feminine face on the verge of smiling. Maybe Lilah was making up the stories about the pots, but this face seemed to be in the midst of learning joy.

From above, rain tapped on the tin roof.

The pale yellow light in the room gave Lilah a sense of peace that felt unfamiliar, maybe tentative, but that she embraced.

"Perfect," she said. "How I'll let any of them be sold is beyond me, but I'd love these for the gallery."

"Let me wrap them up," Robert said, going behind the table to find large pieces of sturdy wrapping paper.

"I'll help you." She took a big square of the paper, too, and smoothed it out on another table. "Wrapping and shipping was my first job when I went to work with my family."

"I'll trust you, then."

"Thank you, Robert. I almost wish I could come work for you. I love your place here, and your work touches me." Maybe even more than Owen's had when she'd first met him.

He grinned. "I'd like that, too, except Bella wouldn't go for it, and I never enjoy when I have to explain stuff to Bella."

LILAH SAW A couple more people that afternoon. She took photos of the man who worked in aluminum and steel, shaping objects from his childhood, including a beehive and a red wagon with paint almost etched into its shiny sides. His work wasn't Lilah's thing, but she thought the items might appeal to her brother.

Next, she visited a woman who welded animals out of rebar. Lilah bought a sheep, a goat and a chicken for Suzannah. They'd be perfect at the inn. She took a few more to send to New York. Folks up there liked pieces like these for their country homes, or even for a small courtyard garden in the city.

Still floating on this unexpected stream of contentment, she drove back to Bliss through gentle flurries. She turned up the music and sang along inside the warm truck.

She ought to ski a little while she was here. She rarely found time in Vermont, which was ridiculous, but she hated leaving Ben with sitters. Maybe he could try a lesson, too.

It would be good for her to find a few pluses for getting in touch with the other side of his family.

She hit traffic in the center of Bliss. Skiers coming down for shopping or a bite to eat. Local residents heading out of town to their homes, hidden in the hollows of the mountains.

Lilah breathed deep as she waited, totally

relaxed, through a traffic light. She was happy. Happy. Who could have imagined?

The worst had happened. Ben's father had finally found him. Owen would never trust her again. He'd blackmailed her into this trip to Tennessee, and still, she felt happy.

As she drove through the small, snow-dusted streets, she realized how much she'd enjoyed the afternoon on her own, exploring the Tennessee countryside. Natural enough. She'd been so busy as a single mom that she'd never taken much time for herself.

It had surprised her how quickly Ben had come to feel at home here, and she was no longer looking forward to the day she had to take him back to Vermont. Not that she would tell Owen that.

She and Ben had made their life in Vermont. They had their own routines, their own home. She'd worked hard to create a safe, happy life for him. Having contact with his father could add to that happiness, but Ben belonged in Vermont.

Lilah skidded a little in the still-falling snow as she reached the fork in the road that led to Bliss Peak in one direction and Suzannah Gage's inn in the other. Lilah headed toward the inn and soon reached Suzannah's white picket fences, reinforced with wire to keep in the goats and sheep and cows.

Movement caught her eye. The goats were stampeding. There must have been at least ten, and when they all got excited about the same thing… She was laughing until she saw a small, dark head, just taller than the goats.

Just one dark head. No tall high school senior hot on his heels. Ben, on his own.

Lilah glanced over her shoulder at the mountain stream to her left. She had to warn Ben before he ran straight into it with his gang of goats. She stopped the truck, not caring that she was leaving it in the middle of the road. Running with careless speed, she took the fence like a hurdler. She hardly noticed the sting as she went over.

She skidded into the herd of goats, readily picking out her son's laughter above their noisy bleating.

"Mommy," he said, veering toward her. "I didn't know you were here."

She knelt, and he ran straight into her, knocking her into the snow, which spilled down her collar and beneath her shirt. Ben sprawled over her, and he struggled to get up.

"I wanted to win the race. I was beating the goats."

And headed straight into icy water. "I saw that," she said, gasping for breath. "Where's Uncle Chad?"

"He's exercising with those big bags of goat food Grandma Suzannah keeps in her shed."

"Exercising? The muscle-bound—I've never heard of a worse idea." She reached up and tugged Ben's hood forward, covering his ears. "Do you know there's a stream right behind us?"

"Can we go see it?"

He hopped off her and grabbed her hand, but she yanked him back. "Ben, buddy, you almost ran straight into that stream. You might have been hurt." How to make him see the danger without traumatizing him?

"Nah," he said, "I'm fine. Is that Own's truck?"

She glanced at the vehicle. The engine was still running and the driver's door stood wide open. "It is. We'd better get it home."

"You're bleeding," Ben said. "Look at your hand."

She lifted it up. She'd taken off her gloves to drive, and there was a cut in her palm. She must have caught a sharp part of the fence as she jumped over it.

"I'll be okay." She scooped up snow and used it to wash her hand, when what she really wanted to do was crush him close to her, overwhelmed by relief that he was unharmed. She'd been right. Owen and his family had ignored her every concern and put her son in danger.

Ben might have drowned or, at the very least, suffered from hypothermia. She pressed her little boy's head to her throat so he couldn't see her fear.

Chad might find himself learning some new moves for the football field when she got her hands on him.

"Mommy, I can't breathe."

She inhaled deeply and stood, taking Ben's hand. "Where's your glove?"

"In my pocket. Gomer keeps stealing it."

She couldn't stop thinking about the danger Ben had been in. "I know you were having fun running with the goats, but if you didn't see the stream, you might have fallen and not been able to get out again. I wouldn't want that to happen to you."

"I wasn't gonna fall in the water. That's just silly."

"Buddy, you need to listen to me." She

knelt in the snow beside her son, who averted his face.

"I'm not a baby, and I want to play with the goats."

Lilah felt a chill that was bone deep. What had happened to her reasonable child? "I don't want you to run out of Grandma Suzannah's house unless someone's with you. You might have been hurt."

"You always say that, and I don't get hurt."

"If I hadn't caught you, you might have."

Lilah noticed that the goats had all veered away from the stream and were making the slow trek back toward the barn, their coats speckled with fresh snow.

"The goats don't like getting wet," Ben said. "They won't go in the stream. But me and Gomer ran, and then they all chased us."

"It's not just the goats, Ben," she said, frustrated. "I don't want you running around in the snow outside Grandma's house by yourself."

"Owen takes me outside," he said.

He was pushing his boundaries, which had vastly expanded. "You are not to leave Grandma's house unless I say you can." That should cover all the possibilities. "Do you understand?"

"You worry too much." He started trudging toward the truck, but Lilah stood frozen in her tracks. She wondered which Gage he'd heard that line from. Shoving her anger aside, she hurried after Ben, suddenly having visions that he might jump in the cab and knock the truck out of park, hurtling it forward.

For a moment she wondered if she might be losing her mind. Maybe she should listen to her son.

She was obsessed with his safety, though. She'd never escape her own dark memories, and she didn't want Ben to ever experience the same pain.

Once they got back to the house, she intended to speak with Chad about his lax child care. What had she been thinking, coming down here in the first place?

CHAPTER TEN

BEN UNDID HIS seat belt and jumped out of the truck the second Lilah turned off the engine. She caught up with him.

"I know you're mad at me, buddy, but I'm still the mom, and I'm supposed to keep you safe."

"I wasn't scared, Mommy."

"I don't want you to be scared. I just want you to think twice." Lilah winced. He was only four years old. "Let's go inside, and you can take a shower."

"Now? Do I have to go to bed?"

She shook her head. "You're shivering, and a shower will help warm you up. And then it'll be time for dinner."

Chad met them at the door of the inn, his features slackening with relief when he saw she had Ben.

"Where were you?" he asked his nephew. "I turned around and you were gone."

Lilah was struck dumb. He'd turned his back on her son.

"Just for a second, Lilah. Really."

She directed Ben toward the stairs. "Chad, can you wait down here? I'd like to speak to you."

"I figured you would."

"Good. See you in a few minutes."

Lilah took Ben upstairs and turned on a warm shower he didn't want to take. She pointed at the curtain. "In you go, buddy."

He sighed, with exaggerated grief. "Okay, Mommy."

Poor kid. She probably could be a bit over-whelming, but she knew what could happen. One second the world was right. The next, her little boy could find himself in hell.

Just as she had.

Chad was waiting downstairs in his mother's kitchen with a cup of coffee for her when she'd finished helping Ben and settled him in the living room with one of his books. She hesitated for a moment. Chad was also a kid. But she had to make her point. It was too important. What if the same thing happened when she wasn't around? "While you were working out with bags of goat feed," she said, "Ben ran down to the stream with the goats. They could have hurt him. He could have fallen into the water, and he could have ended up with hypothermia."

Chad had the good grace to look ashamed. "I'm sorry. I suddenly got this great idea that I could use the feed bags for a better Cross-Fit workout than the tires I've been using. They're heavy, and they—"

She nodded, trying to contain her anger. "You had one job."

Chad bristled. "I have to train for football if I'm going to get a scholarship, and my mom expected me to put the goat feed away."

"Why are you so determined to pretend this is okay? If you had other things to do, all you had to say was that you couldn't look after Ben."

The kitchen door opened. Suzannah entered with an armload of freshly washed linens. "What's going on with you two?"

"The monster mom thinks I let her down with the Ben-man," Chad said, and Lilah prayed that the Gage arrogance would never rub off on her son.

"I can barely speak to you right now," she said. "In fact, I should cool down before I say something I can't take back. You agreed to watch my boy—your nephew. Then you ignored him so completely that you didn't notice he was gone until he and I walked into this house together. He almost ran into the stream with the goats, and you wouldn't have even noticed he was missing." She covered her face with her hands as visions of what could have happened flashed with too much clarity inside her head. She went to join Ben, but Celia was reading with him, so she headed back upstairs, her feet heavy. She didn't want to make any more enemies in this household. They thought she was smothering Ben, but she had to take care of him.

Thoroughly disheartened, she sank onto the top step. Voices murmured from below. Doors opened and closed, but no one came up. Not one member of Ben's new family seemed to care that he could have been seriously hurt, or worse. They were just going about their business as usual.

She went back to her room and closed the door, frustration chasing through her. She let herself cry. Just a little, quietly. She didn't want the Gages to hear her. Or Ben.

"Lilah?"

A dull tap, and Owen opened the door, looking concerned. She glanced up at him, rubbing hard at her cheeks, trying to dry the tears she'd indulged in.

"You all think I'm crazy. I get that, but I trusted Chad, and Ben ended up being at risk. If that's being overprotective, then I guess I am. But I don't see it that way."

Owen seemed to consider her words. "I do wonder if you're overprotective a lot of the time, and maybe I should be more understanding of that." He sat beside her, and she had to shift on the mattress to stop from sliding into him. "But I don't think you're wrong about this. Sometimes Ben sounds as if he's older than Chad, but he's just a little boy. He doesn't know the farm. You're right. He could have fallen into that stream."

She didn't know whether to trust him. "Are you saying that to manipulate me?"

He tilted his head the way Ben did when he didn't understand something. "Why would I try to do that?" He tugged at one of her hands, but she didn't relax. He wrapped his fingers around her wrist, imparting comfort.

"Maybe to make me feel more comfortable, so I'll be less critical of your family?"

"I told them I thought you were right in this case, and I suggested we weren't the best group to judge anyone else's child-rearing practices."

"When did you do all that?"

He grimaced. "Chad and my mom came out to the barn to tell me what happened."

Her temper arced back to life. "They ran all the way to your workplace to vent about me?"

"They went out to do the evening chores in the new dairy barn my mom had built when she started running the place on her own, and Chad texted me that he'd screwed up. I started this way to make sure you and Ben were all right, and they headed my way. We met at the barn. They realized they should fill me in in person because I wasn't likely to be any happier than you."

She smiled, though she was still feeling a little shaky. This was the kind of response she'd expected. Maybe Owen could be a good father. "Why couldn't Chad have told me he felt bad about it? He just acted defensive. All I wanted was awareness that he'd made a mistake, and some hope that it wouldn't happen again."

"He's eighteen, and he was embarrassed. I was a lot less responsible at his age."

What could the past four years have been

like if Owen had always been this caring, this comforting? "Owen, how can I even consider letting Ben come down here by himself? I mean, without me?"

"You have to. Our relationship ended a long time ago. I love my son, and Ben is learning to love me. No matter how you and I end up, Ben belongs to both of us."

"You say that as if there were some chance we could be together." The words stunned her. She hadn't meant to say them. She hadn't even thought them before.

Owen looked equally taken aback. And angry. "Don't embarrass yourself, Lilah, pretending that's a solution."

"I'm sorry. I didn't mean that we would ever be more than we are to each other now. I just—the words popped into my head when I was thinking what might have been if we'd both been different."

He tilted his head as if he were thinking back over their painful past. "Maybe you figure *I* deserve to be manipulated. Possibly, I do. But first you bring in children's protection, and now you pretend you regret cutting me out of your life?"

"I didn't mean we should try being together again." Had she? Was she so pathetic that a moment of shared understanding with this man made her wonder what she'd given up when she'd turned her back on Owen?

"I know how much you love Ben, but don't try to make me believe you could care about me again just so you don't have to allow him time alone with me. You'd hate yourself and me if you did that. It would be like selling yourself."

"Selling myself. You're going too far." She couldn't believe he'd just accused her of being the worst kind of woman.

"Maybe I haven't been blunt enough. I'm tired of you trying to play me. Four years ago, you decided to cut me out of my son's life. You didn't even tell me you were pregnant. Then, the first night you were here, you brought in lawyers and the sheriff and child protection. None of that worked, so your next step is to pretend you want me back."

"How could I trust you when the last time I saw you, you could barely stand? I'm not excusing myself, but I was only looking out for my baby."

"That would be our baby. Ben is mine as much as he is yours. I know you're a survivor. I get that you'll try anything to win, but you aren't winning sole custody of my child."

"I'm sorry I said anything. It was just words, and they meant nothing." She lifted her chin. No need to guard it when he'd already landed a couple of figurative punches. "I was surprised by your kindness and understanding when the rest of your family acted as if nothing was wrong. You seemed to have forgiven me."

"No."

He never lied. She was starting to dislike that honesty now.

She still believed she'd made the right choice for Ben. Owen was clean and sober now. But what were the odds of him staying that way?

"I can't forgive you for stealing my son," he said. "How could I? Ever?"

In some crazy way, she felt abandoned. She understood why he wouldn't trust her. She wasn't a woman who trusted easily herself.

She hadn't considered four years ago that Owen might realize he needed to get sober if he was going to be a father. She hadn't given him the chance to do it for Ben.

She'd thrown good love away. For herself and for her son. She stood. "Thanks for coming up. I'm fine."

Rising, he nodded and went to the door. "I'll come back for Ben after dinner."

Owen and Ben had been eating with them every night.

"I'll bring him home," she said, but then immediately regretted her words. She hadn't meant to call his cabin Ben's home. "I'd like to put him to bed tonight."

OWEN LEFT BEN tucked into his bunk bed and Lilah sleeping in the chair at their son's side, her hair soft and silky on her cheeks, her smile more relaxed than he could remember since she'd exiled him from her life.

Downstairs, he walked into the kitchen, prowling. He rubbed his chin, his fingers stinging as they passed over rough stubble.

His eyes went to the cabinet. The one with the wine. That bottle had to be five years old if it was a day. He should have thrown it away when he'd tossed the Bantry gift of wine.

This bottle was his stash, his backup in case the time came when he couldn't stand sobriety, but it was also his proof that he could have a bottle in the house and not down a drop.

He ended up in front of the cabinet, with

his hand on the small, round pull. His fingers closed. And trembled.

His throat constricted. He wanted it. He needed a drink. If it were vodka, it would have been gone years ago. He didn't like wine as much.

He could like wine tonight. He felt bad about leaving Ben with Chad, and worse about the berating he'd given his brother, but the thing he regretted most was the way he'd insulted Lilah.

One drink. A sip. Maybe he could just breathe in the fragrance of five-year-old, gone-to-vinegar, cheap cooking wine.

No.

Owen slammed his fist against the cabinet and hurried to the front door to put on boots and a jacket and walk out into the cold night. The snow was still coming down, wet now, with thunder and lightning, and he had to slog his way to his truck.

Chaos reigned everywhere in his life, even in this strange weather.

He'd asked his family to meet him at the inn. He'd never told them Lilah's story, but they kept dismissing her concern for Ben. Maybe if they understood, they'd find some empathy for her.

At the inn he turned quickly into the courtyard parking lot, skidding over his mother's delicate yellow stone, splashing enough soggy snow that some of it hit his windshield. He parked as close to the house as he could and then jumped out, hopping across the low wall to the porch.

His mother hadn't locked up for the night, and he found her surrounded by Chad and Celia and Noah at a large, round table.

"The woman is troubled," Noah was saying. "Something must have happened to her, and considering our own pasts, you might all consider showing her a little more compassion. You can't blame her when you don't know her situation, Mom."

His mother nodded. "If someone had stepped in with us, maybe Owen wouldn't drink. Maybe our whole family would be happier." Suzannah bit the tip of her thumb. "I'm ashamed to admit I was such a terrible mother, anyone would have been better, and I'm devastated that my mistakes still make problems for you all. If I could, I would change it all no matter what I had to do."

"Stop, Mom," Celia said. "I don't think being tossed into the foster-care system would have been a blissful alternative. It might have been out of one fire and into a conflagration."

"I'd also rather not hear you'd have been better off if someone took us off your hands," Owen said, drawing their startled attention.

"That's not what I meant." Suzannah shook her head with a hint of her old frantic desperation. "Any kind of mother would have been better than me. Why didn't I see what I was doing? What I wasn't doing for all of you."

"We're not discussing that tonight, Mom." If she didn't relent, he'd have to go chop a cord of wood or steal a good bottle of wine from her cellar. Only Suzannah Gage could see having her children split up and distributed to foster families around the county as an alternative to just protecting them from the man who'd abused them all. "Lilah's done her best for Ben, and she's raised a great child. I don't care if you all disapprove. What I've done, dragging her down here, is bad enough. Maybe you could leave her alone, and let her and me work out how to be good parents to Ben."

"You ask us to be family to Ben—and to her," Chad said. "But she's scared of everything, and it's our duty to tell you she'll teach that boy to be afraid of his own shadow. I won't be surprised if he's scared of Gomer and the rest of the goats after this."

"Lilah pulled Ben out of a goat stampede. He's hardly more than a baby himself, and they're heavier than he is. She trusted you to look after him, Chad, because I asked her to. I feel responsible when you let us both down. You didn't have to say you'd take care of him."

"I was watching him." Chad sounded as defensive as Lilah had described. "I stopped just for a second to see if I could use the goat feed bags for training. You know, dragging it? Lifting?"

"You dumped the kid to bench-press goat feed?" Celia asked, in the same tone Lilah had used.

"Chad, do you know how that sounds? After you pass judgment on Ben's mother?" Owen was uncomfortably aware he'd done the same thing. Maybe this was a second chance for him to stop thinking she overreacted. "If you promise to watch Ben, don't turn your back on him. He's small and curious. Just don't offer if you can't focus on the job."

"Come on, Owen." His mother tapped her

hands on the table. She still didn't like arguments. "Let's not lose our tempers."

"My temper is lost when I think what might have happened to my son if Lilah hadn't shown up."

"She treats us all as if we're conspiring against her, and we're not functionally intelligent enough to take care of a small child," Chad said. "I just want to spend time with my nephew."

"In a frozen stream, apparently, after you bench-press animal food," Celia said.

Owen flashed his sister silent thanks. "Lilah is Ben's mother. What she wants goes before your choices about what's best for Ben. She told me what happened because she was concerned for our child, but you act as if something's wrong with her." And there was, in a way. He'd thought he was going to explain, but they were so angry and judgmental he was changing his mind.

"You're not—" Chad stood up, looking to Noah for backup and receiving only a bland stare. "You're not falling for her again?"

There had been a moment just after she'd assumed he was suggesting they might get back together… Only a moment. "The woman hid my son from me for four years.

Am I likely to forget that? She thought I wasn't safe for him. Now, thanks to Chad, you all are working hard to prove that Ben won't be safe here without her."

"You told him about the stream thing, though, right—that they lead to roads." Celia yanked Chad back into his chair. "That saved me several times when I was a kid."

They were all silent. Celia had often responded to the violence between their parents by running away. Just disappearing.

"He's four." Owen felt his voice rising. "Will he remember about streams and roads? Will he reach a road before he tangles with a bear or falls into the water? If you're looking after him, look after him, focus, people." Which was pretty ironic, considering Noah had already pulled his phone from his pocket. The show must have been over. Owen turned back toward the door. "Give her the kind of break we've all asked for ourselves around here."

"Lilah Bantry." Noah's voice was a mix of surprise and deep compassion. "Little Lost Lilah."

Chad, Celia and their mother looked confused. Before any of them could say a word, Owen turned, ready to shut them all down.

"Cut it out, Noah. This is none of your business. I was going to tell you, but hearing the way Chad talked about her, I thought better."

Noah ignored him. "I knew something was wrong. Her responses feel extreme."

"I said this was none of your business."

"Sorry." Noah put his phone back in his pocket. "I'm a little ashamed of myself because I thought she was acting paranoid with Ben to make a point about you. Anyway, don't you think we'll all get along better if we know the truth about each other?"

"What do you know about truth? What have you ever done that you needed to hide?" Dr. Noah had toed the line better than any of them. His life had been all about control, and repression of the Gage family's negative tendencies.

"What's going on?" Celia asked.

"It's Lilah," Noah said. "She suffered a horrible childhood trauma. I wonder why she never changed her name or hid her past. She had to expect someone would remember sometime."

"I don't understand," Suzannah said.

Owen paid attention only to Noah. "How could she change her name when her family owns an internationally recognized business?

Leave her alone, all of you." He shot them a last warning glance. "Or I'll be the one moving—to Vermont. It's a circus around here."

"Wait, Owen."

Noah again.

"What, big brother?" He turned, ramming his hands into his jacket pockets.

"Lilah should be able to talk about her problem. She shouldn't be hiding it or Ben from life."

"Lilah is none of your business. I know you mean well, Noah, but stay out of this."

"Wait." His mother came around the table. "Are you all right? You're so upset. You won't—"

"Drink?" The wine was on his mind again. How could it not be? Numbness had to be better than guilt and worry. "Good night, Mom."

CHAPTER ELEVEN

"Own, I want to visit you."

Ben's voice echoed around the hollow building, more clinic than barn now, with its open framing and dangling wires. In the middle of tracking some of that wiring high up on a wall, Owen looked down from a ladder that wasn't balanced correctly. He pressed his hands to the wall, intent on keeping his son away from the unsteady metal ladder. "Ben? Where's your coat? And where is Celia?"

His sister had promised to watch Ben.

"Talking all funny to someone on her phone. I wanted to see you. I told her I was coming out here." He looked up at Owen. "She's still talking. Whatcha doing?"

"Looking for wires." Clicking the off switch on his flashlight, Owen stabilized the ladder, at the same time keeping an eye on the power tools spread all over a workbench too near his curious son. "Don't touch anything. Okay?"

"There's lots of wires." Like iron filings to a magnet, he headed for the bench.

"I think I found the ones I wanted," Owen said. "Leave the table alone, Ben."

"I won't touch." He put a tentative finger on the edge of the bench. "You mean this stuff?"

"Ben." Owen started down the ladder. There was a little too much of him in his son. The moment someone told him no, he knew better. Always had. Ben had somehow managed to retain that quality despite Lilah's best efforts to keep him safe. No wonder she worried about him so much.

"Own, what's this?" Ben tapped the back of the power hammer.

"No, Ben." Owen moved faster, skipping a few rungs. Could no one in his family be trusted with his son?

Ben tapped again. "Can I just look at it?" He reached for the round handle that required both his hands to grip, and held the business end of the hammer pointed in the direction of his face.

Owen skidded down the rest of the ladder, which toppled to the side and fell from beneath him. At the same time, he heard the report of a nail being shot out of the hammer, into who knew what, and the concrete floor ended his fall with an unforgiving thud.

Sprawled on the cold, hard surface, he tried to catch his breath. He also tried to turn. Thankfully, Ben began to cry. He couldn't cry if… Owen's arm gave out underneath him, stabbing with unbelievable pain.

"Ben," he said, his voice a gasp, "are you all right?"

"Own?" The little guy's boots slapped against the floor as he ran. "Are you dead?"

"Are you okay?" He managed to lever himself up enough to catch Ben in the circle of his good arm. Ben's hug nudged the injured one, and pain rushed through him again.

He tried to hold Ben a little away so he could see if he'd hurt himself, but the little guy was wrapped around him, sobbing.

"Ben, are you hurt? Are you bleeding?"

He shook his head, and Owen found nothing more than a scrape on the back of his hand "What's this?"

"My hand hit the table when I shot you."

"What?" At last, he realized Ben was crying for him. "Buddy, I'm fine."

"I shot you. With that gun."

"It's a hammer, and you didn't shoot me. I fell off the ladder."

"Let me see." Ben backed up, and this time, he yanked at Owen's shirt, his ice-blue eyes so familiar, so worried, Owen wanted to cry, too.

"I'm good." He took the opportunity to get a closer look at his child. "No blood," he said, with relief. "No puncture wounds."

He shouted a silent thanks and struggled to stand. His head swam with both agony and relief as Ben grabbed at his arms, trying to scramble closer.

"Let me get up," Owen said, looking for his phone but not finding it. "I'll carry you back to Grandma's."

"Okay." Ben rubbed his streaming eyes and nose on his sleeve. "Don't tell Mommy I shot you. She doesn't like guns."

Owen crawled to his feet, bracing himself on his good hand, and then leaned down and lifted Ben, who immediately wrapped his arms around his father's shoulder and hitched his knees into Owen's ribs.

The walk to the inn was a dizzying adventure over rough ground. The important thing—his son hadn't been hurt. He'd have to get the tools to higher ground because, clearly, no one could put a stop to Ben's wandering ways.

"Buddy, can you lean down and open the gate for me?" Owen asked as they reached the fence that barred the goats from the inn's front yard.

Ben leaned down, but his foot slid into Owen's bad arm. Owen managed to turn his gasp into a laugh that Ben shared with a bewildered expression. Breathing hard to keep from being sick, Owen heard the one voice he was hoping to avoid speak his name.

"Owen?" Lilah said from behind him, a hint of "I told you so" in her voice. "You found Ben. Is he all right? Baby, are you hurt?"

"He's fine," Owen said, trying to reach the house before he collapsed. He'd explain later when Ben wasn't around.

"Own's not fine."

"What happened to you?" Lilah was catching up. The fence squeaked on its hinges as she shut it.

"Own fell off his ladder," Ben said, driven to confess. "I was playing with his tools, and I shot him."

"You—what tools?" Lilah came from behind and ran her hands over Owen's body the way he'd examined their son. "You are hurt, Owen. Give me Ben." She scooped the little guy into her arms and looked him over before setting him on the grass. "Are you okay, honey?" she asked again.

"I didn't shoot myself, Mommy, just Own."

She didn't look at either of them, but she reached for Owen's arm, only to stop.

"He had the power hammer," Owen said. No use in coloring the truth. "I'll move everything to higher shelves."

"Own was way high on a ladder, Mommy."

"I see. You were trying to reach him, and you fell off a ladder?"

"Yeah. Does that give me points?"

"You don't need points. I'm not worried that you won't look after him." She turned Ben toward the pale yellow clapboard inn. "Obviously, you didn't realize you should put power tools out of his reach, but I know you'll try your hardest to keep him safe. Ben, let's go ask your grandmother if you can play with her for a while."

"I like playing with Grandma. She lets me cook."

Lilah sent a desperate glance over her shoulder.

"Not at the stove." Owen slid his good hand beneath his bad arm. A sling might be a magical thing.

"Where you going, Mommy?"

"I might take Own to see his brother, Uncle Noah," she said. "Own seems to have an injury."

"Let me see." Ben pulled free of her hand and turned to inspect Owen again. "Is your arm hurt, Own?"

"A little, but you didn't shoot me."

Lilah looked wary again, but she literally bit her lip. "Come on, Ben. Let's go talk to Grandma. Owen, my car is unlocked." She gave him a stern glance that promised they'd discuss specifics later. "If you want to wait for me."

"Don't give my mom details until we know what's up with my arm." He was never sure what his mother could handle.

"I won't have to tell Suzannah." Lilah sifted Ben's fine, curly hair through her fingers, pointedly reminding Owen their son was always happy to share information. "But she still might get really worried in a hurry."

"Explain a little, then." He tried to lift his injured arm and noticed it jutted at an odd angle beneath his long-sleeved, flannel shirt.

A wave of dizziness floated over him again. "Just broad strokes."

"Okay." Turning, she hurried Ben in front of her.

Owen went to her car and slid into the passenger seat. He put his head back and hoped the nausea would ease. Sooner than he'd expected, the driver's door opened, and Lilah slid in, accompanied by a scent that went straight to his head.

She still used the perfume he'd been the first to give her. Though, who knew if another man had given her the same fragrance since?

He glanced at her. Focused on starting the car, she didn't even look his way. Her features were slightly different from the time when they'd been together. More refined, almost fragile. Her jaw was soft and strong and delicate. How many times had he followed its sweet curve with kisses?

She turned suddenly, pausing as she reached behind them into the backseat.

"Why are you staring at me?" she asked.

"To take my mind off my broken arm." And because he couldn't help himself. She was still beautiful, still a mystery and a challenge to him. And she loved his son so much.

Who could have guessed that would make him feel as if he needed her again?

"Don't make me nervous."

"I make you nervous?" Interesting. He'd been the one to tell her they weren't going to mean anything to each other, but he liked the idea that she might not be as self-contained as she pretended.

She reached back again and came up with a soft blanket, which she tucked around him without actually touching him. For some reason, he didn't protest that he didn't need her nurturing.

"Every time you're nice to me, I can't help wondering if you're plotting your next move with Ben," she said.

With that, she bumped him back to earth, and he swallowed a groan, aware of the throb in his arm again. "We both believe the worst about each other. It's bad for Ben, long-term, if we can't be friends."

She turned her face to the windshield, and he wondered what went on behind that expression he couldn't read.

She didn't want to be friends.

Neither did he, but he wasn't sure he was happy to be antagonists any longer.

And Lilah's beautiful face gave nothing away.

If only he could feel that same certainty. Even now, she believed she'd done right, breaking off their relationship, keeping Ben away from him. But every day they grew closer, and every day, Owen wanted more. More explanation, more understanding. More of the truth about Lilah.

SOMETHING ABOUT THIS accident had changed the atmosphere between them. Lilah wished she could read Owen's mind. Funny, she hadn't wished for that four years ago, when she needed to know whether he'd be able to stop drinking.

She hadn't had to read his mind then. He'd been unflinchingly honest.

But Owen wasn't the same man. He wasn't trying to earn love, to believe he even deserved it. He'd been sober for a couple of months, longer than he'd managed in the past. But she'd lost his trust. He would lie to keep her confused and off balance. To keep her from taking Ben home to their safe life.

"I don't know where Noah's office is," she said.

"On the square. Go straight into town. He's about halfway down the east side of the courthouse."

"I've never noticed his sign."

"He's subtle." Owen's voice cracked a little, as if he were laughing at her or trying not to groan again.

"So are you these days."

He didn't answer. Didn't pretend to misunderstand her sarcasm.

"I'm afraid you're going to need surgery," she said. His arm was a safe topic.

"I am, too."

"Can Noah do it?"

"He's not a surgeon, and we don't have the equipment for something like that in town. That's why I'm building the clinic."

"What if Ben had been injured like that? I hate the thought of driving him in pain all the way to Knoxville because you don't have services here."

"Are you dreaming up another reason to keep him from spending time here with me?"

She felt herself blushing. The heat was uncomfortable, but less so than the awareness that she would have done just that when she'd first arrived in Bliss. "I'm not all about manipulation, Owen."

"We have Life Flight. They land on the lawn behind the courthouse."

"Oh. Good." She glanced at his arm. He

hadn't moved anything except his head since she'd started driving. His face was tinged with gray. "Are you cold? I can pull over and tuck that blanket more securely."

"I'm fine. I'm not going into shock."

"You're superhuman?"

"We'll find that out when Noah tries to set this thing."

His voice went a bit hoarse, and she touched his shoulder without thinking. "I'll stay with you," she said.

He eased away, as far as the car would let him. "That's not necessary. I'm all right, and you're the last person to take care of me."

"Why are you so raw now?"

"Raw?"

"Angry again. Is it because of Ben?" The accusation lay there in his rejection of her honest effort to comfort him. "I thought we were moving beyond that."

"Then we should deal with it, because I'm having a hard time trying to pretend it's in the past. What you did is always in my head."

"I was afraid for my son. When I became pregnant, I was happy. It was shocking and a little terrifying, but I wanted my baby, and then I realized I was Ben's shield against the bad things in the world. To keep him from going through what I did. I needed to protect him, both from men like my abductor and your drinking. I'd have done much worse than lie to you to do that."

He was silent a moment, in too much pain to bristle at the accusation against him. "We can't keep him in a bubble. He wouldn't be happy, and in the end, you'd regret making him afraid of life. I believe that much about you, because I remember how happy you could be despite your past."

"And if I said I'm sorry about the time you lost with him?"

"Are you?"

Her hesitation betrayed her, but she could not lie. "I wish I were, but would you choose an—" She didn't want to call him an alcoholic. "A man with your problems to take care of Ben now?"

"I'm asking why you didn't explain. How am I supposed to understand?"

"You had to change for yourself, Owen, not for me, and not for the baby I was carrying. I needed to be certain that if you did stop drinking, it was for good."

He swallowed as if the truth really were a bitter pill. "I get that you're saying you'd do the same thing again. And I'd still force you to come here. I'm ashamed of how cruel I've been to you, and I'd like us both to be good parents to Ben, but honestly, I'm not positive you wouldn't cut me out of his life again."

"What are you saying?" That he'd never really change? He'd never be a safe father for her son? How could he say that again, even after he'd spent time with Ben? "You've made him love you, Owen. You can't let him down."

"I'll never let him down." Owen braced his arm, his breathing strained. "At least that's what I'm telling myself as often as I tell you, but how can I promise? And how can I trust that you won't decide it's time to walk away again? We both know I'm one bad decision away from a drink, and I always will be."

"Why isn't Ben enough?" Why hadn't she been?

"He is. You were what I wanted back then, Lilah, more than anything. Except I had to drink. I don't feel that way now. I want it, and it's a battle to resist at times, but I'm working hard to control it."

Her body ached with the pain of the past. "Why don't you get help? I've never understood why you don't just ask for help."

"Rehab didn't work, and every time I leave

an AA meeting, the bleakness makes me want to drink more."

And that was an answer. He wasn't ready to accept help. He didn't think he needed someone else's assistance. "I'd make the same decision under the same circumstances." Usually, that thought was all she needed to erase any wisps of guilt. She tried to feel relief, but, for the first time, it wouldn't come.

With gratitude, she spotted Noah's brass sign on a brick building opposite the courthouse. "Here we are. Wait. I'll help you out of the car."

He ignored her. The second she stopped, he opened his door and eased out, swaying a little as he straightened.

"I told you to wait," she said. "You aren't superhuman."

"I can't take anything for the pain," he said through gritted teeth.

"Because of addiction?" She hadn't thought of that. "You don't have a choice. You can't get through the pain of knitting a broken bone with determination."

He shook his head.

"Wait and see what Noah says." Lilah offered her arm, but he focused on the building, his jaw clamped shut as if he didn't see her.

Startled at the sting of his rejection, she opened the door and waited for Owen to start up the stairs ahead of her in case he toppled. How she hoped to catch a man several inches taller and many lean pounds heavier than her she couldn't say.

At the landing, she reached around him and opened Noah's office door. A young woman looked up from the receptionist's desk.

"Owen," she said, assessing him with surprise. "What did you do to your arm?"

"Hi, Lynsay," he said. "I think I broke it."

The waiting room was empty. Heartening. He wouldn't have to wait long.

"Noah—Dr. Gage—is with a patient, and he has two waiting. That's all our treatment rooms. I'll see if I can slip you in ahead of the two he hasn't seen yet."

"Don't go to any special trouble."

"They're well visits. You look like an emergency."

"Lynsay, have you met Lilah Bantry?"

The receptionist nodded a measured greeting. She'd obviously heard gossip. "Nice to meet you."

Lilah smiled, pretending not to notice the other woman's curiosity. Everyone in the

misnamed town of Bliss treated her with suspicion. She should be glad they were willing to side with Owen unquestionably. He'd
inspired loyalty, and that must have meant
people liked him. Even if they didn't trust
him to stay sober, they took his side without
question against an outsider.

"Have a seat," Lynsay said. "As soon as
Noah lets me know he's ready for the next
patient, I'll notify him you're here."

Owen sat, resting his head against the
sand-colored wall behind his metal chair.
The office wasn't extravagant, but Noah
had a good reputation in the town. Lilah had
heard from more than one shop owner that
he'd saved his fiancée's stepmother from giving birth prematurely last fall.

Lilah found herself checking the time over
and over on the big clock behind Lynsay's
head. The minutes trudged past as if they
were mired in the red clay of these mountains. Finally, a console on the desk buzzed,
and Lilah exhaled in relief.

"Just a sec." The receptionist rose, straightening her scrubs. "I'm sure he'll see you,
Owen."

"He doesn't have to put me in before the
other patients who got here first."

"Oh, you're a tough guy," Lynsay said, with a sense of familiarity that troubled Lilah.

She wished she could feel that much at ease with him, especially when he needed help. Even more troubling, she felt a little— jealous.

Lynsay had hardly disappeared through the door when another woman came out, nodding at Owen and Lilah as she left the office. Then the door opened again, and Noah headed toward them. His concern got Lilah right in the heart.

His love for his brother reminded her of the distance she'd put between herself and everyone else she loved.

"What did you do?" he asked, already kneeling in front of Owen to gently manipulate the arm. "Do you mind if I cut your sleeve? I think it'll hurt less than trying to roll it up."

"Not out here," Owen said, clearly in pain from his brother's touch.

"Sure."

Standing, Noah helped Owen to his feet with a hand beneath his other elbow. Lilah started to stand, but Owen shook his head.

She sat back down, deflated, anxious.

The door closed behind the two men. Lynsay busied herself at the desk for a few minutes, but finally, she looked at Lilah, folding her hands together.

"Your son is beautiful," she said.

"You've seen him?" She hadn't noticed Lynsay before.

"Sure, with you and Owen around town. I've known Owen since he was a child, and Ben couldn't look more like him."

"I know." She wouldn't change a single thing about Ben, but she had wished more than once in the past few weeks that the resemblance between father and son wasn't so obvious.

"Do you think you'll be moving down here?" Lynsay asked, as if it were the logical solution to Owen and Lilah's problems.

Lilah reeled inwardly, but she managed a casual shrug. Owen's friend didn't need to know how loaded that question was.

CHAPTER TWELVE

"I THINK I can set it. I'll send the X-rays to an ortho I know, and he'll decide if you need surgery." Noah did a double take. "What's wrong?"

"I think I'm going to be sick. Can you hand me one of those bags?"

Noah reached for one of the green bags and shook it out in front of Owen. He took it with gratitude.

Surgery. He hoped not.

His brother stood back. "I'll stop in my office for a sample of some pain meds. And then I'll give you a prescription, but, Owen, you have to be careful with them because they're narcotics."

"Always the big brother," Owen said, trying to be wry and in control. "I'm not taking a narcotic."

"You need one. You can't gut your way through bone pain."

"I have no choice." Owen stopped talking

to allow a wave of nausea to recede. He'd been the one guy on the football team who vomited instead of toughing out extreme pain.

"You can choose to be responsible. You are responsible. I wouldn't suggest it if I didn't believe you can handle it."

"I don't believe." Owen glanced at the door behind Noah as if Lilah might hear through the heavy wood. "I haven't proven trustworthy in the past."

Noah frowned. "You've never admitted that in the past."

"I never had so much to lose. Lilah's made it clear she believes Ben won't be safe with me. Children's services threatened to put him in a foster home while they decided if either of us was good enough to have him."

"She only did that when she and Ben first got here. I might have done something as unforgivable if you'd forced me to bring my child down here from the life I'd made for him."

"I won't take your pills."

Noah stared at him, trying to think of a way to convince him.

"Noah, my head is full of all the dark days and nights I've spent, not knowing how I got

somewhere, not knowing if I'd hurt someone. Wishing I could feel like any other person. Wishing I could be like anyone except
Odell Gage."

"You're nothing like Odell."

"You escaped that gene. You take one
drink and that's plenty for you. I take one,
and I start lining up several more. It was a
matter of time before I became Odell, and
I think Ben is finally the reason I have a
chance to take a different path."

"You have to be the reason, Owen. You
can't use someone else as your crutch."

Frustration made a dent in the pain. He
wiped sweat from his forehead and then from
the top of his lip. "You aren't hearing me. I
want to be better for my son."

"I'm not being purely selfish about finishing the clinic on time when I tell you that
you won't be able to work if you don't handle this pain."

"Let's get on with the X-rays."

"Hold on. I'll be right back to get you."

"Noah?"

His brother turned with his hand on the
doorknob. Owen paused, staring at the
bag again. Talking made his nausea much
worse. When the moment passed, he looked

at his brother. "I'd take some ibuprofen if you have it."

"Okay. I'll send Lynsay."

Lynsay brought a prescription dose and then helped Owen to the X-ray machine in a room off Noah's office. About halfway through the scans, Owen reconsidered his stand on controlled substances. If he couldn't get through X-rays...

"Last one," Noah finally said, and the machine shot one last scan. "Doing okay, brother?"

"Couldn't be better."

"Lynsay will take you back to the treatment room while I email these shots to the orthopedic surgeon I mentioned."

"Thanks."

"Then we just have the cast."

"Do you have a bullet I can grip between my teeth?"

LILAH TRIED NOT to stare at the door. She'd never seen Owen like that, pale with pain, yet angry and determined.

After hurrying away from her desk to look after Owen as if she were Florence Nightingale, Lynsay had returned and was rescheduling the other patients' appointments. It felt like hours before Noah showed up again, alone.

"Where's Owen?" Lilah asked.

"Back in the treatment room. We've done some pictures, and I expect to hear from the ortho anytime. Owen's refused to take a prescription for pain meds."

"He already told me he wouldn't take them when we were driving over here."

"I admire his courage," Noah said, "but he's suffering needlessly. I'm giving you the prescription, and I'll call the pharmacist to tell him you're getting it filled. If you'd check in on Owen tonight…"

"You're acting as if Owen and I are together. Nothing could be further from the truth. I'm not sure he'll let me help him." She stared at the printed script, ashamed because she'd given Owen ample reason to believe she didn't wish him well. "And I don't think he trusts me. He might be more willing if you ask your mom or Chad or Celia."

"He'd never admit weakness to them," Noah said. "And he's going to think he's weak if he needs these. We've all let him know we don't believe he can stay sober."

"I've done the same. I kept his son from

him, and then I brought in the authorities to try to find him unfit."

"Which didn't work out for you," Noah said. "We can compare notes on the way we've mistreated my brother, or you can accept that he might be more willing to believe you understand he's hurt and he needs help. We've given him a lifetime of accusations."

Lilah looked into Noah's eyes, marveling that the entire family had the same icy gaze, except for Suzannah. "You think he'll be all right if he takes the painkillers?"

"He doesn't want another addiction. He hates the idea, so, yeah, I'm willing to give him the benefit of the doubt. And I don't like the way he looks right now. You share a son. You know him well, so you can find a way to talk to him."

"I don't know why you think that."

"I'm trying to say he loved you once. You have some pull with him still, and I don't think you want to hurt him again."

"I never wanted to in the first place," she said. She was admitting the truth to the wrong brother, but felt such a relief to finally say it out loud.

"Good." He backed out of her personal space, already turning toward the door to his treatment rooms. "Just drop by his cabin tonight and tell him I asked you to check in. I'll keep him here long enough for you to go get that filled."

Lilah had seen the pharmacy on her visits to town. Grabbing her coat and purse, she hurried out of his office, grateful for something to do.

"WHEN WE GET BACK, don't let Ben jump on you. He was worried he'd hurt you when I left him," Lilah said, "and he'll want to cuddle."

"I'll remember to duck." The ibuprofen hadn't made much of a dent in the pain, but at least he'd stopped feeling sick. Owen adjusted his sling. He might just make it through this after all. "He'll be calm once he knows I'm all right."

Lilah adjusted her grip on the steering wheel. She rarely showed her nerves, but she'd been flexing her fingers for most of the drive. "Maybe he should stay at your mother's with me until you're feeling better? I'm not sure how you'd handle bath time."

"No." Owen felt her tense at his sharp tone. "Sorry," he said, "but you never miss a chance to try to move me out of his life."

"I'm not doing that. Look at your arm, and be reasonable."

"Ben and I can handle whatever he needs. I can still make his dinner one-handed, and he takes his own shower or bath. I'll be there with him."

She didn't answer at first. She swallowed so hard, he saw the muscles in her throat move. "Okay, but call me if you need help. Or have Ben call."

"What do you think is going to happen? I'm not helpless." He suddenly remembered her suspicions about his painkiller of choice, and resentment flooded him. "Or are you thinking I'm going to drink? I won't self-medicate, and I'd never put Ben at risk."

"Hold on, Owen. I didn't think that. If you won't take the prescription your brother wanted to give you, why would I assume you'll drink?"

"I don't know how you think, Lilah. The past four years prove that." Her kindness today made his resentment of the past more difficult to handle. Combined with his physical pain, his anger pushed hard and left him with an urge to lash out.

"You don't have to know what or how I think. We're just two people caring for a child we made together, but we have no deeper connection."

They were both playing a game. Ducking and weaving to avoid each other. Trying to understand her had turned him into an amateur psychologist. After all, he was so good at dealing with his own problems.

"You're afraid," he said.

"If I were afraid, I wouldn't have survived after the abduction."

"You're capable and responsible enough to run your family's store. I investigated after you came here. I know how successful you've been. You're a good mom to Ben, except you wrap him in a cocoon he's constantly trying to escape. You pretend you're over what happened to you, but you're terrified it could happen to Ben. That's not healthy, Lilah."

"It's a good thing we're almost to your place, or you might end up walking."

"If we'd kept matters business all those years ago, neither of us would have had to consider we made mistakes." Like they should be doing now.

"You don't know anything about me. You've forced me to let my son live with you. I don't like feeling separated from him just because you have to feel you're in charge.

You can't make all these other assumptions based on our unnatural relationship."

"Ben's my son, too."

Those four words. Everything came back to the two of them having an equal right to that sweet little boy who loved them both.

"We're at an impasse." She brushed at a strand of hair blowing across her forehead from the car's vent. "You want me to pretend I'm okay with the pretend life I'm living here, but I don't want to share Ben. It's just been the two of us all his life. And every time he's alone with one of your family, he gets into trouble. Tell me I'm wrong about that."

"He's experiencing freedom he's never had. Of course he's going to get scraped up or bruised now and then."

"Scrapes and bruises are one thing. But nearly falling into an icy stream and shooting off a nail gun are much more serious. Ben could have ended up really hurt."

"I'm not saying you're wrong about the nail gun, but you make me feel as if I'm no different from that criminal who took you."

Her breath hissed through her teeth. "I hate you for even saying that. I've worked hard not to see that animal in every man I meet. If I'd ever thought that about you, I wouldn't have come near you."

Outrage and fear filled her voice, and it ricocheted around him, making him realize how cruel he'd been. She did make him feel like her abductor, but that man had scarred her forever and should have been off-limits for any argument.

"I'm sorry, Lilah. Why don't you let me out?" Before he made everything worse.

"Don't be ridiculous. I'm not putting you out on the side of the road."

He almost insisted, but the intense pain in his arm reminded him he was already exhausted, and he was being an idiot, running from his own bad behavior, instead of just apologizing.

When she reached his cabin, he got out of the car, thanking anyone who could hear his silent gratitude that he'd broken his left arm and could still use his right to open doors and fend for himself.

"I'll go get Ben from your mom's and bring him back," she said, half out of the car.

"Thanks." He leaned against the hood to steady himself. "Lilah?"

She stared at him, her gaze bleak.

"I'm sorry," he said, meaning it more than

he'd meant anything he'd said to her since he'd found her again.

It might have been the cold air that made her eyes water. She bit her lip, nodded and got back in the car.

LILAH SHUT HER DOOR and turned the car around, hearing gravel spew behind her. She glanced back at Owen, who remained stone still.

Tears ran down her face. She didn't care.

She only cared for Ben. Her love for him, savage, bottomless, as protective as every mother's, made her vulnerable. She'd been reckless and unafraid when she met Owen. The worst had already happened to her, so why worry?

And then she'd had Ben. The worst would be something happening to him.

Owen couldn't have been plainer about his opinion of her now. She hovered. She worried. He wasn't that kind of parent, and she was tired of him and his family judging her while they kept putting Ben at risk.

But that simple "I'm sorry." And the look on his face. As if pain had scrubbed him clean, and he couldn't hide anything. He had been sorry he'd brought up the vicious pig who'd tried to destroy her when she was five years old.

For the first time, they'd shared a truly honest moment, and that connection made her vulnerable. Owen was Ben's father, and she'd truly loved him. She'd missed him, longed for him, needed him.

And there had been moments, while she was pregnant, and even after Ben's birth, when she'd wanted to get in touch with him and tell him the truth. She'd thought that maybe their beautiful son could have made the difference to Owen.

He did seem to be changing since they'd been here. Until tonight, on that drive home.

At Suzannah's inn, Lilah sat in the car, rubbing her eyes until the tears finally dried. She switched on the car light and glared at her own owlish gaze. A few minutes' quick work with makeup fixed her up.

She went through the porch door into the dining room. Suzannah, spreading fresh cloths on the tables, stopped. "Honey, is my son all right?"

Lilah met Suzannah's frightened gaze and almost cried again. "He broke his arm, but Noah set it. He's fine."

"Where is he?"

"At the cabin. I came to get Ben, and take him home—I mean—over there."

Suzannah tucked the tablecloth she was holding against her belly. "You argued? He never was good at handling pain. Once, he broke his ankle playing football—he was terrible at the sport, but his father insisted—I never knew Owen had such a temper. He was always a quiet boy, but everything he'd held inside for years came busting out of him when I tried to help him while he was wearing that cast."

Lilah brushed over the truth. "He's testy, but he's probably suffering."

"Don't worry. If he can't take care of Ben, he'll let us know. That boy cuts to the chase for Owen. Since Ben's been here, he's stopped trying to pretend everything's all right."

It was a night of firsts. Lilah felt something in common with Suzannah. "You think so? He has a lot of pride."

"But he loves that boy. He wouldn't do anything that might hurt Ben." Suzannah narrowed her gaze at Lilah, as well. "Are you all right?"

"Fine." Lilah refused to let herself back away, but the moment of bonding evaporated,

and she was uncomfortable with Suzannah's
need to nurture.

"You could ask him to let Ben stay here."

"I did, and he said no. You both take it for
granted he has the right to choose," Lilah
said, breaking the détente.

Suzannah unfolded the cloth she was holding and threw it over the table. "I'm trying
really hard not to get in the middle of whatever's going on between you. I love Ben. You
love him, and so does Owen. We all love
Ben. We'll all do what's best for him."

"You can't believe Owen is best for him.
Not really. You see him dragging in here,
looking as if he hasn't slept more than a couple of hours a night. You know what keeps
him awake."

"I do know. I see his lights on in the cabin
until late at night. I see him wandering the
farm in the spring and summer. But I know
when he's been drinking, and he hasn't since
before Thanksgiving."

"How long before?"

Suzannah didn't answer.

"He told me, Suzannah. A few weeks. It's
not over. He's just trying hard again. He's
tried over and over to stay away from alcohol, but he always fails."

"He's been under a lot of stress because he knows if he drinks, he'll lose the clinic contract. And then, add the stress of finding out about Ben." Suzannah lifted her chin. "But he still hasn't given in. He still hasn't taken a drink."

"He forced me to come down here."

"I know." Suzannah wadded the tablecloth in her hands. "He treated you horribly, but I think he didn't believe you'd bring Ben on your own, and he was desperate."

"That makes it all right?"

Suzannah shook her head. "That makes it a bad decision on his part after he learned you'd been hiding his child from him."

"Because I thought he posed a danger to my son. I'm tired of explaining myself, and I'd think you, of all people, could understand my fear."

"I wasn't a good mother. My children suffered because of me. I wish I'd been as strong as you with their father, but I know Owen. He's not Odell."

"Now, but if he drinks again? If he keeps drinking? Those are my fears, and not even Owen can honestly know for sure they'll never become fact."

"I believe my son loves his child, and he's

trying hard to be a good man. And a good father."

What was wrong with this family? "I'll go get Ben."

"I've made you angry. If you don't mind my help, Lilah, I'll go over tonight and check on them before Owen goes to bed."

Lilah was tempted. Every instinct urged her to accept Suzannah's suggestion, but Owen's accusations in the car replayed in her head. "He'd know you offered," she said. "I have to be sure he'll ask for help with Ben if he needs us."

"Good girl." Suzannah took a deep breath as soon as she said the words. "I'm sorry. I didn't mean that in a condescending way. I know you must be desperate to keep your son out of that little cabin and safe by your side. It's just that Owen is just as desperate to keep Ben with him, and neither of you is really wrong."

Lilah stared at Suzannah. Being called a good girl would normally offend her, but she believed Suzannah meant it as a compliment. She let it go and headed for the stairs. "Is Ben with Celia?" she asked over her shoulder.

"Last time I saw them both."

Again, that crazy attitude of "who really

knows?" She climbed the main stairs and went down the back hall to Celia's room, hearing Ben *vroom*ing a car.

Celia laughed. "You ruined my beauty shop, buddy."

"I don't need a beauty shop in my town."

"Yeah. You're right."

They'd built a small village out of cars and tracks and little houses that Celia must have dug out of the treasures she'd kept from her own childhood. Owen's sister saw Lilah first and clambered to her feet.

"Hey," she said. "How's Owen?"

Ben jumped up and ran to Lilah, stumbling over his cars and his shoes, which he'd taken off and dropped on Celia's floor.

"He's fine." Lilah scooped her son into her arms, finding comfort in his warm, sturdy hug. "Fine," she said again, looking into his worried eyes, ice blue like Owen's and all his siblings'. "He has an excellent cast, and I have a marker. You can draw on it. Ready to go over to the cabin?"

She should get an academy award.

"Ready." He wriggled to get down, and she set him on the floor. He ran immediately to his shoes.

"Lilah," Celia said, "I'm sorry about earlier. I only looked away for a minute."

For pity's sake, the common theme was going to drive her insane.

"Celia has a boyfriend," Ben said, as if a boyfriend and poisonous insect were the same kind of thing. "She was talking all smoochy to him." He grinned up at Lilah. "Grandma said that word. Smoochy." He laughed like a teenager hearing an off-color joke. "Smoochy."

"Sorry," Celia said again, with regret that seemed sincere. "I really am."

"Everyone in this household has lost him at some point," Lilah said. "I'm getting used to it."

"I mean it, Lilah. I'll be more careful."

"I guess you will. Chad is."

"You don't like us much," Celia said.

"Not true. I just love my son."

"I love you, too, Mommy." He clomped over in his untied shoes for a hug. Lilah hugged him and reached for his laces, but he was off again, running back to Owen's sister.

"Love you, too, Auntie." He grabbed her in a stranglehold, and she laughed over his shoulder.

"How lucky am I?" she asked, hugging

right back. "You're my favorite boy in the whole world."

"Except for your boyfriend."

"Oh, no. I like you even better than him." Celia sat back to tie first one shoe and then the other. "Boyfriends come and go. Nephews are forever, buddy, so you and I are always going to be best friends."

"Best friends," he said, laughing as if he liked that. "Auntie Celia is my best friend, Mommy."

Celia looked up, her face alight with unfeigned love as she hugged Ben close to her again. "But I'm not smoochy, and I never talk smoochy. You remember that, skunk."

He giggled from deep in his chest and hugged his aunt again. Lilah melted a little. Her boy had owned her heart since before he was born. "Come on, buddy." She put out her hand. "Own's waiting for you."

Celia laughed at the name Ben had given her brother. "See you tomorrow," she said.

"Night." Ben paused to wave with enthusiasm from the bedroom door. "Don't eat pancakes before Own brings me."

"I won't."

Ben ran down the hall toward the stairs. Holding the rail, he carefully made his way down. "Mommy, can Auntie Celia come visit us at home?"

"Sure. If she wants to."

"I'll ask her."

Suzannah was waiting at the bottom of the stairs with Ben's coat. "Night, big guy," she said. "See you in the morning, first thing. Take care of your daddy."

"Own is fine." He glanced up at Lilah, whose heart broke at her baby's silent plea for reassurance.

"Perfectly," Lilah said, taking his coat from his grandmother and helping him put it on, "except for that cast. Wait until you see it, Ben. It's a pretty shade of green. I voted for purple."

"See you in a while, Lilah." Suzannah hugged Ben, and Lilah could almost imagine Owen in Ben's place until she remembered Suzannah hadn't been like this when he was little. Lilah wanted to ask how she could have neglected her little boy, but it wasn't her business. It would never be.

Ben climbed into his car seat, and she buckled it before she drove back to the cabin. Owen was waiting at the door. He lifted Ben with one arm, and they hugged each other, showing their love without words. Ben had cared for Owen as if he knew from the start he was his father, and Owen had loved Ben from the moment he knew he had a son. She was sure of that.

Their feelings for each other were uncomplicated and all too real.

"It's cold out here," Lilah said, shivering. "Let's go in."

Owen set Ben down, but their son clung to his father's leg. "I didn't hurt you, Own?"

"I fell, Ben. It had nothing to do with you. Did you eat dinner with Grandma?"

"Grilled cheese and milk from the goats."

"Goat's milk?" For some reason, that surprised Lilah.

"Perfectly safe," Owen said.

"I'm just surprised he liked it."

"And then we had cake. Chocolate." Ben rubbed his belly. "I like cake, Own."

"So do I. I wish your mom had brought some home."

"I could go get you a slice," Lilah said.

Owen grinned at her, as if their earlier argument had never happened. "No, thanks, but I do think I could use your help with bath time." He eased the green cast upward in his sling. "Not sure I'd manage to keep this dry."

"Are you feeling all right?" His face was paler since she'd left him.

"I'm good," Owen said with a faint look of surprise.

She realized she was worried about him. Eyeing her as if he could read the emotions unsettling her, he patted the back of Ben's head, his large hand almost covering it. "This guy's already late for bed."

Lilah gathered herself. "Come on, buddy. Let's visit the bathtub."

"Shower, Mommy." He put up his hand to take hers, pausing only for a jaw-breaking yawn. They climbed the stairs together, and she helped him into the shower. He told her to go away. He was growing up, her boy.

"I'll bring your jammies and leave them on the counter," she said.

"Okay. Shut the door."

As she gathered Ben's pajamas, she ignored a slight compulsion to run downstairs and check on Owen. The bathroom billowed steam as she slipped his jammies on to the counter and glanced at the shower curtain. Even in a bath, Ben tended to fling water, but the curtain was closed, and Ben was chatting with one of his toys.

"Don't forget to brush your teeth when you get out," she said.

"Mmm-hmm."

She stood in the hall a moment and left the door open a crack. What to do next? She could lurk outside the bathroom to stay out of Owen's way, or do the exes-who-get-along type of thing and go back downstairs. Besides, he had to eat something. Whipping up a quick dinner for her son's one-handed father wouldn't hurt her.

Nevertheless, she walked down the stairs as if she were sneaking up on her nemesis. At the bottom, she ended up stumbling upon the sight of Owen, sitting in a chair, resting his head on his good hand. He looked up, his face ravaged by pain.

He looked horrible. She went to kneel in front of him. "Why are you doing this to yourself?"

"Leave me alone."

Her natural instincts roared to life. *Snub me? Fine, I'll walk away.* For once, she shut those instincts down.

"You're in pain. Ben will see. He blames himself already."

"He'll be asleep soon. Why are you pushing me to take the drugs when you know I have a problem?"

"Because you know you have a problem, and you won't overuse. Noah wouldn't even give you enough to let you get in trouble."

"You think I don't know where to get whatever I need?"

That set her back on her heels. "I have two choices. Believe you love Ben, and you're an honorable man, or believe your addictions will still get the better of you. Tonight, because you're taking care of him, I have to believe you're in control."

He set his jaw. She watched his chest rise and fall with several hard-taken breaths.

"What are you so afraid of?" she asked. "Help me understand, or this could be a problem for us."

"I know who I am and who I've been. I'm afraid of who I might be." He rubbed his hand over his mouth, and his expression was raw, his eyes hollow. "Still my father. Always. My father."

Her throat felt tight. That fear cut through her. "I'll help you." She took the pill bottle from her pocket. "Your brother gave me these. I'll give you one now. You call me if you need another."

"How does that work, Lilah? You hid my son from me for four years. You've been looking for a way to prove I'm unfit, and I'm going to give that to you by taking drugs? A man with addiction issues?"

"I can't argue any of that, but I hate seeing you in this much pain for no reason. Let's try to get along tonight. I make no guarantees down the road, but for now, do the responsible thing, and manage the pain of your broken arm so you can take good care of our son."

Owen swept the back of his hand across his lips, which were dry. Still, he cracked a small smile. "Your meting them out to me isn't the worst idea."

She shook a pill from the envelope in her hand and passed it to him. "I'll get you some water."

"Thanks."

He stared at the pill as if she'd handed him poison. He was so afraid, and he knew himself better than she'd ever known him. She had no idea what it was like to be addicted to something. How often did he think of drinking even when he wasn't hurt?

But she couldn't stand by and watch him suffer. How would he take care of their son if he was in pain? If his brother thought he could handle these narcotics, then she—and Owen—had to trust Noah's judgment. She brought water, and when he reached for it, she caught his wrist. He looked up at her, startled, and she remembered how they'd been once, caring for each other, eager to be together. They'd valued each other.

She kissed his forehead, not with the crazy longing of the old days they'd spent together, but with a whole heart. With the bond of a man and a woman who shared a son they both loved. She respected Owen for fighting his own anguish, and she wanted him to understand he could trust her—for help and empathy.

"You won't be taking the medication for long. Just until the pain eases enough for the ibuprofen to work."

He took the water and turned her hand, holding her still. "Thanks," he said. "I'm not sure anyone except Noah in my family would have the faith in me to do this."

With her free hand, she took the envelope back out of her pocket. He had to be able to live with temptation.

"No," he said. "You keep them." He met her eyes, straight on. "It's not that I don't trust myself." He shook his head. "I guess it is, but I don't want you wondering about this any more than I want to. I'll ask you if I need another one."

"Why don't I sleep here tonight?" She swept the worn couch with a wary eye. "You must have extra sheets and a pillow?"

"No." He released her hand, and swallowed the pill with the water. "I'll call you if I need help with Ben, but you don't need to sleep here. I'm not an invalid." He set the water glass on the table beside him. "You should get back. There may be more snow, and the road will get bad."

Lilah accepted the distance he put between them. She felt safer on the other side of it. "Okay, but you're the one who reminded me I drive every day in a Vermont winter."

He touched her hand again. "Not when you're worried about Ben."

She kissed him again, enjoying the warmth of his cheek and the prickle of stubble. It was one kiss too many. She shouldn't feel so happy about being close to him. Without another word, because words always got them in trouble, she hurried to the door. "Say good-night to Ben for me."

She'd never let anyone else do that before.

CHAPTER THIRTEEN

DURING THE LAST WEEK in January, Owen and his team completed the framing and drywall installation on the clinic. The committee who'd pushed the clinic proposal through a reluctant town council had arranged for a celebration.

Lilah had come to the cabin early to help him and Ben get ready. He hated being so grateful for her support, but all that big talk about managing one-handed had been just that. Big talk.

"I don't understand," she said as she helped Ben zip his parka. "This committee put together a party before the building is finished?"

"This clinic's a big deal. We're getting medical care this community has never had. My brother is already talking to prospective staff."

"So the committee is spending money on a party just because you've framed the rooms?"

"And wired the building and finished the drywall."

"Are they spending clinic money?"

He shook his head. "It's potluck. All the families are bringing tables and chairs and a few dishes. Mom already had Chad set up our contribution, and she's providing soda and coffee and water."

"I helped Uncle Chad," Ben said.

And he hadn't been eaten by goats or leaped headfirst off a mountain. A big day for the Gage family.

"It'll be good for the community. The more snow we get up here, the harder the local residents work. We'll all appreciate a nice break and some fireworks."

"What are fireworks, Own?"

"Like explosions in the sky. You've never seen fireworks, buddy?" No Fourth of July? No New Year's Eve? And most of his family lived in New York City? "You've never taken him home to see the ball drop in Times Square?"

"I didn't like those crowds when I was his age." Lilah busied herself with her own zipper.

How could he have forgotten? She'd been lured from her mother in a crowded store. A knock at the door startled them all. Ben went over and tugged it open, using both hands on the doorknob. Chad waited on the threshold, grinning at his nephew.

"Ready to go, bud?"

"What are you doing here?" Owen asked.

"I thought you could use a hand. I'll help you carry everything." Chad caught sight of Lilah.

Ever since the goat incident, Chad had worked on weaseling his way into her good graces. Owen studied her, too. Beautiful, graceful, now totally focused on her son, who'd burst out the door behind Chad to hop around the mud puddles in the driveway. Lilah watched him, making sure he didn't jump in any. She raked her pale blond hair over her shoulder, unaware they were watching her. She looked deceptively fragile, her beauty compelling. Chad seemed fascinated.

Owen felt an uncomfortable, unwelcome surge of jealousy. Idiotic, but Lilah's kindness had reminded him how it felt to be the center of her attention. Their extreme antipathy had seemed to fade.

He had to admit that during his pain-filled nights he'd been forced to acknowledge that Ben would be happier if he and Lilah could find a way to put the past behind them.

Each time that thought crept inside his

mind, he'd brushed it aside as quickly as he could, but watching Lilah, he couldn't help thinking it again.

Four years ago, he would have fought to keep their relationship alive if he'd known Ben was coming.

"I can pull the grill over with one hand," he said to Chad. "But the cooler's in the back of the car."

"You were going to drive over?" Chad's mocking tone drew Lilah's attention. "What did you pack in the cooler?"

Owen thought about pounding his little brother into the new foundation when they reached the clinic. "I put in juice and some healthy snacks for Ben and veggies for all of us, as well as hamburger patties and a salad."

"You're going to force the kid to eat carrots and grapes when he could have funnel cakes and hot chocolate? I heard Allen's Drugs is bringing their funnel cake machine."

The pharmacy normally ran it as advertising for their soda fountain during the county fair or the fall festival.

"Maybe a funnel cake for everyone would be a great idea," Lilah said, smiling.

"I like cake," Ben said. He'd hopped close enough to the door to hear them talking.

Owen shook his head. "We'll see if we have room after we eat the food we brought."

His brother considered for a second, but then he headed to the grill. "I'll pull this."

Ben looked everyone over, sensing an undercurrent. Then he took off.

"Wait, Uncle Chad. I want to come with you."

Off he skipped, and Owen shook his head at Lilah. "I think my brother may have a crush on you."

"I've noticed. I'm thinking if I ignore it, it will go away. I won't be robbing the Gage cradle anytime soon."

"He's only a few years younger than you." But he couldn't deny an embarrassing sense of relief.

"A high school senior?" She grinned. "That broken arm of yours has robbed you of your good sense. I'm decades older than Chad in maturity, if not years."

True, but she made him think of how she lived, afraid and alone. Distancing herself from loved ones because she was safer inside her bubble. "You choose to be older, Lilah. You work hard to stay ahead of risks. Maybe I took the fun out of your life."

"Ben changed the way I have fun. I don't

need to go back to the kind of playing we did before I was pregnant, Owen." She pushed her hand beneath her hair at the nape of her neck and lifted it, as if it were annoying her. "Don't worry about your brother. First, the idea is creepy, and second, he's only trying to prove he's a man, like you and Noah."

"I'm not jealous," he said. He wasn't sure he'd ever lied to her before.

She looked bewildered. "I didn't think you were."

"Why did you think you had to tell me not to worry about him?"

She shrugged, and her hair slid over her shoulder, a flash of gold in the gray, snowy day. "I thought you might be worried I'm still trying to get back at you, and that I might use Chad to hurt you."

"Didn't even occur to me." He must have been losing his edge.

They drove the short distance around the fields to the new driveway he'd had made for the clinic.

They got out of the car, and Owen placed his hand in the center of Lilah's back, as they looked for Ben. At the far end of the parking lot, a small bluegrass quartet, bundled up like snowmen, began to play the music that had been born in these mountains.

The rhythms reached inside Owen, who'd always known them. And in front of them, Ben waited. Owen smiled at his son, who stared fascinated at the banjo player's flashing fingers.

"Lilah."

Owen turned with her as a voice called her name. Christine Laverty, who owned a small antiques shop on the square, had parked behind them. The music had drowned out the sound of her pulling up.

"I didn't expect to see you here, Lilah." She stopped and stared at them both. "Oh," she said. "You're the one who—"

"Who what?" Owen prompted her. With an abusive, drunken father who'd seemed proud he was a monster, Owen had suffered the town's censure from the day he'd entered kindergarten. That was fine but no one was going to treat Lilah or Ben as if they'd done something wrong.

"Your mother told me you had a little boy, Owen." Christine stared at her hands. "Whose mother never told you he existed. But I never put you together with Lilah.

We've been dickering on some pieces in my shop."

"What did you want to tell me?" Lilah asked.

"Um—I found another one of those chairs you—"

"If you want her to buy a chair from you, now would be the time to cut the judgment." He turned Lilah away from Christine.

"Wait." Lilah slipped out of his grasp. "Maybe I deserve it," she said to him as she turned back. "I am the one, Christine, and I do want the chair. I'd also like to believe you won't spread gossip that might hurt our son."

Christine's face was bright red, and not from the cold. "Owen, I'm your friend, too. I see that you're—" she paused, staring at Lilah "—making changes. I don't want to help someone who's treated you as if you don't deserve your own child."

"Then sell to Lilah, because you'll be helping yourself, and don't make this situation worse for Ben." He nodded toward his boy, standing by Chad near the clinic, still tapping a boot-clad toe with the band. "That's my son, and he doesn't know anything about the past. I hope he won't until his mother and I explain."

"Sorry." Christine passed Lilah a business card she fished out of her quilted jacket. "Here's my number again. Let me know if you want the chair. I'll see you around, Owen."

Lilah didn't move. Her shoulders were set as if she were bracing for a blow. Her hand drifted slowly to her side, and the card seemed to slip from her fingers. Owen bent and picked it up from the muddy gravel. "Let it go," he said.

She turned back to him. "I never thought about you or Ben going through this because of me."

"I'm trying to stop being angry with you about it, Lilah, but I'm dumbfounded that you thought I wouldn't mind not knowing I had a child."

"You weren't ever supposed to know," she said.

"Look how easily I found out. I'm only surprised it didn't happen before now."

"I didn't know you wanted a child. We never talked about being married or starting a family. I thought I was on my own—especially after you said you didn't want to stop drinking." She lowered her voice. "Not that I believe you're anything like your father. I wish I'd never said that."

"Let that go, too." He had to stop paying attention to that same fear. He wouldn't let himself become a man like his father. "Come on. Chad has his own friends to hang out with. Let's get Ben."

She held his gaze with an unspoken something in her eyes. "Thanks," she said, "for defending me. You didn't have to, and I wouldn't have expected you to."

He started to say he'd done it for Ben. His instincts compelled him to reestablish the distance between him and Lilah. She'd hurt him more than he cared to admit, and he wasn't up for another round of rejection. But, for Ben's sake, he nodded, and started walking toward the boys and the bluegrass band.

As they caught up, Ben lifted his arms in the air, a signal Owen already recognized. He scooped up his son, one-handed, and Ben hitched his legs around Owen's waist.

"You'll have to walk in a minute, buddy." Lilah adjusted Ben's knitted cap, which had gotten twisted in his struggle to get his balance on Owen's hip. "Owen can't hold you like this for long."

Her sweet, floral scent wafted past Owen, and he smiled into her eyes. She looked away, seeming a little panicked, while a pink stain rose up the column of her throat.

"I smell the funnel cakes. They must have set up already," Owen said.

"They're behind the other side of the barn," Chad said. "I mean clinic, where the door was, under the loft."

Ben clapped his hands. "Funnel cakes. Yeah!"

Chad tagged along for the treat on Owen's dime. They sat together at one of the picnic tables the drugstore management had lent the town for the day.

Chad helped Ben eat his golden-brown, sugar-dusted, fried cake. Afterward, standing on the bench beside Owen, Ben used Chad's napkin to wipe his face.

"You got sugar, too, Own." He wiped Owen's chin, snagging a bit of paper on stubble Owen hadn't shaved this morning or yesterday. Ben touched it. "Ouch," he said. "You gotta get your own paper off."

Owen rubbed at his chin, but was surprised to find Lilah focused on his face, too. Even more surprised when she looked away as if she didn't want to be caught staring at him. As if she cared again.

He hugged Ben close. What did they look like? A normal family, enjoying the winter day? Two estranged parents, uncomfortable at being stuck with each other?

LILAH'S TENSION MOUNTED as the day wore on. Slowly. She wanted to be with Ben. She wanted things to be easy with Owen, but she didn't understand him. Angry and resentful? That, she understood. Thoughtful, protective, welcoming—she didn't want any part of that. His kindness woke old emotions that she'd put to bed with great effort.

Take his quick response to Christine Laverty in Lilah's defense. Christine hadn't deserved that. She had taken his side with the loyalty of a friend. Funny, when he thought he had few friends in this town.

Why would he defend the woman who'd kept him from knowing his own son?

The realization of what she'd done dug ever deeper beneath her skin. Every time she'd felt guilty about Ben's having no father, she'd blithely assured herself she'd done the right thing. Owen's own qualms about his alcoholic father had shored up any doubts that managed to wriggle through in the past four years, but since the day he'd broken his arm, she'd begun to understand how hard he was trying not to be the man who'd terrorized his own family.

After they'd sampled all the food they could, they went inside for the games. Lines of moms and dads and children snaked around the building, throwing sandbags through the mouth of a fish painted on a wooden stand, knocking down milk bottles, fishing in a big glass bowl for gift certificates from merchants in town.

"Uncle Chad's going to fish for me," Ben said, dragging at her hand. "We need to find him before everybody wins everything."

"He's probably still eating somewhere." Owen adjusted the sling that pulled at his neck. "Buddy, your nose is running." He pulled a tissue out of his back pocket and passed it to Ben.

"You came prepared," she said, watching as Ben took the tissue and blew.

"He was a little stuffy this morning."

She hadn't even noticed. She knelt beside Ben on the cold cement floor and tipped up his chin. "Do you feel all right?"

"I want a prize. Chad says he always wins."

He looked fine. Eyes clear, breathing fine now. Just a bit of a runny nose. Maybe it was the construction dust in the building. She stood, peering around for Chad's head above the others.

"This place is getting more crowded," she said.

Owen slid his arm around her waist, apparently remembering she didn't like crowds. But when she looked at him, his gaze startled her.

She turned to see what had caught his attention. A guy in overalls and a flannel shirt, a tractor-emblazoned ball cap on his head, had hauled a vintage silver flask from his pocket. As he took a drink, she glanced back at Owen, whose jaw had tensed.

"Sorry," he said, his expression guilty. "Some things I can't help."

He turned toward one of the office areas, but he didn't let her go. He was only guiding her, with the affection of a friend. She was frightened, and yet his touch reassured her. He wasn't the monster she'd feared. The discomfort in his crooked smile told her he didn't want to long for that man's drink.

"My mom said she was putting our table beside the office I've been using," Owen said as if nothing had gone wrong with their sweet little pretend-family day. "This way."

Ben danced at their sides, and Owen moved away, as if he thought that being close to each other suddenly felt wrong. It did to her, as well. And he was probably thinking she'd bundle Ben into her rented car and flee to Vermont.

She tried to balance instinct and good sense. The man was an alcoholic. He wouldn't ever stop wanting to drink. He just had to tame the need.

All too aware of the glances thrown their way, she wondered if he noticed, as well.

"Don't get lost, Ben," he said, as their son paused for a long, hard look at some older children knocking down bowling pins with a ball.

"I can do that," Ben said.

"I'll bet he could." Owen went to the back of the line, reaching for Ben's hand.

Lilah fell in beside them, willing to pretend that everything was okay. As long as Owen didn't give in to his demons, everything would be okay for their son.

"He's so full of funnel cake, we should

probably let him work off the energy." She noticed Owen's sudden, quick scan of their interested neighbors. "They really keep a close eye on you."

He shrugged with a wince at the sling. "I guess it hasn't been long enough since I last made a spectacle of myself."

"You may not be the problem. They seem to have circled the wagons to keep you safe from the wicked big-city woman."

"They're making any number of assumptions," he said. "It happens in a place with a population of less than five thousand during off-season months."

"They'll get used to the idea that you have a son." The simple reassurance, which she meant sincerely, rocked Lilah. She'd also grown used to the truth she'd hidden for so long. Owen was Ben's father. He was critical to Ben's happiness, and she'd managed to stop resenting him for having a say in her child's future.

Mostly.

"I don't care what they think or say about me," Owen said, "but I don't like the idea of anyone talking around Ben."

"Talking 'bout what, Own?"

Owen shut his mouth in a thin, tight line, but Ben's smiling anticipation soon had him grinning. "About what a great kid you are." He leaned down to scrunch up Ben's knit cap. "'Cause you really are."

Ben wrapped his arm around Owen's leg for a second and then shuffled ahead of them in the slow-moving line.

"I'll probably never understand why you did what you did," Owen said, "but that is the best little boy in the whole world. I feel lucky I get to love him."

Hardly breathing, Lilah allowed herself to look at the man who'd meant everything to her, who now meant so much to her son. Somehow, she'd have to make room for Owen in her life.

"I'm lucky, too," she said.

He looked down at her, his gaze steady, until it fell to her mouth, and suddenly she was aware of—everything. The light in the building, the voices of men and women and children walking past, her breathing, each slow beat of her heart.

She hadn't sent Owen away because she'd stopped loving him. She just hadn't wanted Ben to be in danger from a man who hadn't even trusted himself. He'd been sober now for such a short time. But how much time would have to pass before she could trust he wouldn't drink again?

CHAPTER FOURTEEN

AT THE END of the night, the clinic committee had planned a fireworks display. Fireworks over snow couldn't be more beautiful, and Owen knew the perfect spot to watch from. He found Lilah and Ben in the kitchen area of the barn—the new clinic, he reminded himself. He sidled up to her. "Come with me," he said, taking her hand.

"Where are we going?" She reached for Ben, who sneezed as she pulled him off the counter. "I wonder if he is getting a cold," she said, slightly worried, wiping his nose with the tissue she pulled out of his pocket.

Owen glanced at his son, who looked fine. "When Chad was a little guy, his face would get red, and his eyes looked tired when he was sick."

"It's usually the same with Ben." She pressed her cheek to his forehead. "I don't think he has a fever. How do you feel, buddy?"

Ben grinned. "I think I need another funnel cake," he said, burrowing his hands between them.

Laughing, she kissed his head, and Owen's smile faded. What if they belonged to him, these two? The woman and the boy. What if they were his family?

It wasn't only Ben who mattered to him. He had loved Lilah, and he hadn't wanted to leave her. He'd never understood the way they'd parted, and tonight he dared let himself wonder what a new life would be like if they could start over again.

He turned them with his hand at the small of Lilah's back. "Let's go before someone else grabs our spot."

If he told her how he felt she wouldn't believe him. He'd been too harsh. She was too willing to believe the worst about him, and maybe he had given her good reason.

He steered her and Ben toward the clinic's front door. "Wait," he said, as they crossed the parking lot. "I'm stopping by the cabin to pick up a quilt. We might get chilly up there."

He went in and got the quilt off the couch. Without thinking, he glanced toward the kitchen cabinet where the wine still waited. Dutch courage. Maybe he'd know what to say to Lilah if he eased the lock on his emotions.

His mouth went dry. He wasn't that weak. He couldn't afford to be that weak ever again.

With one last glance at that closed, cherry cabinet door, he balanced the quilt, which was unwieldy to carry with one hand. Lilah took it as he went back outside. What would she think if she knew the temptation that still shouted in his head, even when he was happy and ever so slightly hopeful?

He tried to push traitorous thoughts of the wine out of his mind as they walked straight toward the ridge that formed the western border of Suzannah's farm. Before they reached the trail, Ben started running.

"I know where we are. Uncle Chad took me up this big hill." He put some space between himself and his parents.

"Not too far," Owen said, only to hear the same words, almost in an echo from Lilah.

They both smiled, and he had to wonder if he looked as self-conscious as she did.

"Let's go a little faster," Lilah said.

"Good idea."

Ben slowed as he reached the top. Lilah handed the quilt to Owen and picked Ben up.

"Here we are," he said as they reached a small flat section of snow and pine needle–

covered ground that seemed to jut out over
the valley below.

"Don't run away, Ben. You have to stay
close to us up here."

"It's like daylight, Mommy."

The moon hung over them, full in the clear
sky after the drizzly day.

"But there are shadows, and you might
not see the edge." Lilah set him down and
then took the quilt and spread it. "I hope we
can see to get down again. We should have
brought a flashlight."

"We can use our phones," Owen said.

"I see a bird's nest." Ben headed over to
the low-hanging branch to investigate.

"Don't touch," Lilah said.

"I know. Chad told me they're full of
germs and you'd get mad if I touched them."

"I'll have to thank Chad for his helpful advice." But Lilah's smile was soft and sweet
and indulgent.

"Come, sit down." Owen nodded at Ben.
"He'll be all right."

"Every time someone by the name of Gage
says Ben will be all right, something horrible happens."

"One goat stampede," Owen said.

"And a toppling ladder."

"That happened to me."

"Because Ben was going for the power tools."

He sat and patted the quilt. "He'll be fine. He'll come sit with us when the fireworks start."

He'd barely spoken the words when a whoosh sounded and the first explosion of color blossomed above them. He looked at Lilah, whose eyes widened.

"Wow," she said.

"Oooooooh." Ben strolled to the quilt and leaned against Owen's bent knee. "Wow, Own. Pretty."

"It is pretty."

"Sit down," Lilah said and tugged their little boy between them.

"I'm cold, Mommy."

Owen picked up one corner of the quilt, and she grabbed the other. Together they wrapped the quilt around themselves and Ben. Ben climbed into Owen's lap and slumped back against his good shoulder.

Lilah scooted closer, as well, and for that moment, they really did form a small family, clinging together beneath the glittering streamers of light showering down from the sky. Owen glanced at Lilah and caught her looking up at him. Her smile was like fireworks.

He locked his emotions inside. Longing for her, for the family he'd dreamed one day would be his own. It could only ever be a dream. They'd achieved a much-needed peace in the past few days, even though he knew it was a fragile one, as well. Ben was happy sharing his time with both of them. And even happier when they were all together.

If he rocked the boat now, he could capsize it.

"OWN? OWN, WAKE UP."

Ben sounded congested. Owen turned over, flinching at the pain in his arm, and found his son leaning on the side of the bed, prodding him.

"What's wrong, buddy?"

"My throat hurts, and I can't stop coughing." As if on cue, he started hacking.

Owen sat up immediately. He pressed the back of his hand against Ben's forehead, but he couldn't tell if his temperature was up. Maybe that was a skill learned over time.

"I think I'll call Uncle Noah," Owen said. He wasn't about to call Lilah and have her think he didn't know how to take care of a common cold. "Let's get you back in bed, and I'll go downstairs and bring you a drink."

"I want to go with you. Don't leave me alone."

After a trip to the kitchen for water, Owen tucked Ben back into his bed and called his brother.

Noah answered his phone right away. "What's up?"

"I think Ben's sick. He has a sore throat, and he's coughing." He stopped. "Sorry for waking you up."

"No problem. Does he have a fever?"

"I don't think so. I can't tell." Noah's question made him feel even more inept.

"Then he probably doesn't. You should get a thermometer."

"I know. Wish I'd thought of it before tonight."

"Do you have any children's acetaminophen?"

"That, I have. Mom told me I should pick some up when I told her Ben was coming."

"Give him the dose that's right for his age and weight. Is his breathing normal?"

Owen turned on the lamp on Ben's nightstand and watched his son breathe. In and out. In and out.

"I think it's normal."

"Do you want me to come over?"

"Sort of," Owen said. "But not really. I think he's okay."

"You should call Lilah. She'll be upset if you don't, and she knows Ben better than you do. Sorry if that hurts, but she'll have been through this before. Plus, I'll bet she can tell about his temp."

"You're probably right."

"You're not admitting defeat if you ask her for help."

He was, but maybe it didn't matter if it was for Ben. A cold shouldn't create all this drama. He'd scare the little guy. "All right. Do you mind if we bring him in tomorrow?"

"If you need to, that's fine. Just phone the office for an appointment. I'll tell Lynsay to book you right away."

"Thanks, Noah."

"Call me back if anything worries you."

"Okay." He disconnected the call. "Hold on, Ben. I'll be right back."

"I feel better, Own."

"Do you?" He looked back from the doorway. "I talked to Uncle Noah, and he said I should give you some medicine."

"Yuck." Ben wrinkled his nose and slid farther down beneath his bedding.

After a grin at his son, Owen went downstairs and got the acetaminophen from the kitchen. Without thinking, he'd tucked it into the cabinet with the wine. He glanced at the bottle, still sealed shut. Then he closed the cabinet door and hurried back upstairs to his son.

He measured out the dosage and gave it to Ben with a chaser of water.

"I'm going to call your mom."

"Yay," Ben said with less than his normal exuberance.

LILAH THREW ON a sweatshirt over her flannel pajamas and ran down the stairs. Then she ran back up and grabbed the thermometer from her makeup bag. Suzannah came into the hall as she was heading back out.

"Something wrong? Did Owen hurt his arm again?"

"He thinks Ben's sick." She started impatiently for the stairs. "I can't talk now, Suzannah."

"Call me if I can help. I'd be glad to go with you."

Her uncertain tone got through to Lilah. Suzannah didn't know if she'd be welcome. "I appreciate the offer. Really, I do, but I'm sure it's just a cold. He had the sniffles earlier."

"You look panicked."

"I know. It's crazy." Lilah yanked her sweatshirt down as if she were reaching for her composure. "I'm a little crazy where he's concerned, but he's so important to me, Suzannah."

"He's lucky he has you." She patted Lilah's arm awkwardly. "Please call if I can bring anything or do anything."

"Thanks."

She bolted down the stairs and out to her car, but she didn't start it right away. She needed a second to wrestle her emotions into submission. She didn't want to scare Ben, and Owen had sounded shaken up.

He'd told her to come straight up when she reached the cabin. She found them sharing a book in Ben's room. Ben coughed, and Owen smiled at her, but with relief that made her feel like the calm one.

"Hey, buddy," she said. "How are you feeling?"

"My throat, Mommy." He pointed a finger at his open mouth. Owen got up to make room for her on the bed. She went over and peered at Ben's throat. Behind her, Owen held up a lamp.

"I didn't think to look," he said. "I gave him the acetaminophen, like Noah said."

"It just looks a little inflamed." Relieved, she smiled at her boy and then pressed a kiss on to the tip of his nose. "A little red. And I don't think you have a fever, but we'll just take your temperature anyway." She ran the thermometer across his forehead.

Ah. Instant relief. "98.8," she said.

"That's high?" Owen asked.

She laughed at his concern for a change. "Not a bit. He may have a little cold, but we'll keep an eye on him for a couple of days, and he'll be fine."

"I'm glad you came, Mommy. Can you stay with me tonight?"

She looked to Owen for her answer. He hovered in the doorway in flannel pj pants and a dark T-shirt, his hair standing on end and his eyes wide and hollow. He lifted both hands in a gesture that made her feel bad for him.

"It's just a cold," she said. But maybe she should insist on staying. This was Owen's first experience with a sick child.

"Feel free to stay," he said. "Do you want to sleep in here? Or I can make you a bed on the couch."

"I'll hang out with Ben." She grinned. "You wouldn't happen to have some coffee?"

"This late?"

She started to explain she had a sudden craving for caffeine, maybe out of relief that Ben seemed fine. But then he nodded.

"I know what you mean," he said, and she got an unwelcome insight into what it must be like for him when he needed alcohol. "I'll make coffee. I'm glad you came, too."

She was grateful he turned away before she could say anything accusatory about the drinking. He hadn't announced he was heading for the nearest fifth of vodka. "I'm glad you called," she said. "It's nice to see you in my shoes when it comes to parenting."

Maybe understanding each other's experiences could be good for both of them.

His footsteps pounded down the stairs. Ben rolled over, pulling the blankets with him.

"Read to me, Mommy."

She picked up the book Owen had set down and began to read. Within a minute, Ben was sound asleep again. Poor little pumpkin. Lilah tucked him in. He grumbled a bit but burrowed deeper into his bed.

She turned off the lamp and went to the door, but she left it half-open in case he called for them.

The coffee was still brewing when she arrived downstairs. Owen turned from the kitchen counter.

"I'm sorry about all this. I wasn't sure what to do."

"Are you kidding? I'm glad you called." She went to the cupboard and took down two mugs. "I finally get the feeling we can do this together."

"I actually wondered if you might head out of here the second I told you he was sick."

She set the cups beside the coffeemaker. "Why would I leave now?"

"Because I took him to the top of a mountain, and we sat in the cold. That probably made things worse."

"I keep trying to tell you and your family I'm not nuts."

Owen brushed his unruly hair across his forehead. "I feel a little nuts right now."

"I appreciate you trying to take responsibility, but I was with you. I knew he sounded stuffy. If I blamed you because he picked up a germ, I'd have to blame myself. I'm just glad it's nothing serious."

"Noah said to let his office know if we want to bring him in tomorrow."

"Right now I don't think we'll need to." She put her hand over his arm. "It's okay."

"I can finally admit we've all been rough on you about being overprotective. Too bad the others can't see me tonight. You'd have to pass me the award for worrying."

"The first time Ben got a cold, I took him to the emergency room." She shrugged. "Maybe it's the moment you realize how dependent on you they are."

"Thanks." Owen turned his hand over and caught hers. "You both matter to me. My son is lucky you're his mother."

She looked up and got lost in his eyes. Funny how that ice could emit heat. "What are you saying to me, Owen? You aren't just talking about Ben right now."

He nodded, tugging her closer. "I wouldn't

choose living like this, Lilah, sharing Ben in separate homes, separate lives."

Her chest felt as if a giant hand gripped and squeezed. She wanted to stop him. She didn't know how. If he said anything else… "Owen, no."

"No, what? Let me talk for once."

She wanted him to talk about the feelings his eyes were intimating, and she wanted him to remember she was the woman who couldn't find a way to trust him again. "You're reacting to your scare about Ben. Too much happened tonight, and you need sleep."

He touched his index finger to her lips. "I'm saying what I should have when you threw me out nearly five years ago. I'll try to be the right man. I won't drink. I care about you. More than that, I believe we might find our way back to each other if you're telling the truth about only sending me away because you thought I wasn't safe."

"That was four years ago. Our time has passed, and you're sober now because of Ben. But how long will it last?"

"I'm asking you to give us a chance."

She pushed his hand away. "I'm still the woman who hid your son from you, and you're still the guy who wants to drink. I saw that today."

He nodded. "I want to, but I'm not drinking, and I finally understand why you kept him from me. You were afraid for him, and you did your best. That's what I'm offering you, too. I haven't touched a drink in months, and I don't intend to. I know I can't have a life and an addiction."

"No, Owen."

"Because you're still afraid?" he asked.

"Absolutely." She turned away from him. "Ben loves you, and he deserves parents who don't hate each other. If something went wrong between us again, I might hate you. I certainly wouldn't forgive you."

From behind her, he slid his arm around her waist. "I did hate you. At least I thought I did. I tried to. But I don't."

She turned around. "Owen, this is crazy. Our son comes before any feelings you and I might think we're feeling because I've helped you when you broke your arm, and you've made me see you love Ben the way I always needed you to."

"I'm not asking Ben to give me another chance." He lowered his head. His mouth was so close to hers. So warm.

"You can't ask me either." She wanted to pull away, but she couldn't force herself to move out of his arms.

"I am asking you because neither of us wanted to care again, but we've been good together. We answer what's missing in each other. I understand why you worry so much about Ben because I felt so afraid tonight that he might be really sick. And you saw the way I looked at that farmer and his flask today, but you didn't panic. You gave me compassion and understanding."

"Because you're my son's father."

"I don't believe Ben's your only reason for caring. I was not his father when you fell in love with me, and you sent me away because I had a problem, not because you didn't love me."

"That's my secret," she said, "and I never meant for anyone else to know how much I still cared."

Could she let herself care like that again?

He brushed her lips with his. Kissing him was like coming home. She relaxed in the circle of his arm around her. She sank into the sweetness of his tender affection. This man owned parts of her that no one else had ever reached.

And she wanted to give him everything—her tomorrows, her son, her trust. She wanted Owen to take her love again.

"No." She pulled away. "Nothing's really changed. You were a good man with a thirst that ruined your life. I can't stop you from seeing Ben, but if we were together, the first time you drank, I'd leave you. And Ben would know the difference between having two parents, and having a mother who could never forgive his father for betraying him and me."

"I'm not drinking. I won't make you worry about a drunk guy ruining your life."

"You don't come with the guarantees I need."

He caught her, sliding his hand beneath her hair at her nape. "You needed guarantees before. You're stronger now."

"I'm not strong enough." She leaned her cheek against his wrist. She wanted a happier ending, a fairy-tale promise he could keep. "I'm telling you I cannot take a chance." Tears burned her eyes. "Not on you."

Because how would she survive when the end came? And how would she help Ben survive?

She turned away. She couldn't go far tonight, but in the morning, she'd pack up her son and take him home to Vermont.

"I'm going back to your mom's," she said. "If Ben wakes up and wants me, he can call."

Owen didn't answer. His bleak expression required no words. The compassion he needed from her no longer existed because Ben mattered more. She couldn't give her son a temporary family that was bound to shatter the moment something in Owen's life made him turn back to alcohol.

CHAPTER FIFTEEN

HANDS WERE AT her throat, on her shoulders. One covered her eyes and then slid over her mouth. This time might be the last time. The horror would end because he was killing her.

Wait—out of her horror came the vaguest hope. She wasn't five. This might be a dream. If it was a dream, she could wake herself. With sheer willpower, Lilah rose from her pillows, gasping, barely restraining a scream. Every time was the same—the nightmare always returned to let her know when her life was a mess.

Panting, she looked around Suzannah's cozy guest room. Embers in the fireplace barely gave off any light, but a darkish blue morning sky peeked around the corners of the window shades. She hurried to open them and then turned to make sure no one else was in her room.

The bedposts loomed. The shadows of

the armoire and the dressing table threatened her.

She grabbed her college sweatshirt from the end of the bed, where she'd left it when she came back from Owen's last night.

She had to get out of here. She needed air.

She tiptoed down the stairs, anxious not to wake the other guests or Suzannah, who'd been asleep when she crept back in a couple of hours ago.

Little Lost Lilah learned to handle her demons. Again and again. Over and over.

But that was all right. Little Lost Lilah's little son would never have demons to face.

She headed for the kitchen, hoping to find a last cup of coffee in the pot. No luck there. She plugged in the kettle and found a tin of Monk's Blend leaves. Thank goodness for Suzannah's thoughtfulness as a hostess.

While she waited for the water to boil, she wandered through the spacious dining room, where the small, lit table lamps pushed out darkness. She opened the blinds in here, as well.

Lilah inhaled one more time. Everything was okay. She'd packed her things before she went back to bed. She'd made flight reservations for this evening. Packing Ben's things wouldn't take more than an hour, and they could get out of Bliss.

"Bad dreams?"

She turned, almost knocking a chair to the floor. She caught it and clenched her fingers around the wooden back. "Suzannah, I didn't mean to wake you."

The older woman belted her robe. "No problem. I get nightmares, too. It's not Ben?"

"No. He's okay." Her mouth was crazy dry. "He has a cold, but it's nothing serious. No fever."

"That's the news I hoped for. Tea for two?" Suzannah asked. "Or I could start the coffee." She shot back the cuff of her robe and checked the time.

"I put on the kettle."

"Oh, good. Can I make you something to eat?"

"I'm not hungry."

"No." Suzannah's smile was too aware. Either Owen had called her—doubtful in the extreme—or she really did know what it was like to be chased by nighttime demons. "We'll just sip our tea and reassure ourselves."

"You sound like a therapist."

Suzannah laughed. "Probably from seeing one for such a long time. We all have our flaws, Lilah, and I'm still making sure mine don't become major character traits ever again."

She might be assuming too much. "What did Owen tell you?"

Suzannah seemed to weigh her options. Lilah couldn't believe he would have called her last night.

"He didn't actually tell us at all. One of the other children got curious about you and did a little research."

She baffled Lilah. "You aren't talking about last night?"

"You never hid your name."

"What?" Then Lilah understood. "The kidnapping. Someone finally searched my name. Which sibling was it?"

"Does it matter?"

"I don't care who went prowling into my business, but I don't want any of you to speak to Ben about it. Someday I'll tell him when I think the time is right."

"I'm worried about you," Suzannah said gently.

And she didn't even know the whole truth about the abduction and its affect on Lilah even now. "I'm fine. You might as well know Ben and I are going back to Vermont today."

"Why? Because you don't deserve a life with a decent man who cares for you?" Suzannah tightened her belt again. "I assume Owen is the reason for your sudden retreat? You two bonded over your slightly ill son. Owen finally realized his feelings for you still exist, and he scared you by talking about them."

"I'm not like you. I know I'm not to blame because a criminal tried to destroy my life."

"I have plenty of reason to blame myself," Suzannah admitted. "You were a child. You were brave enough to free yourself. I was an adult, and I had four children who depended on me. I wasn't even brave enough to free them, and I love them so much I can never make it up—what I owe them. You have a child now. You know that Owen can be a good father. Please, don't take that from him."

"You know how many times Owen has failed at staying sober. Even with me, he'd say he wasn't going to drink while he was in New York, and then he'd get completely wasted. I can't remember how many times." An image of that man with the flask yesterday and Owen's hungry look popped into her mind. "Suzannah, I won't live with an alcoholic, and I won't let Ben get used to having his father in his home just long enough to be scarred when I have to make him leave."

"Maybe Owen wouldn't be so—troubled—if I'd been stronger. Like you are."

Lilah couldn't disagree. "Owen thinks I'm weak, but I'm trying to make sure my choices for Ben give him a better chance at a happy life, without my fear or Owen's addiction."

"But what if you make him afraid, Lilah? Keeping him wrapped in cotton wool is no way to teach him how to weather the bad times."

"I understand that's what you think I do. Maybe I have overreacted a few times since we've been here, but I'm taking care of Ben the best way I know how."

"So is my son."

"Even now, when you know I've just been reliving a crime committed against me, you're making a pitch for Owen?"

"For my grandson." Suzannah turned toward the kitchen. "Because I'd hate to see him choose to hide. Three generations of men, hiding from their troubles. You don't want that any more than I do." She looked straight into Lilah's eyes. "Or Owen."

"I don't really want that tea after all. In fact, I'm fine, just tired." Lilah went to the stairs. "I'll see you in a little while."

Every member of the Gage family seemed to feel they had a right to advise her on what was best for Ben.

What a laugh. The most dysfunctional family in Tennessee, setting themselves up as judge and jury.

She should have tried harder to keep Ben out of his father's reach. She just hadn't realized Owen, who hadn't wanted to stop drinking, would ever be sober long enough to care about his son.

OWEN WOKE, STARTLED to see sunlight in his room. "Ben?" He rolled out of bed and stumbled along the hallway. "Buddy, are you awake?"

Ben's bed was empty.

"Buddy," Owen called, heading down the stairs, "how do you feel this morning?"

But he wasn't downstairs either. The whole house was empty, as empty as a black hole, sucking all the energy out of him.

"Ben?"

He ran back up the stairs. Ben's coat and hat and gloves weren't on the floor, or in the chair at the end of his bed. Owen grabbed his phone, still lying on the nightstand. He hit Lilah's number.

The second her answer cut into the ring, he asked her, "Is Ben with you?"

"He's not with you?"

"He's not here. His coat's gone. Go downstairs right now and find out if he's having breakfast. I'm getting dressed."

"If he's not downstairs, I'm calling the police."

"Hurry," Owen said and hung up.

He dressed as quickly as he could, grunting with pain. Then he searched the outside of the cabin before he ran through the barn.

Lilah didn't call. He called her.

"He's not here," she said. "I already called the police. A guy named Layton said he's coming, and he'll bring searchers."

"He's the sheriff."

"How many searchers can he get?" Her voice broke. "I'm going to look through the clinic."

"I just did. I'm coming to meet you through the fields. You head this way. Maybe we'll find him."

"All right, but hang up so I can call your mom and have her get Chad out here. He's been in the woods with Ben more than any of us."

Celia and Chad and Noah gathered friends. Searchers came from town, along with Sheriff Layton and his colleagues. The woods were filled with voices calling for Ben.

A panic-filled morning passed into an afternoon of sick dread. With each passing minute, the weather worsened. As clouds came up, bloated with snow, and the wind began to whistle through the trees and over the hills, Owen's hope faded. He pretended for Lilah that he was certain they'd find Ben, but inside, he felt sick dread.

News vans rolled up. Noah spoke to the reporters and kept them away from Owen and Lilah. The clinic committee had a communication tree that they used to raise more volunteer searchers.

They didn't find a sock or a shoe, not a mitten, or even a lock of curly brown hair. Ben had disappeared.

Owen kept his eye on Lilah. Her worst fear had come to life. She wasn't speaking, and she wasn't crying. Grim fear gripped her gray features. He couldn't help her because every time he went near her she pushed him away.

She wasn't the only one who assumed this was his fault. He couldn't even say why he felt as if he'd brought this down on their heads, but he should have known Ben had somehow left his house.

As darkness and snow fell together, the search groups gathered in the field in front of the inn. Owen knew what was coming from the look on Sheriff Layton's face.

"No one's seen anything of him, Owen, Ms. Bantry. We have to call off the search for the night. It's too dark to do anything else. With the snow, we're putting all these people in danger."

"I'm telling you, we'll find Ben by a stream. If we give up tonight, he'll be out in the cold—he won't survive the night alone in the woods." Owen's voice hitched, and Lilah grabbed his arm, as a whimper escaped her throat. Owen's body screamed with pain. He wrapped his arm around her, and she finally let him hold her. He tried to share his strength with her, even though every cell of his being clenched in panic.

The sheriff shook his head. "I want to help you out, but one of the searchers could fall in the water or off a cliff in the pitch-black out here. We can't keep the volunteers going all night."

Owen stared in disbelief. "How am I supposed to care about anyone except my son? And why don't you care about him?"

"It's my job to care about everyone." Sheriff Layton looked at Lilah. "I'm sorry," he said, in the mountain's soft twang. "I want to find your son, but I can't risk more lives. We'll start again as soon as it's light enough."

"I'm trying to understand." Lilah trembled so hard, her voice shook with every ragged breath.

"I'm not giving up," Owen said. "Come with me if you want, Lilah. Some of the others will keep searching with us."

"Of course I'm coming with you." She looked around at the faces that surrounded them.

The men and women who'd been combing the mountain for hours talked among themselves. Some went toward the parking lot in front of the inn, but most stayed put.

"We'll take the road over by Tanker's Falls," Noah said, walking away with Emma's hand in his.

"And I'm going toward the ski lifts," Chad said. "They hypnotize Ben."

"Wait." Owen lifted both hands. "I'm not sure how many of you heard me tell the sheriff earlier, but I taught Ben to follow a stream if he ever got lost. If you hear water, go toward it, and call for him."

"Will do," Chad said.

Noah nodded, his face stony.

Owen wanted to punch something. "What if he heard us last night, Lilah?"

"That's what I think," she said. "I should have stayed with him."

"And we never would have talked. He left, rather than face an argument between his parents." Owen knew how desperate Ben must have felt. How many times had he done the same thing when he was a kid?

"But what if someone took him? What if we're wrong?"

"That person would have had to come up the mountain and down a twisting, unpaved road. It would have to be someone who wanted Ben and no one else. I'm afraid we're the problem."

She cried, and he tightened his hand around hers.

"We've already been to my favorite places,

to all the places I've shown Ben. I don't know where else to go."

"Let's just choose a direction we haven't taken." Her voice was so tight, it was hardly recognizable. "Which way do the goats head when they break out? He's certainly traveled with them more than once."

A smile hurt his mouth. He felt as if he were doing something wrong, smiling when his son needed help. "I'm sorry," he said. "If I'd just let you go…"

"You knew I was leaving? I'm sorry. I should have told you. I think Ben must have figured out that's what I'd do, as well. He knows me even though he's only four."

He increased his grip on her hand. Lilah's thick mitten and his leather glove might have formed a barrier between them, but he felt her body's warmth, and it made him grateful because her words filled him with cold.

He tugged her closer. "Careful. Don't trip over a root." His advice made her groan as they both thought of Ben tripping over roots and holes and rocks, into icy water. Taking a deep breath, he shouted his son's name. "Ben! Ben, buddy, come to me if you can hear my voice!"

"Please, let him hear us," Lilah said. "Ben?" Her shout was a broken cry that shattered Owen.

"We have to find a better way to make things work for us," he said. "We can't risk this ever happening again. He's just a little guy even though he acts so mature."

Lilah wiped her mouth with her free hand. "I know you think I've made him into a mini-adult, because I didn't want anything to happen to him—"

"But you never lost him in the woods in Vermont."

"This is no time for an 'I told you so.' I wouldn't do that."

He stared intently at the darkened woods, following the beam of his flashlight with concentration. After today he'd have a hard time defending himself from accusations that he wasn't good father material. "Let's not argue now." Owen pointed at the path that curved in front of them. "After we find Ben, we'll discuss custody."

"Custody? When you didn't even notice Ben leave your house? I try to give you a break, but you use it to bring up custody?" She came to a dead stop in the muddy path. "I don't have to give you anything, and I won't give you my child. Do you think I don't know how to disappear?"

Her threat rattled him as if someone had taken him by the head and shaken him like a toy. At that moment, a whistle cut through the cold night. He turned toward the sound and followed the streak of red into the sky. A flare.

"That has to mean—" Chad had headed in that direction, believing Ben might have gone to the ski lift that bordered on Gage property. Had his younger brother planned ahead enough to take a flare?

Owen didn't finish his thought, and he didn't wait for Lilah. He ran across the rough ground, tripping, nearly falling so many times he was surprised he stayed on his feet.

He ended up splashing through one of those streams he'd been terrified his son might have fallen into. Lilah, gasping, came rushing up behind him.

He didn't care. He couldn't stop for her. She wouldn't want him to.

"I just need to see Ben," he said, hearing his own words and the desperation in them.

Owen stumbled as the ground rose up to the top of the hill where Chad had just lit another flare.

"We're coming," Owen shouted.

"He's safe," Chad yelled back to them.

Lilah uttered a sound that tore at Owen's guts. But he didn't turn back, even though every instinct urged him to help her, to comfort her.

She didn't want his comfort. She wanted nothing from him except their son.

So he had to get to Ben. That was the only thought that made sense. He needed his son in his arms. He needed to hear Ben's voice and feel the weight of his sturdy, small, impatient body.

Owen struggled up the hill, grabbing one-handed at branches, skidding through snow and ice he could barely see in the bouncing illumination of his flashlight. At the very top, he waited, holding back a heavy shrub to let Lilah through.

At the same moment, they saw Chad, holding Ben on his hip, but Ben was cradling his arm in the same way Owen had after he fell off the ladder.

"Wait," Chad said. "Don't panic. I think he broke it, but he's all right."

"Baby." Lilah pushed past Owen and slammed into Chad and their son. Ben's good arm wound around his mother's neck.

"Mommy," he said, crying. "My arm…"

"Let me see." She touched gently, and looked back at Owen, tears running down her face. "Can you call Noah and tell him we're coming?"

They both took off their outer clothing and wrapped it around Ben, who cried harder. Owen stood there, feeling like an outsider, now that he was so close, but Lilah came first with their child.

Before he could reach for his phone, Ben looked up as if he hadn't known his mother wasn't alone. His eyes went wide in the light, and then he blinked, leaning backward to release his arm and hold it out to Owen.

"Daddy."

That word. It was magic. A gift. Happiness and trust.

Pure bliss.

Owen couldn't speak, but a sound came from his throat that made Chad and Lilah turn to stare at him. He didn't care at all that he was crying. He held out his arms.

"Son."

It was all he could manage. Lilah held Ben out and let him go, but the look on her face cut Owen like the sharpest blade.

He knelt, holding on to his boy with his

cast, but as Lilah came near, he also reached for her hand, as if he could hold her, too. Hold them both and keep them here. In his life.

Where they both belonged.

Lilah pulled away. "I'll call Noah."

CHAPTER SIXTEEN

OWEN CARRIED BEN, while Chad lit the way for them with the flashlight. Lilah pulled out her phone and called Sheriff Layton to tell them they'd found their son.

Her voice still shook, but with relief now.

"Does he need an ambulance?" the lawman asked.

"I spoke to Noah," she said. "We think Ben has broken his arm." Naturally, in these woods. In the dark. Because she couldn't keep her voice down in an argument with his father last night. "Noah's going to meet us. Ben has been in the cold all day, but he was walking fine. We'll make sure his hands aren't frostbitten."

Chad pulled Ben's gloves off and shone his light on them. They were healthy and pink, and Ben wiggled his fingers.

"Gomer came with me, but I lost him, and then I had a doggy, Mommy. A big, white doggy. He was so warm. I followed him for a while, but I got tired, and then we sat under a huge, old log." He held his uninjured arm wide, whacking Owen in the nose as he measured his temporary sanctuary for them.

Thank goodness he hadn't taken a nap with the big dog. With hypothermia, he might never have woken up again.

"That sounds like Mr. Tucker's Great Pyrenees," Chad said. "He probably thought Ben was a sheep or something and tried to herd him back to the farm."

"I'm not a sheep. Daddy, will Grandma be mad I lost Gomer?"

"I'm mad at Gomer. He went home without you," Lilah said, but then remembered she had the sheriff on the line. "Sorry," she said. "I just wanted to let you know we found him." Her son was alive. He hadn't fallen down a bottomless pit. No backwoods criminal had carried him away from her forever. She couldn't be sure if his arm was broken or not, but he didn't seem to be in as much pain as Owen had been. "Can you let the rest of the searchers know we found him?"

"I'll do that," Sheriff Layton said. "You get some rest. We'll talk tomorrow."

"Thanks, and, please, thank everyone else

for us." All those generous hearts, out searching for her son in the cold.

Her son wouldn't have wandered off and the searchers wouldn't have been at risk if she'd just had the good sense to stay put in Vermont and dare Owen to try to take Ben.

Ben's relief at being found seemed to dissipate, and he leaned against Owen again as they made their slower descent through the woods, snapping brittle, cold branches, and sliding on the composting piles of wet leaves on frozen ground.

Lilah avoided even looking at Owen's broad shoulders. She'd never imagined she'd see him cry the way he had when Ben called him daddy. She didn't want to remember that moment or the tug of his hand on hers.

She was going home, and her injured son would be coming with her. She wouldn't let him near this place again.

Lilah was sure Owen knew exactly what she was thinking. His instincts rarely failed him. His father's abuse and his mother's neglect had made him a survivor, too. And she'd all but threatened to disappear with Ben, somewhere Owen would never find them…

His hand had groped for hers, and he'd held her as if he needed her, but he wanted Ben.

Too late. Just as she'd almost been too late, removing her son from this stinking wilderness. It might be the place Owen couldn't help loving best on earth, but it had been one crazy risk after another to Ben.

As soon as they reached the clearing outside Suzannah's inn, the family poured across the fields, crying out Ben's name. Noah and Emma, Suzannah and Celia, all crowded around, clamoring to touch Ben's collar, or his sleeve, or pat his damp knit cap.

Lilah pulled off her own cap and replaced Ben's with it. As she shoved his under her elbow, the Gages eased her out of their way.

"Where have you been?" Suzannah asked in a high, strained voice that sounded nothing like her usual determined cheerfulness.

"How did you find him, Owen?" Celia asked.

"It was Chad." Owen nodded to his brother. "He guessed right about the ski lift."

"I wanted to ride the chairs," Ben said. "Daddy, can we ride the chairs now that I didn't get dead?"

Silence answered him. Every face turned to Lilah.

Their collective, unspoken question was obvious. How did a four-year-old learn about getting dead?

Lilah's greater worry was that he didn't seem that alarmed by the prospect.

"We'll ride the chairs sometime," Owen said. "When my heart's back in shape, and after we talk about running away."

"You and Mommy were fighting." Ben's sober glance trailed over Lilah's face before he looked back at his father. "I don't like fighting."

"Fighting?" Suzannah asked.

Celia took her mother by the arm and steered her toward the inn. "Must be time for us to go inside. I'm sure Lilah and Owen want Noah to look Ben's arm over before they get him to bed."

Noah agreed with a nod and led them onto the inn's porch. He examined Ben's arm while Owen held the little boy and made funny faces as Ben began to cry. At last, Noah wrapped the small arm in an elastic bandage for support and straightened. "I don't think it's broken," he said. "The wrist is swollen, and he's in some pain, but I think it's a sprain." He glanced at Chad with a smile. "You must have panicked."

"Me and everyone else in Bliss today," Chad said. He grinned at Lilah. "But it was a lucky day, and he's all right."

She nodded. "This time."

"I'm meeting some guys for a movie," Chad said, clearly disappointed in her answer, while everyone else stared at her with suspicion. "Ben, buddy, don't ever do that again. I don't like being scared any more than you like fighting."

Lilah had to admire his ability to get to the point.

"Why were you scared?" Ben asked. "I was the one who got lost."

"You had the Tucker's dog to keep you from being afraid. But we just didn't have you," Chad said. "Scary, so don't do that again."

"Okay." Ben sounded reluctant. Then he brightened. "Or I can find you and you can run away with me."

"Perfect." Chad scrunched up the top of Ben's borrowed cap and sent Lilah a commiserating smile above the boy's head. "That's the only way to do it. So don't forget next time. Come get me before you run away, and we'll go together."

He headed out of the house, and the others

began muttering their goodbyes. At last, even Suzannah went upstairs, and Owen picked up Ben and turned toward the door. "Come with us and say good-night, Lilah."

He led the way, carrying Ben with Lilah following behind them, planning her announcement in her head.

"Chad's a good kid," she said, instead of "I'm taking my son home, and you will never see him again."

"He has his moments, but deep down, he has a heart and a sense of responsibility."

"Daddy, I'm tired." Ben yawned. "Mom, do I have to take a shower tonight? And brush my teeth?"

"Absolutely," she said. "But I'll help you with your wrist."

"I want Daddy." He held up his arm. "Look, Daddy, we match."

She nodded, unable to speak after the twist of the knife in her heart. Ben loved his father, but Owen would just have to get used to either visiting in Vermont, or living without him. When Ben was older, he could decide if he wanted to come back here again, but she wasn't ever returning. Her life lay elsewhere, and she was tired of considering anyone else's opinions when she made decisions about her son.

"DADDY, I THINK Mommy's mad at me."

Owen helped Ben pull his pajama shirt over his dark curls.

"She's not mad." Not at Ben anyway. "She doesn't want anything to happen to you, and she was afraid when we couldn't find you."

"I wasn't scared, except when I got tired, and then the doggy stayed with me, and I was fine."

"That's not enough when you're the mom or dad," Owen said, trying to find a way to explain. "When you're a mommy or a father, and you can't find your son, you start to think bad things that scare you. We were afraid you might fall down or sprain a wrist." He gently touched Ben's bandaged arm. "And we might not be able to find you."

"I wouldn't like that." Ben yanked at the hem of his shirt. "But I still don't like when you fight."

"I don't either, son."

"Do you like my mommy?"

Heaven help him, he more than liked her. He wanted her to stay here in the mountains that owned him, body and soul. He wanted to share all the little towns she'd enjoyed discovering, and he wanted to show her the trails to his favorite spots where they could talk together about the things that mattered most to them. Above all, he wanted a chance to make a family with her and Ben.

But what mattered most to Lilah was getting away from here.

"I like your mommy. A lot."

"But you were mad at her, and she was mad at you."

"I'm sorry you heard us argue."

"I want to be with both of you. I get sad when she wants me, and you want me. Why can't we all stay together?"

"Good question, buddy." Owen squeezed toothpaste onto Ben's toothbrush and handed it over. "We'll talk about it tomorrow," he said, as Ben yawned wide enough to break his jaws. "I promise you."

"Okay, Daddy." He started brushing.

Owen leaned down to scoop up Ben's wet towel and the rug that was always more like a swamp after Ben's shower time.

"Daddy?" Ben looked up, toothpaste dripping from his mouth on to his shirt.

Laughing, Owen cleaned his chin. Every

time Ben called him daddy, he felt like shout-
ing for joy. "What's up?"

"I love you."

Owen knelt and hugged his son as tight
as he could. "I love you, too, buddy. With
all my heart."

When Ben finished brushing, they walked
together to his bed. Once he was under the
covers, Ben quickly turned on to his side and
closed his eyes. Owen dimmed the light as
he stepped through the door. He looked back
in a rush of gratitude that his son was safe
and asleep in his own bed.

He tossed the towel and rug into the laun-
dry room and cleaned the bathroom sink before he made himself go back downstairs.
Bracing for the argument to come, he was
not surprised to find Lilah at the door, grip-
ping her scarf in fisted hands.

"No raised voices or frightening my child
tonight," she said. "We aren't discussing
this. I'm taking him home tomorrow, and if
you want to fight it, you'll have to explain
to him."

Of course. "I'll let you go tomorrow, but
believe this—I will have my son back in my
life. You aren't taking him for good."

"Ben and I live the way I want to from now on."

He stared her down. Today had frightened her. He was relieved they only had to deal with a sprained wrist. But tomorrow they were going to discuss the cold, hard facts of Ben's new life, and that included shuttling between Vermont and Tennessee.

IN THE MORNING, nothing had changed. Lilah woke to the unutterable relief of knowing her son was safe. Knowing that he'd be safer, and so would she, when she got him home.

No more considering Owen's feelings. No more worrying that Ben's grandmother or his aunt or uncles would forget to look after him.

No more worrying that Owen would find she'd somehow let herself care for him. She didn't want to see these hills through his eyes. She didn't want to share her life with anyone except Ben. The second she'd let someone else in, Ben had hurt himself. She packed her things and put her bags in the car, going back inside to thank Suzannah for her hospitality.

"You're leaving?" Owen's mother wiped her hands on a dish towel as she turned from the sink. "I don't understand."

"I just can't stand being here anymore. Ben has been chased by goats, he almost injured himself with power tools, he was neglected by Chad and Celia when they were looking after him, and then he spent a day lost on a mountain."

"Chad found him, too. And everything else has just been childhood stuff. Children get hurt now and then. They run away. All mine did. He's fine."

Lilah closed her eyes for a second and steeled herself with a deep breath. "That's some comfort, Suzannah, but I'm taking him home."

"What about Owen? And us? We love him, too."

"Then you can visit him in Vermont."

"He never scraped a knee in Vermont?"

"I'm not discussing my son with you, Suzannah. Thank you again for letting me stay here. Thank you for wanting to get to know Ben. You can come to us anytime you want to see him."

Suzannah opened her mouth to speak, but stopped herself.

"Goodbye, then." Lilah nodded, uncomfortable with her sudden urge to hug the other woman. Owen's mother had been kind to her, and it was obvious she loved Ben.

"I understand fear," Suzannah said. "Do you think I don't wonder, every time I look at a man who interests me, if I'll end up hiding from him so he can't hit me—or worse?"

Lilah froze, her hand on the kitchen door. "I'm not talking to you about this."

"Odell once held a gun to my temple in the middle of the night for three hours. Owen doesn't know that. Neither does Noah or the younger children. I never told even my therapist or the ladies in my support group. You know why?"

"I don't want to know." Because she could feel Suzannah's fear. It crawled down her own spine. She knew Suzannah had kept quiet those three hours because Odell might have hurt one of the children if she'd made a noise and woken them. Lilah knew because Timor Blanton had said he'd go back and take her little brother if she made a noise when they were in stores together, or stopped at a gas station.

"I never told anyone because that was the moment I knew Odell owned me. If he shot me, one or all of my children would come to save me, and Odell would have killed them, too. I'm humiliated because I stayed with him for ten years after he pushed that gun into my head."

"Why didn't you leave the first time he turned his back?"

"I told you before I wasn't like you. Owen said you ran into traffic one day so someone would stop and help you. I never trusted anyone to stop for me."

"I wanted to die," Lilah said, surprising herself because she'd never admitted the truth out loud. "So if they hadn't stopped…"

"I ache for you because you didn't want to die. I think you were that desperate to live."

People had stopped for her. Enough of them to scare Timor off. He'd jumped in his own car parked nearby and sped away. Where she'd found the courage to make that one desperate bid for safety, she didn't know, but it had worked. She took a step back from Suzannah, unwilling to admit she might possibly be right.

"But now you think anyone who's close to you might hurt you like that man did." Suzannah stared down at her hands. "I understand that. You were in trouble. The people who should have protected you didn't. You can't trust anyone, so you won't let Owen be part of Ben's life."

"I'm not like that. This is about Ben's safety. Goodbye, Suzannah. I know Ben would like it if you'd come to visit us in Vermont."

She drove toward the cabin, her hands sweaty on the steering wheel, her mouth parched with dread.

The house looked so still, she feared for a second that Owen had left with Ben, and she'd never see her baby again.

Wasn't that what she planned to do to him?

She parked in front of the door and got out, hurrying up the steps. How many times had Ben opened the door for her as she reached it? Not today.

She rang the bell.

No one came, and the minutes stretched out endlessly.

"Owen," she called. Silence was the only reply. "Ben?"

The sound of the lock being turned brought her a jolt of relief. Owen opened the door. He hadn't slept. Dark circles framed his eyes. He didn't smile. "We're ready." He backed up to let her in.

"Where's Ben?"

"In the kitchen."

She moved in front of Owen. Ben had pulled a chair to the glass door, and he leaned on it, his back to her, staring out at the mountains where he'd scared her half out of her wits the day before.

"Ben?"

"What, Mommy?"

"Time to go. We have a plane to catch this afternoon."

"No."

Ben had never said no to her—at least not since he was two. "We need to go, buddy. I have to return the rental car, and we have a reservation."

"I want to stay here. I like it here."

Owen's eyes were rimmed with red when she glanced his way. He swallowed hard, but went toward their son.

"Ben, I'll come see you as soon as I can. Everything's going to be all right."

"Will Grandma come? And Uncle Chad? I like it here, with all of you."

"But Mommy needs to go home right now for a while, and you can come back. This is always going to be your other home."

A niggle of guilt wormed its way into her conscience. She didn't intend that to be the case.

The bare, bony trees climbing up the ridge

outside reminded her again how afraid she'd been yesterday when she couldn't find her little boy. Taking Ben home to Vermont was the only answer.

"Time, Ben. Now."

He dragged his feet as he went to the couch where his coat and gloves and scarf waited. He and his father looked like twin images of misery.

This wasn't her fault. Being a parent wasn't easy, and until Ben was old enough to understand he couldn't run as if he were one of the goats he loved so much, they wouldn't repeat this experiment.

Owen picked up Ben, who wrapped his arms around his father's neck. They were sweet together, the man and the boy. Lilah pressed her hand to her chest where an ache begged her to change her mind.

Why not try this again?

Because I can't keep Ben safe here. This is not where we belong. And I can't trust Owen to keep his promises.

Owen opened the front door. He walked through it, carrying their son. Without acknowledging her, he went to the car and helped Ben into his seat with one skilled hand. He'd learned how to care for Ben.

But he hadn't learned that you couldn't take chances with a little boy's happiness.

"You're welcome to come to Vermont anytime," she said as he straightened from the car.

The warmth of the past few weeks had fled, and he eyed her as if she were a stranger.

"My lawyer will be in touch," he said.

"So we're going to fight?"

"For Ben?" He lifted his stubbled chin, masculine and strong. "I'd fight even you for Ben, Lilah, and I never let anyone down in my life the way I let you down."

"I don't know what you mean."

"I wanted to be the right man for you back then," he said. "Now, I'm glad I didn't make the mistake of thinking I was."

His coldness froze her. Goose bumps tingled on her skin. "I have to go." She opened the driver's door.

Inside the car, Ben was crying. Not hard, not like a child. He cried like he did everything else, with a soul too old for his little boy self. His soft weeping tore through her.

She shut the door and started the engine.

"Daddy." Ben struggled to turn around in his seat. He waved frantically at his father, who stood there, waving back until they turned out of his driveway, on to the road that passed by the inn.

Owen looked like a man trying to pretend a fatal injury was only a flesh wound, and Lilah felt weighed down with guilt.

"Ben, I'm sorry. We've been gone so long. It's time to go home."

"Mommy, I'll be good if you let me stay. I won't run away. I'll stay right where you tell me. I don't want to go home yet."

She kept driving, hitting the gas a little as they passed Suzannah's place.

It was like all those years ago. She was escaping, and she couldn't get out of here fast enough.

BEN KEPT A stony silence on the plane and even after they got home. He refused her help getting ready for bed, and when she went in to his room to kiss him goodnight, he was crying again.

"Ben, buddy, I'm sorry about all this. You'll see your father again when he comes up here."

"You don't want him here."

"I want you and your daddy to have time together."

"You can call him and tell him to come

here." He took a deep breath that ended in a sob. "Please."

His begging went on for what seemed like forever. She didn't know what to do with the tears pressing behind her own eyes. For the first time, she doubted herself, questioning whether she was doing what was best for Ben.

Her parents had tried to keep her safe. They'd let down their guard for just a second. She'd let her guard down by allowing Owen back into her life.

"Daddy. I want my Daddy."

She sat back on her knees, clueless, guilty. She knew his ache. She'd missed Owen that much after she'd sent him away. As if she'd excised part of herself.

"Ben, honey, give him a chance to come visit."

"But I want my daddy now. I want to go on the chair lift. He promised."

"You knew we had to come home sometime."

"Because I was bad?"

"No." She hated that whole bad-boy thing. He'd never heard it until he went to day care. She should have hired a nanny.

"I won't be bad anymore. I promise."

Another thing she'd tried to avoid. Having Ben blame himself for something that wasn't his fault. "You didn't do anything."

"I ran away. That made you mad at Daddy and me." He rubbed his fists in his eyes. "He didn't even call me tonight."

She shook her head. It couldn't be this way. She couldn't do this to him.

"We'll call Daddy, and you can ask him when he's coming to visit you."

He brightened. "Right now?"

She felt her jeans pockets for her phone, but it wasn't there. "You stay here. I'll go downstairs and find my phone, and we'll call him."

After Owen talked to Ben, they'd discuss how he'd visit Ben in Vermont.

WHEN THE PHONE RANG, Owen stared at it from across the room. The room seemed darker than usual, and the kitchen counter looked farther away.

A trick of the wine. A mere trick.

He ignored the sound. There wasn't anyone he needed to speak with. Except Ben.

What if Ben had somehow persuaded his mother to let him call?

Owen struggled to his feet and started

across the room, but his foot hit something, and he nearly fell. He glanced down. The empty wine bottle. That stuff was like vinegar anyway.

He grabbed his phone. It was Ben. Lilah's number, but she wouldn't be calling. "Buddy," he said. "How are you?"

There was silence. Long silence. He dragged the phone down and stared blearily at the screen. It was definitely Lilah's number.

"Ben?"

"Owen?" Her voice was faint.

She had the nerve to sound injured with that one word. As if he'd done something wrong. He hadn't touched that bottle when Ben ran away, and he hadn't touched it when his son came home, barely injured after a day in the frozen woods, even though his relief had demanded a nice, numbing drink.

Shame struck him. "What do you want?" he asked.

"What have you done?"

Seriously? "I felt a little sorry for myself, and I opened the wine."

"Why would you do that?"

"Why did you leave?"

"Because my son got hurt in those mountains, and I can't count on you."

"Yeah. Well, I wanted to forget about your opinion of me."

"Forget?" Her voice rasped. "You wanted to forget me and Ben and your whole life. Your future. None of it mattered to you."

"You matter." He didn't mean to say it again. He was furious she'd thrown his feelings in his face, and she'd only made him more determined she'd never take his son from him again. "You both matter, but I will get him back."

"You just made sure we'll never come near you again." She threw the accusation at him.

He took a deep breath. "Do you think I don't know that? I wanted to hurt you and myself, because I am your worst nightmare. And my own."

She gave a small gasp. Of rage? Couldn't be regret. "Then you won't fight me anymore for Ben."

"You got that wrong. I forced you to bring Ben here, and I'm not proud of pushing you around, but we began to make a relationship out of what we feel now. I was as frightened as you when Ben disappeared, and just as relieved when he was safe. I thought we'd pulled together with our shared love for Ben, and I got this image of us as a family in my head—and the suggestion made you run for your life."

"Are you blaming me? This is my fault?"

He was blaming her. She'd been easy to blame. But he'd just proved her every decision had been correct—because he'd wanted that drink. "I'm trying to be honest with you. I thought I knew how to handle the worst if it ever came again, but losing Ben…and having you be the one who took him away from me, because I asked you to try to love me again? I wanted to stop thinking." He stared inside his own dark soul. He'd wanted that drink. "It wasn't the right choice. But maybe this is just who I am."

"So you're never going to stop drinking?"

He didn't know how to answer. Drinking hadn't worked. He couldn't forget. He'd been an idiot and a fool, and he finally understood he'd never be able to run from his grief again. He kept making his own problems, and then making them worse.

"I want to lie to you right now and promise I'll never touch another drop."

"No." She stopped speaking, but he heard her breathing. Hard. "No matter what you say, I won't believe you anyway, and that means I can't trust you with Ben."

"I guess I deserve that, but you don't get to decide whether I see my son. You left me once because I wasn't good enough for you." How could she believe anything else, now? How could he make her believe she might be wrong? "I stayed away because I thought you were right, but this time I do know what I'm losing, and I will find a way to stop this mess I keep making."

He heard a rustle against the phone, and a sniff, as if she were trying not to cry. "I knew I couldn't believe you, and I'll make sure Ben isn't ever alone with you."

"I never drank when Ben was here." His insides churned with those bitter swallows of wine and the deepest regret he'd ever known.

"I won't ever make it easy for you to see him again. I only called because of him. He's been crying since we left. He thinks he did something wrong, and that's why he can't see you. When you're sober, you had better call him back."

"I will."

"And only when you're sober."

"Lilah, I know you don't believe me, but…" He stopped. Making promises when his word was worth nothing. "I'll call Ben and explain."

"Don't blame this all on yourself. He knows I'm the one behind our leaving Tennessee, and he'll just blame me more, if you try to take the fault. It'll only confuse him."

"We'll work this out."

"I'm through trying to work things out. I'm sorry for Ben, and I don't want him to see this as punishment, but we won't be coming back to Tennessee, and he will not be alone with you again. Ever."

"I'll talk to him tomorrow." This time he let her hang up. There was no point in fighting to make her believe she should give him one more chance.

He had to find a different way. He had to heal his wounds without the benefit of alcohol before he made Ben and Lilah dread him like he dreaded the sound of his own father's name.

He might be too late with Lilah.

CHAPTER SEVENTEEN

LILAH HAD LEFT her phone on the desk in the shop's office. When it rang one Thursday afternoon about a month after she'd left Tennessee, she was with a customer. She couldn't help thinking every call might be from Owen.

Because she was a fool, and as much as she didn't want him to call, she longed to hear his voice. She didn't trust him to take care of Ben. She knew he could never care more about her than he cared about the next bottle in his makeshift bar, but she couldn't stop thinking about him.

She didn't want to believe she could care for a man like Owen.

Nevertheless, they'd arranged for him to visit this weekend with Ben. Owen's attorney had forced hers to agree Ben would return to Tennessee and that Owen would come get him, but she hadn't heard a word about travel plans.

"I'll take this desk," Mrs. Peterson said, ignoring the phone's chime and rubbing her hand over wood that looked and almost felt like soft brown butter. "Go ahead and tell me the price. You know I've been looking for one just like this for the past three years. Do your worst."

"I can work something out for you." Lilah turned the tag over. Mrs. Peterson had probably kept her in business the first year she'd been in Vermont, and she'd loved the items Lilah had shipped back from Tennessee. "I can offer you forty percent off, to thank you for everything you've done for the shop."

The other woman raised both eyebrows. "You've changed, my sharp-eyed friend, but I won't argue. Let's run my credit card before you change your mind."

They finished the purchase, and Lilah walked Mrs. Peterson to the door. Then she tried not to run to the office to check her phone. The missed call had been from Owen. Her pulse thumped despite all her best efforts to be sensible. Owen and his family had accused her of paranoia, but she'd always been right about him.

Yet, still she missed him. She was haunted by the memory of his bleak expression, watching her drive away. What might she have done in his shoes? And hadn't she taken her favorite defensive position, running away?

He'd called Ben every day since they'd been back in Vermont. She'd spoken to him, and he'd been sober. Which didn't mean he stayed that way after he hung up, but she actually hoped that was the case.

She hit the voice-mail icon. "Lilah," his voice said, "I just wanted to let you know my mom's coming to Vermont to pick up Ben. Celia will bring him back on Sunday night. Mom's flying out of Knoxville at about three this afternoon, and she has your address. Let me know if any of this is a problem."

Of course it was a problem. He'd interfered with her plans again, and she wouldn't be able to see him to make sure he wasn't drinking. She had to let her son spend time with a man who might start boozing the second Ben fell asleep.

That evening, Ben was bouncing all over the house while she packed his bag. She'd barely finished when the doorbell rang. Ben rushed ahead of her and dragged the door open.

"Grandma." He threw himself into Suzannah's arms.

She hugged him, her eyes squeezed shut with joy. "I'm so happy to see you, Ben." As she looked up at Lilah, her good spirits drained away. "How are you?"

"Fine." She searched for a way to ask the question most vital to Ben's happiness and finally gave up on being subtle. "How is Owen?"

"Stone-cold sober since you talked to him on the phone after you left." Suzannah's expression suggested her own sense of guilt. "I check all the time. I don't want him to lose access to his boy."

"You check?"

"I visit him at odd moments. You understand why he does what he does?"

Lilah rubbed Ben's soft curls. "Go get your coat and hat, buddy."

"Okay. Don't leave me, Grandma."

Lilah quailed. He missed his father so much. "I'm going nowhere without you," Suzannah said, "but we need to hurry. We have a flight home, little guy."

"Has Gomer busted out again?"

"Not without the aid of his little henchman."

"What's a hintman?"

Even Lilah smiled—maybe in relief at

the break in tension between her and Ben's grandmother.

"I'll explain on the way to the airport," Suzannah said. She waited until his feet disappeared up the stairway. "I'm sorry about Owen, and I realize he's responsible for himself, but you might give him a break, considering what his father and I did to him as a child."

"This again? Did he send you to start a campaign for him?"

"He'd kill me for even bringing the subject up."

Lilah glanced toward the stairs, listening for Ben. "I know his father treated you all terribly, and I also realize you neglected Owen and the other kids. But he's Ben's father. He makes his own choices."

"I made mistakes," Suzannah said, "that Owen is still paying for."

"He should speak for himself."

"He told me to stay out of his business and leave you and Ben alone. I'd like to do as my son asks for a change, but what if my experience could help, rather than causing more trouble for the people I love?" She literally wrung her hands. "The thing is, Lilah, I think we can know each other in the way women do who've been abused. You and I both endured harrowing experiences, but we survived. Same as Owen. The difference is, we both decided how to handle the fear we still feel. Owen doesn't want to feel."

"You're not a psychologist, Suzannah, and we got nowhere with this conversation that night at your house."

"This situation makes what I have to say more important. You're part of our family now, and we all miss you, like it or not. You're stuck with interference." Suzannah looked at her with compassion. "You were only a child when you were attacked. You're still reacting as that child would. You've been hiding since then."

"I was not afraid after the kidnapping," Lilah said. "You don't know me. If anything, I was reckless, especially when I met your son. And Ben is not a crutch to help Owen stop drinking. I hate every minute my son spends with yours."

"You don't." Owen's mother acted as if she possessed the wisdom of the ages. She looked into Lilah's eyes, and Lilah found she couldn't tear her gaze away.

"Suzannah, this problem is not between

us. I don't need you to analyze me. Besides, my lawyer tells me I can't talk about it."

"You and Owen should work this out together," Suzannah said as Ben's feet pounded overhead. "You need to make your own decisions."

Fortunately, Ben came flying down the stairs before Lilah had to offer Suzannah the same blunt suggestion Owen had—to get out and stay out of her business.

OWEN LOOKED UP from the wooden goat he was carving to check the time. With the cast off, he'd started working on a birthday present for Ben. He'd expected his mother to call, saying they'd landed at least an hour ago. She wasn't answering her cell phone either.

He crossed the small workroom to the fireplace and tossed in another log. It landed with a splash of red embers, and he prodded the other logs until the flames began to lick around the new fuel.

Laughter seemed to rise on the winter wind that always buffeted the small building. Owen hurried to the door in time to see his mother jogging across the lit field from the road, with Ben dancing at her side.

"Daddy," he called, running to leap at Owen. "Your arm's okay."

"Yours, too. Everything's perfectly okay now." Owen hugged his son close, love and deep gratitude for this little boy lighting him up. Over Ben's shoulder, he looked at his mother. "I tried to call."

"I know." She wiped at her forehead. "But I figured you'd ask me what I said to Lilah, and I thought I'd save us both that conversation."

He grimaced. "I told you to leave her alone."

"She told me that, too." Suzannah stopped quickly, looking embarrassed. "Not in so many words, but we both knew the thought was there."

Owen reached behind him for the door and pulled it shut. "I'll take him back on Sunday night, Mom." He patted her shoulder to reassure her. "Thanks for trying to help me out, but I need to handle this."

"I wish you both would so that Ben doesn't have to keep making this trip." Suzannah turned, waving her hand over her shoulder. "I'm not saying another word. Not to either of you. Why would you consider the wisdom of someone who's made plenty of mistakes herself?"

He'd made enough of his own, and treating Lilah like a hostage had been one of them. Another was pinning his sobriety to someone else's welfare. He'd always said AA didn't work for him, but he'd gone to a meeting the night Lilah had called him from Vermont. Turned out, AA did work, if you committed.

He pressed Ben's head to his chin and kissed the little guy's silky hair.

"Glad to see you, buddy."

"Let's go see the goats, Daddy. Gomer probably missed me."

"We all missed you, buddy."

"You can take a picture of me with Gomer. If Mommy sees I'm all right, she might not be mad at Tennessee anymore."

"Mommy's not mad at Tennessee. I did something I shouldn't have done, and your mom is just worried about you."

"You don't do wrong things, Daddy." Ben put both hands on Owen's face and stared into his eyes.

He could lie to look better in his son's eyes. He could try to explain he was a drunk who couldn't stop drinking or that he'd finally taken charge to make the right decisions for himself. To make his own life better. So that the people he loved could depend on him, and he could feel worthy of their love.

"I did do something wrong, buddy, but I'll try not to do it again. I don't want to hurt you or your mother. I want to make you both happy from now on. You're not in trouble, and Mommy doesn't have to worry that I'll make mistakes while you're with me."

Ben stared a little longer. Finally, he frowned. "I don't get it."

Owen hugged him tight. "You don't have to. All you have to do is race me to see Gomer." He set his son on the ground and tugged the sides of his knit cap around his ears. "Careful of the uneven ground, and don't run into the stream."

"I won't." And Ben was running as fast as his legs would carry him, laughing with happiness that floated into the chilly night air around him.

Owen loped along in his wake, his determination a thing of certainty rather than hope. No more pinning his future on the strength of his feelings for Lilah or his family or a job he needed, or even Ben. He had to be his own reason for getting his life back on track.

He and Ben spent the weekend starting on

a tree fort that Ben would be able to play in come the spring. They took pictures, which Owen sent to Lilah without comment. He began to wonder if she'd lost her phone when she didn't respond with a caution about letting Ben play with the hammer and nails and splinter-filled boards.

She didn't respond at all, but she did call Ben on Friday and Saturday night and heard about their progress. Ben told her Owen would be bringing him back on Sunday.

"Can he stay for a while?" Ben asked after he'd relayed the news. He frowned a little at whatever she said. "Oh. Okay. I love you, Mommy." He shoved the cell phone Lilah had placed in his small backpack into the zippered pocket on the front. "Daddy, are you too busy to visit me?"

"What?" Owen turned from the dishes he was washing after their meal. "I'm never too busy for you."

"Mommy said so."

Wishful thinking on Lilah's part. "She doesn't know I'm not as busy as I was when she was here."

"Then you can stay in Vermont? Mommy's making my favorite cookies. You'll like them."

Cookies were certainly an enticement. "Not this time." He was through forcing Lilah to put up with him. "But before too long, when I take you home, we'll see if Mommy minds if I stay for a while."

He had to prove to himself and to her that this wasn't one more attempt that would fail. Every night, after Ben went to bed, Suzannah came down to stay with him while Owen went to AA meetings in a basement room at the courthouse in town.

Sunday afternoon, he boarded the flight with Ben, who fell asleep almost as soon as they pulled back from the Jetway. When they landed, Ben slept through the ride home, but he recovered his energy enough to bolt ahead of Owen to the front door of Lilah's tidy Cape Cod.

She met Ben, as eager as Owen had been to have her son back with her.

Owen watched the two of them, hugging, happy to be together, Ben filling her in on everything he'd done in a stream-of-consciousness spiel that pleased Owen.

"Mommy, did you make my cookies?" Ben suddenly asked, as if remembering he hadn't eaten in a few hours.

She nodded. "But you can only take one

off the plate, buddy. I have dinner ready for you, too."

He ran off, shucking coat and hat and gloves.

Owen waited, not expecting an invitation to come inside. "I'd like to say goodbye to him before I go."

Lilah stood aside. "Why are you here? Is something wrong?"

He eased past her, strangely aware of her nervousness, of the way her gaze lingered on his face. He hoped he was hiding the hunger he felt, looking at her, searching for forgiveness, for some remnant of caring that he might not ever deserve again.

"Nothing's wrong," he said. "Except between us." He braced himself to be thrown out. "Do you think we could talk after Ben goes to bed? I can come back whenever you say, if you don't want me to wait now."

She measured him with cool blue eyes. She didn't look worried, but that didn't surprise him.

"You're welcome to eat with us," she said, but she looked away. "I'm not sure what Suzannah told you…"

"That she interfered. I'm sorry she did that, but I didn't come to apologize for her."

"Daddy, you want a cookie? Mommy's are the best."

Owen looked to Lilah, still searching for a cue as to how he should behave in her home. It would be so much easier to blame her for all this mess if he didn't have a conscience.

"Your dad can have a cookie after dinner," Lilah said.

Ben slammed his hands together, his eyes shining. "You're staying? You're friends again?"

Owen's first instinct was to protect Ben with a lie, but that wouldn't help if they went to court over his custody. He'd never understand how they could be friends and still fight each other. Owen's attorney had warned him that the judge in their case might ask to speak to Ben, so there was no keeping the possible battle from his small son.

"We'll always be friends," Lilah said, startling Owen so much that he didn't know what to say. "Because of you, Ben. Try not to worry." She managed a smile, but the corners of her lips seemed to tremble. "Let's eat. I made Ben's favorite spaghetti again."

"Daddy's favorite, too." Ben danced ahead of them.

After a second, without glancing Owen's way, Lilah followed their boy.

Owen did what he meant to do from now on. He put one foot in front of the other and moved forward.

LILAH HARDLY BELIEVED her own performance. She got through dinner, offering Owen Parmesan cheese and coffee and smiles that barely went skin deep. At last, Ben began to yawn, and when she suggested bedtime, he demanded his father help him with his shower and his unpacking.

Lilah cleaned the kitchen, listening to footsteps overhead. Her fear was a living thing, expanding in her chest until it seemed to flow through her body.

She fought it. She had the upper hand here. Owen was at her mercy because she'd already established his weakness.

If only she didn't care what her desperate actions did to Ben. If only she didn't wish this could be their life, taking care of the son they'd made when they'd loved each other. Sharing a home and hopes and dreams.

"Lilah?"

She turned, pretending she hadn't been

twisting a damp dish towel until her hands and fingers were sore.

"Is he asleep?" she asked.

"I wonder if he's catching another cold. He slept on the plane and all the way from the airport."

"He must have run like a wild child while you had him," she said.

Owen smiled as if he liked that idea. "He was born to live in those mountains." He closed his mouth, and even she could see he wished he hadn't spoken the words. "I'm not trying to pressure you," he said.

"What do you want? You were always honest. Just tell me what's on your mind."

He nodded, shoving his hands into the pockets of his jeans. "Now that I'm here, I feel as if I've learned from my mother, like I'm trying to say things I shouldn't."

"You don't have to." She cleared her throat. "You're going to fight for Ben in court. You've only been unkind that once to me, but you have to make me seem like the unstable one because you want Ben as much as I do."

Owen's head went back as if she'd struck him. "What are you talking about?"

"I'm sick of the negotiations, too."

"And they're getting us nowhere." He pulled his hands out of his pockets. As if he couldn't face her, he moved to push the chairs in at the table. "But I didn't come to threaten you or blackmail you into coming back."

She sagged with relief, even as her heart broke a little. "You're giving up?"

"Never." He turned then, his face fierce. "I came to tell you I won't give up. Maybe I misunderstood what was happening between us in Tennessee. I thought you were learning to love my place. I thought you were remembering that you cared for me."

She had been. She cared for him, and she'd finally had to be honest and admit to herself that his home enchanted her. From the snow-crusted hollows to the mountains with their wet, shiny granite and dark winter trees. "It doesn't matter how I feel about—"

"I thought you were learning to trust me."

"You know I did." She remembered her anger. "Until you drank again."

He stepped in front of her, confronting her with a broken expression that cut her deeply. She had to clench her hands to stop herself from touching the face that looked so hurt, and hurt her, with his pain.

"Lilah, my name is Owen, and I'm an alcoholic."

She stopped breathing.

"I'm not your psychologist or your—"

"You're the woman I loved." He took a deep breath that didn't seem to ease his tension. "The woman I love. Maybe I never stopped loving you. There hasn't been anyone else, no matter how much I wanted to forget you."

"No." She put up her hand to cover her face. "This is some new trick. Because you think it's the only way you'll get Ben back into your life."

"I'm not that unkind," he said. "Not anymore. I wouldn't do that to you or to him."

She wrapped her arms around her waist. "I don't understand."

"I tried to stop drinking in rehab because I loved you." He shook his head. "That didn't work. I tried to stop because I was shaming my family. I realized no one cared about my family's shame as much as my older brother and I did, so I drank some more. Then I tried to stop because Noah got me a job that would restore my reputation and give me a chance at a better life. I didn't drink for a couple of months, and when I learned about Ben, I thought I'd never drink again because I'd do anything, give up anything, I'd offer anything I have, to be his father."

She remembered that night on the mountain, under a sky of fireworks, believing things could be better than before, that she could trust Owen with Ben and with herself. "Then why did you do it?"

"You took Ben away, and I knew you'd never willingly bring him back. I didn't have it in me to force you again, so I knew we'd have to go to court and fight like two people who'd stopped loving each other."

"I just wanted to keep him safe until he was old enough to understand how dangerous the mountains are." She shrugged. "Until you drank that wine."

Owen smiled at her gently, but she saw the despair that he tried to hide. She even saw his amusement at her expense.

"Don't you hear how crazy that sounds?" he asked. "I grew up in those mountains. How many children have survived the normal bumps and bruises of childhood, even when they run away from their parents' arguments?"

"I'm not crazy." She bit out the words. "But I'm not going to live any life that puts Ben at risk. You would have been welcome here anytime."

"Lilah, I don't live here. You came to escape me. Your life here excludes me. My family is in Bliss. My job is there."

"And you expected me to uproot my life."

"One last time," he said. "I hoped you'd want to come live with me, and with all the people you met. They felt familiar to you from the moment you met them. Even I could tell that," he said, and she remembered them all. The worn faces of the artists, the beautiful hope, their welcoming invitations and the dickering they'd done over exquisite objects that drew her back there now, as the works of art arrived, piece by piece, at the gallery.

"Every artist you met," Owen said, "my family, my mother and my sister and brothers—you came to care for them all, even when you tried not to. And you remembered how it felt to care for me."

"Until I heard the familiar sound of your voice when you've been drinking."

"I thought I'd lost you both. I can't explain—

the relief of him being safe, and then immediately, you were running for cover. You told me that being with me put him in danger, and I couldn't disagree. I knew you'd fight me every step of the way. I couldn't face the battles and the accusations. Not from you."

He straightened, shame fleeing his face as suddenly as it had come. In its place was a certainty that startled her. Unexpected, but real as the ground beneath her feet.

"I ran in my own way," Owen admitted, "but I'll never run again. Not because I'm proving something to you. Not because I want the job that still means a new life. Not even because of Ben, and I'd die for him. Just as you would, Lilah."

She swallowed. "I would die for him, but I won't be fooled by a man as desperate as I am to be his parent."

"And I won't lie to you." Owen shrugged, his body language showing that he'd offered her the truth, even if he couldn't find words to make her believe. "I am sober. I've gone to AA, and this time, it's because I know I need help. I will be sober. And when I've been sober long enough to make you believe this is who I am from now on, I'll come back to you and ask you to try to love me again."

The promise shocked her. And then his words registered. How many times had he refused to promise anything? But then the rest of what he'd said registered.

"You're leaving?" Joy should have been her response. Instead the ground seemed to open up. "You're giving in?"

"Not a chance." He tipped up her chin with one finger and held her gaze. "We've managed to work out visitation between us. Unless you want to change it, our current arrangement about Ben works for me. We can both fire the lawyers, or you keep yours fighting if that's your choice. But I want you and Ben in my life. Both of you."

"Both?" Some of that magic from the night on the mountain came back to her. If only she dared hope. If only she dared risk believing in the new man who stood before her.

"When you're ready," he said. "When you can trust me again, you tell me."

She told herself to resent his arrogance. But how could she, when this was the certainty she'd wanted from him from the second she'd known she was carrying his child?

"I don't trust easily," she said. His drunken voice, accusing her, wasn't easy to forget.

"There's no deadline."

He started toward the hallway but came back, and she glimpsed the old Owen, the swagger and the sweetness, as he curved his hand behind her head and smiled at her with staggering tenderness.

"I won't push you," he said, just before he touched his firm mouth to hers in a gentle kiss that promised more. "I'll be waiting if you're brave enough to try again."

Brave enough? She watched him, willed herself to stand perfectly still and not follow him. Not speak to him. She didn't want to fight, and she didn't need to prove her courage to anyone.

He grabbed his coat off the stairs before he opened the door and stepped over the threshold into the cold. Snow swirled around him out of the darkness.

"Owen," she said, too full of a confusing mixture of longing and dread to understand herself.

He looked back, flakes of snow already glittering in his dark hair and on his shoulders.

"How do you know you won't drink again?" she asked.

"I don't."

His bleak face somehow gave her hope.

He still wasn't making empty promises. He wasn't threatening her. He was just honest.

The door closed, and he was gone, but he'd left a storm behind. Raging inside her.

CHAPTER EIGHTEEN

"MOMMY, WHY ARE you so sad?"

Lilah turned from the stack of clothing she'd sorted from Ben's dresser. Perched on the edge of his bed, with a plastic airplane in his lap, he studied her.

"I'm not sad, baby," she said. It wasn't exactly a lie. She was unsettled. At loose ends. Her life felt open-ended. She gathered the little jeans and shirts he could no longer wear and stood, balancing them in front of her. "We should have done this a long time ago."

"Throw my stuff away?"

He sounded offended, and she laughed. "And my stuff, too. We have a small house, and it's filled up with things we can't use anymore."

"I don't get it, and I'm hungry. I want pizza."

"Then let's get out of this house and go have a pizza."

"I want pizza from Tennessee."

She pretended that wish didn't trouble her.

Ben seemed more attached to Tennessee than he was to his own bed in his own home. But it wasn't just the place he missed.

"I want my daddy, Mommy."

"I know you do, sweetie." There'd been several visits. Ben always came back exhausted, happy to see her and more than ready to go back to his father in Tennessee as soon as possible. "He's coming on Thursday so you can hang out with him before you both leave on Friday."

"I want to show him more of my favorite things to do. He likes my school. And duck bowling."

"He'll like everything you do."

"I wish you weren't mad at him all the time." Ben set his plane on the small table in the center of the room.

"Buddy, I'm not mad at your father." Her young son, the very best part of her and certainly the best thing that had ever happened to her, had put her on the defensive. "I'm a—"

She choked off the word before it could escape, but it screamed in her head with the strength it had gathered all the weekends she'd spent alone.

Afraid. Just as Owen had said. Even Suzannah was right.

She was afraid of Ben getting hurt in those hazard-filled woods, terrified he'd get lost again, and she'd never find him. She was afraid she'd love Owen with all her heart, and he'd throw her love away, and she'd never find herself again.

One last harsh truth finally cut through the cocoon of detachment she'd tried to cloak herself in. She was more than a little gutted that Ben might love his fun-to-be-with father more than his overprotective mother.

Those woods and all the so-called normal things that had happened to Ben in Tennessee threatened her. What if Ben preferred his life there? She might lose control. And it wasn't just Ben's safety that concerned her. Being in Tennessee herself, close to Owen, brought back all those other feelings she'd kept so long at bay.

She had been reckless—for her—when she'd known Owen, but pregnancy had transformed her into the frightened survivor, that five-year-old girl who'd somehow found the courage to escape her abductor.

Childproofing and alarm systems and her preference that Ben's friends come to their house for playdates instead of his going to theirs. Had she been standing still for years? So locked inside the fear of doing something that might jeopardize Ben's safety that she'd done nothing at all?

She'd told herself she was protecting him from a father who might show up in his life and then disappear because he loved drinking more. Owen had admitted he still felt a powerful urge to seek out the oblivion he found at the bottom of a bottle, but she'd found her own refuge in the bland, stultifying environment she controlled to ensure Ben's safety.

Neither of them could be hurt because they'd loved unpredictable, unreliable Owen if they never had anything to do with him.

"Mommy, are you okay?"

"Huh?" She backed into the dresser behind her before she even knew she was moving. Ben's concern, plain and inescapable in blue eyes exactly like his father's, got through to her. "I'm fine."

Fine, if she never wanted to love again, if she was happy to stagnate in a life with no highs or lows, and none of the blinding joy she wanted her child to feel one day when he grew up and met the person who made him complete.

But she had kept him safe, whispered the quiet voice in the back of her mind.

So why had he flourished in the weeks since he'd met his father? Why had he gone from being shy of strangers and slow to leave her side to an extroverted runaway?

Because Owen had given him confidence. Owen and his assumption that Ben could get himself out of trouble around the farm with a few simple lessons. Owen and his family of scatterbrained siblings and an interfering mother. Owen and his love.

"I'm going to make Daddy a picture," Ben said.

She nodded. "A picture of what, baby?"

Ben turned his father's reproving gaze on her. "I'm not a baby."

"So I notice." But he was barely past the toddler stage. Maybe she'd made the right decisions until now.

"Daddy knows I'm a big boy. He lets me do stuff."

Maybe she hadn't.

"What kind of picture are you going to make for Owen?"

"Me and Gomer that day we got lost." He

ran to the tray of drawing paper on his shelf
and grabbed crayons and a blank white piece
of butcher paper. "When we were climbing
the mountain before Gomer got tired and
went home."

The day he'd run away to escape her argument with Owen. He'd tried to get back on
his own. Like his father, Ben hadn't given
up that day. He'd kept fighting to find his
way home.

Owen had said he was fighting for a home
for all of them, together. He'd stumbled along
the way, lost some important battles, but he
had never given up—not when he'd tried to
be sober because she'd asked him to. Not
when he'd tried because he needed to build
the clinic for his town. Not even when he'd
tried to stop drinking for their son.

Owen might have given in for a moment,
when she'd taken Ben from him a second
time, but he'd come back swinging.

She was the one who'd ducked straight
back into the safe world she'd made where
she tried so hard to forget love and pain and
fear. And the deep happiness she'd felt that
night on the mountain, just the three of them
beneath a dazzling canopy of fireworks—a

happiness that was fighting to be recognized inside her right now.

"Draw your picture, ba—Ben." She corrected herself this time. "And maybe we can take it to Daddy after you finish?"

"Tonight?" Ben clutched the paper and crayons to his chest.

She immediately lost her nerve, but for the first time she didn't run for safety. Instead she took a lesson from her son and from Owen.

She wouldn't change her mind. No woman should keep putting up a fight to feel nothing at all.

"I have to talk to my friends at work about taking care of the shop," she said. "Maybe we can go tomorrow night. I have things I'd like to tell Owen."

It was time to run toward life, instead of trying not to live at all.

OWEN CAME OUT of the courthouse basement door. The meetings helped keep him on track, but he had yet to walk through those doors at the end of one and not think how badly he wanted a drink.

Tonight as he walked out, breathing in the crisp, cold air, he had a hallucination. When he lifted his gaze from the icy ground beneath his feet he saw Lilah and Ben sitting on a bench across the road.

He'd never had hallucinations, even when he drank.

"Daddy." With a shout, Ben launched himself off the bench. Lilah jumped up after him.

So a hallucination could actually be a dream come true.

"What are you doing here?" He crossed the road and caught his boy as always, in midleap.

Lilah laughed at them, her gaze frightened, her hands twisting together in front of her heart.

"I thought for the first time since I was five years old, I might have to run into traffic and see if the only man I will love all my life would be there waiting for me."

He held on to Ben, who stared goggle-eyed at his mother. Owen tried to speak, but he couldn't believe she'd come to him. He couldn't believe the two people he loved most in the world were here, where he could touch them and talk to them.

And love them.

"I'll always be wherever you need me,

Lilah." He held out his hand and cradled the tender curve of her cheek. "Are you real?"

"Oh, I'm real, and I'm determined to try again. Can we see if we still love each other?"

He leaned down, kissing her with reassurance and gratitude, and love that he'd had no idea would ever be returned. "I'll spend my life answering that question."

"You're too mushy," Ben said. "Stop being smoochy."

And that was how to start a brand-new life together.

EPILOGUE

"THE GROOM'S WAITING at the bottom of the stairs with the best man hopping at his side." Suzannah had sneaked back inside the inn once Lilah's own mother had taken her seat on the bride's side of the tent erected in the yard.

"I thought they weren't supposed to see me before the wedding." Lilah adjusted her veil for the fiftieth time. "Could you help me with this pin, Suzannah? It's digging into my skull."

"You're not afraid of bad luck, are you?"

That question was like throwing gas on a fire. Lilah was so determined never to be afraid of anything again.

"You asked that on purpose."

"You bet." Suzannah took the hairpin and tilted Lilah's head. "Ben and Owen have gifts for you that they want you to have for the ceremony. Go down there, and then make your entrance."

"You'd better explain to the guests we'll be running a touch late."

"Will do. I think this is right. Does it still hurt?"

Lilah touched the whisper-soft, translucent veil. "No. Thanks. Can you help me pull it back?"

Suzannah uncovered her face. "Don't forget to have Owen pull it forward again, and hurry with those two, or your dad will come looking for you."

She ran down the back stairs, and Lilah hurried down the ones that led to the dining room.

Owen and Ben, chatting with their heads together, stopped speaking immediately. Owen straightened, towering above his son, his stunned, adoring expression telling her everything she needed to know. Ben put his finger in his mouth.

"Pretty Mommy," he said.

She laughed. "I think I just had my favorite moment in the wedding," she said.

Owen beckoned her to hurry. "I'm sorry we're late with this, but Butch was running late."

"Butch Dayton?" She hurried down the

rest of the stairs, peering outside through the wide windows. "The pig-iron sculptor?"

Owen took a brown paper bag out of his pocket. "He changed his medium for this. Sorry about the froufrou wrapping paper."

"Wait'll you see, Mommy." Ben jumped up and down, landing on his father's well-polished shoe.

Owen took a beautiful oval locket of beaten silver out of the bag, dangling it by a delicate platinum chain. He opened it and cradled it in his shaking palm. Lilah touched the photo of him and Ben in their wedding clothes, lovingly embraced by a heart insert.

"Perfect," she said, barely managing a whisper. "How can I thank you?"

Owen hugged her tight. "Marry me," he said.

"Put on the necklace," Ben said. "You have to wear it when you and Daddy get married."

She turned, and Owen fastened it for her. Then she knelt to pick up her son, uncaring of his flailing feet as he hugged her.

"I gotta go, Mommy. I gotta take Daddy to the end of that long white rug."

"And I gotta go because I gotta marry you," Owen said. "And then love you more and more every day of my life."

"But wait." She tugged his head down and kissed him. "I love you." And with no fear at all, she made all her vows in her heart right then and there. She could speak them all day, but this moment, with just the three of them, was the one that mattered most.

* * * * *

LARGER-PRINT BOOKS!

GET 2 FREE LARGER-PRINT NOVELS PLUS 2 FREE MYSTERY GIFTS

Love Inspired®

Larger-print novels are now available...

LILP15

YES! Please send me **The Montana Mavericks Collection** in Larger Print. This collection begins with 3 FREE books and 2 FREE gifts (gifts valued at approx. $20.00 retail) in the first shipment, along with the other first 4 books from the collection! If I do not cancel, I will receive 8 monthly shipments until I have the entire 51-book Montana Mavericks collection. I will receive 2 or 3 FREE books in each shipment and I will pay just $4.99 US/ $5.89 CDN for each of the other four books in each shipment, plus $2.99 for shipping and handling per shipment.*If I decide to keep the entire collection, I'll have paid for only 32 books, because 19 books are FREE! I understand that accepting the 3 free books and gifts places me under no obligation to buy anything. I can always return a shipment and cancel at any time. My free books and gifts are mine to keep no matter what I decide.

263 HCN 2404   463 HCN 2404

Name _____ (PLEASE PRINT) _____

Address _____ Apt. # _____

City _____ State/Prov. _____ Zip/Postal Code _____

Signature (if under 18, a parent or guardian must sign)

Mail to the **Reader Service:**
IN U.S.A.: P.O. Box 1867, Buffalo, NY 14240-1867
IN CANADA: P.O. Box 609, Fort Erie, Ontario L2A 5X3

MMLPBPA15

READERSERVICE.COM

Manage your account online!

- Review your order history
- Manage your payments
- Update your address

---

*We've designed the
Reader Service website
just for you.*

Enjoy all the features!

- Discover new series available to you, and read excerpts from any series.
- Respond to mailings and special monthly offers.
- Connect with favorite authors at the blog.
- Browse the Bonus Bucks catalog and online-only exculsives.
- Share your feedback.

Visit us at:

ReaderService.com